Conspiracy of Silence

Also by Decima Wraxall and published by Ginninderra Press

Bloom

Stolen Fruit

Flame

Glimmers of Light

Decima Wraxall

Conspiracy of Silence

Conspiracy of Silence
ISBN 978 1 76109 481 1
Copyright © text Decima Wraxall 2023
Cover image: Melissa Wraxall

First published 2023 by
GINNINDERRA PRESS
PO Box 3461 Port Adelaide 5015
www.ginninderrapress.com.au

1

Drops of moisture beaded our resident's brow. I said, 'How are you, Lottie?'

She struggled to open her eyes. 'Not…so…well, Sister.'

I checked her vital signs. Slight temperature. Blood pressure normal – I'd expected it to be low. Decades of experience warned me that something was amiss. A query in my glance, Elsie's nod. It could be serious.

I said, 'We're sending you to hospital, Lottie. Check things out.'

She nodded. 'Whatever…you think…best, Sister.'

At casualty, triage staff ordered immediate surgery. Her laparotomy revealed a purulent, intestinal ulcer.

Later, her GP congratulated us on our insight. 'If you hadn't acted promptly, Lottie might well have died.'

Wattle Grove prided itself on being a safe home for residents in their twilight years. Well-tended garden courtyards were a place to drowse on sun-drenched mornings. Spring brought a honey aroma of golden blossoms, and the perfume of red roses. Magpies fluffed damp black and white wings, droplets sparkling from fountain pools.

Weekend RNs (registered nurses) met the challenges of dementia and frailty with compassion. Angela, West Wing morning; Elsie and Merle, afternoon RNs; Doone, our night sister. 'Valued member of our team and the profession,' Matron said. She was only a call away from problems. We shared laughter and tears, part of every day. A Chinese philosopher put our role succinctly: loving and caring for our neighbours' grandparents as our own.

One resident was unconscious, expected to live no more than hours. Her husband sat in silence, nursing his four-year-old granddaughter.

She pulled at his arm. 'When can we go home, Pa?'

He hugged her tighter, face mournful. 'Shh! Soon.'

Medical experts tell us that hearing is the last sense to go. It comforts patients to hear a loved one's voice, even if they are unable to respond.

'It would be lovely if you spoke to your wife.'

He shrugged. 'What's the use? She has nothing to say.'

A while later, he arrived at my desk. 'She's gone.'

His granddaughter piped up, 'Does that mean Gran's kicked the bucket?'

Pa managed a chuckle, despite his grief.

Our oldies had survived two world wars and a major depression. Some, like Tom May, had received the highest award for bravery, the Victoria Cross. His story was far from the only one of survival and courage, under the worst conditions. Yet the majority of folk said, 'We were no heroes.' They'd put their safety on the line during the Second World War. In peacetime, they lived quiet and dignified lives, raised families and contributed to the community.

Nursing and domestic staff represented a veritable United Nations of cultures and creeds. Our differences enriched relationships, brought lasting friendships. Some had seen their children into adulthood, marry and leave home. Mine were still young.

In 1973, I'd begun the East Wing morning shift, on weekends. 'I'll stay six months,' I told my husband, Neville. 'Boost our travel funds.'

About to fulfil a lifetime's craving to explore foreign shores, Neville organised travellers' cheques, arranged cash. 'Deutschmarks are the best-value currency.' He booked airline tickets, opened a London bank account, paid a deposit for Embassy House Hotel, at Queens Gate. A Toyota camper van awaited. 'We'll pick it up after a week enjoying the joys of the capital.'

I laughed. 'You've left nothing to chance.'

'You know me, sweetie. I never do.'

Naomi, nine, was already with her godparents, a bus ride away from her primary school. Our son Cedric, three, looked forward to a holiday with his grandparents. A week before departure, I took him to my parents' farm in the northern tablelands of NSW.

The following morning, Mum's phone jangled. 'It's for you.'

Surprised to hear the voice of my brother, Druce. 'Neville's in Bankstown Hospital. Renal colic. Pain so excruciating, he bent the metal sides of the casualty gurney.'

My disbelief. Shock. Our travel dreams trembled. In days, we were due to fly out.

Druce told of whispered conferences outside the screened cubicle.

'H–how is he…?'

'They've brought the pain under control.'

My parents exchanged worried glances.

The receiver crashed into its cradle. 'Neville's in hospital…kidney stone.' I gulped. 'He's OK now. But…doctors say no trip.' He'd be devastated.

'Oh dear. I know how you've been looking forward to this,' said Mum.

'I'll return to Stacey Street. See if there's anything to be done.'

Fearing the worst, I threw things into a case. Concerned faces, and hugs, saw me onto the express train. Cedric remained with his grandparents.

My concern shuffled with guilt. Missing our trip should be of secondary importance. But I wasn't yet ready to accept the loss of my dreams.

Pale from the affects of pain and lack of sleep, Neville set his jaw. 'I'll go overseas if they have to carry me onto that plane.'

I shivered. 'If only there were enough time for surgery. Suppose the pain returns?'

He looked grim. 'An intravenous pyelogram showed my stone's on the move. It should pass easily.'

'How can you know that?'

Our GP shook his head. 'No trip. For God's sake, man, you know what the pain is like.'

Neville set his jaw. ' Going overseas is non-negotiable. My wife is a registered nurse. Give us a script for pethidine. She'll cope with any emergency.'

I seized the keys to our great escape: a plastic bag full of syringes, meth wipes and six ampoules of pethidine; paperwork legalised the possession of classified drugs.

Our plane taxied along the runway. Was this real? So many times I'd waved Neville goodbye, on location with Film Australia. Jaunts to Perth, Bunbury… His excitement over Istanbul, Turkey, for the seventy-fifth anniversary of Gallipoli.

Botany Bay slipped beneath our wings. Sunlight glittered on backyard swimming pools. The rural scene morphed into waves of desert sand. Shiny rivers, threads of silver in barren landscapes.

Neville chatted to a fellow passenger.

The stranger said, 'Your wife will no sooner be out of Australia than she'll want to return to the kids.'

I thought to myself, mate, you don't know me.

A stopover in Hong Kong. Neville loved to bargain. We splurged on a new diamond ring and wedding band, to replace cheap ones, all we could afford at the time of our wedding, a decade earlier.

Luxury of the Grand Hotel. An aroma of Chinese spices enhanced every exploration. We drooled over excellent meals. A trip to the famous peak was ticked off Neville's to-do list.

Borne aloft on the wings of a Qantas jet, we headed for Europe.

I gasped over my first glimpse of European snow-capped mountains, a breathtaking vista. 'Wow!'

Excitement mounted. We flew into Heathrow. Or 'Thief Row' as it was dubbed at the time. Two men were jailed for stealing luxury goods from wealthy passengers.

Neville's face shone. 'On English soil at last.'

The right documentation for pethidine, and raised eyebrows, saw me through border control. An endless walk retrieved our luggage.

On the Tube, men wore bowler hats and carried furled umbrellas, relics from another era.

Neville squeezed my hand. 'Sideways seats on the train. That's different.'

We drifted in a state of bliss.

'Sweetie, we've made it.'

A black London taxi sped us to the Embassy House hotel, at Queensgate.

We enjoyed a baked lamb lunch, followed by a peaches and cream dessert. My body teetered from exhaustion, uncertain whether it was midnight or noon. We couldn't stifle our yawns.

Neville grinned. 'Fancy a brief lie down before we hit the high-lights?'

The treasures of antiquity awaited eager eyes, my head craved pillowed comfort.

We blinked awake eighteen hours later.

London names were as familiar to us as our own. The old board game, Monopoly, taught fifties kids the magic of that British capital. Euston Station, Pall Mall, Trafalgar Square, Bond Street… A visit to Madam Tussaud's Wax Museum was high on our list. We admired an African woman in all the splendour of unique fabric design and a matching turban, a wax model of perfection. Until she moved.

The Tower of London, engendered chilling thoughts of Anne Boleyn and her slender neck. The Victoria and Albert Museum proved a treasure house of wonder and delight. Houses of Parliament presented a mixture of history and impressive architecture.

Neville drooled over Hamley's Toy Museum, a dreamworld for a middle-aged man into model trains. At the National Art Gallery, Neville admired the originals of two Turner paintings on his favourite theme: trains.

I gazed at *Rain, Steam and Speed*, and the *Great Western Railway*. 'They're superb examples of his work.'

Travelling round England. Neville returned from the loo, chuckling. 'We've seen the last of it.'

'What?'

'That pesky stone. It tinkled into the urinal. My neighbour in the cubicle shot me a speculative look.'

'I'll bet.'

We had a good laugh.

At Shottery, Stratford-Upon-Avon, we explored Anne Hathaway's childhood home, a half-timbered cottage, dating back to the sixteenth century. As carefully as any lady's coiffure, tons of wheat straw had been shaped into a thatched roof. It had mellowed to a soft grey, doubtless a recent replacement: thatched roofs only last twenty or thirty years.

William Shakespeare had married Anne Hathaway in November 1582, eighteen to her twenty-five. She was three months pregnant, a common situation at the time. To avoid scandal, the nuptials were performed out of their parish. The guide said, 'June was the official month of weddings, a time when everybody indulged in sheer luxury: their one bath a year.'

Neville chuckled. 'Unbelievable.'

An old-world garden breathed the fragrance of roses, wallflowers, sweet peas, herbs… 'Tended by members of the Hathaway family for thirteen generations. The garden is now under the protection of the Shakespeare Birthplace Trust.'

Original blue heirloom patterned plates and dishes gazed from a solid oak sideboard. 'These items represent the period from 1520 to 1911.'

Sturdy oak beams, polished by smoke and time, had acquired the hardness of steel.

Neville whistled. 'Just look at those oak pegs, affixing crosspieces of timber. Old ships used the same system.'

An original love seat, darkened to ebony, took my attention. 'I can picture Will holding hands with Anne. The flickering candlelight.'

'Not expensive wax candles,' the guide told us. 'Theirs would have been reeds, rolled in mutton fat.'

The table glowed with the patina of over three hundred years. 'The polish used was a mixture of turpentine and beeswax.' She shared the table's secret: an unpolished side.

An image emerged. Anne kneading bread, a dab of flour on the tip of her nose. Blowing wisps of hair away from face. Brow damp in the hot kitchen.

The guide, 'Burning bundles of dried gorse heated the bricks. Once hot, they retained the right temperature to bake the bread.'

Perhaps Will crept up to kiss the nape of her neck? I pictured her chuckle, 'Be off with you. Check the oven.'

Our guide said, 'She closed the oven entrance with a solid elm door. Scrubbed the surface, and turned the table. Ready with a long-handled wooden spatula to lift out the fragrant loaves. Notice this slatted cupboard beside the second fireplace? It allowed woodsmoke to cure their bacon, unique to the area.'

Polished brass gleamed. 'This is a long-handled plague pan.'

The idea of 'plague' seemed quaint to me, in our modern world of antibiotics and vaccines.

'They put hot embers inside, sprinkled with aromatic herbs. Perforations in the lid allowed the delightful aroma to seep through. Folk believed it aided recovery of the sick. They carried it throughout the house, leaving a wonderful fragrance.'

Burton-on-the-Water, a model village. Neville wandered around, entranced. 'I could build something similar in our yard back home.'

But I'd never fancied a railway in my garden.

The proprietor of the souvenir shop glanced at the calendar. 'Why, it's almost the first of June.'

Recalling our visit to Shottery, Neville joked, 'Doubtless, you'll all be getting ready for your annual bath.' Expecting a chuckle over old customs.

Eyes bulged beneath bushy eyebrows. 'How dare you! We bathe regularly, thank you very much.'

His lady assistant, echoed outrage. 'Indeed.'

Neville endeavoured to explain. Every word made things worse. We beat a hasty retreat. Laughing through our tears.

A visit to Giztrell House was on Neville's agenda. 'Since it's our family name. I've always been curious to see it.'

The estate was named after Gitzs baronets who had owned land in the area since about 1500.

Being an outlaw of this famous dynasty didn't stop Neville ringing Lord Giztrell to arrange a visit.

Told Neville's surname, a posh voice replied, 'You have excellent credentials.'

A time was arranged for the following morning.

I dreaded the visit. 'But…but…you're no blood relative . You inherited your mother's married name. Edmund Giztrell wasn't your father.'

Neville shrugged, not a man to be put off by a minor detail. 'I want to see what might have been.'

That evening, Neville mentioned his plans to cider drinkers in the Five Bells pub.

The idea of phoning a lord seemed outrageous to ordinary English mortals. They shared a glance and continued drinking.

The gatehouse was bigger than our Stacey Street cottage. Black Angus cattle grazed on rich fields. We parked our hired Toyota campervan outside the Victorian Gothic revival mansion. An architectural nightmare, not beautiful as one expected.

In days before it became a National Trust property, Lady Giztrell led us through the huge entrance. We passed statues and a grand staircase. Outside, on the back veranda, she indicated cane armchairs. Feet away, stinking animal skins buzzed with blowflies.

I thought, this is the ultimate aristocratic insult. Humiliated? Neville took it all in his stride.

Lord Giztrell dragged out his trusty Debretts. Everyone of any importance was listed in that book, like breeds of cattle or dogs. His lordship said, 'I don't see your name listed here.'

Neville gave a dismissive wave of his hand. 'We don't worry about such things in Australia.'

I was mortified.

Instead of explaining that his mother had been married to Edmund Algernon Giztrell, son of Sir Cornelius, Neville offered no explanation, doubtless raising their suspicions. Who were these interlopers from the Antipodes? If only Neville had thought it through. I guess he felt ashamed of not being Algernon's son, born long after his early death.

Lady Giztrell took us around her garden. She told of the ironwork removed for the war effort in the 1940s. Cleverly, she led us towards the exit.

Neville showed her our hired Toyota van, told of our proposed trip to Europe.

'Oh, it's a hireling.'

Neville drove off, mission accomplished. Our hosts remained none the wiser. I wriggled with embarrassment, overjoyed to have the visit over.

Back at Stacey Street, Neville would later mention the visit to his cousins. A brief pause in the conversation was their only reaction. Strange, I thought, how often truth is taken as fiction.

At Cowes in southern England, Neville made friends with Nance and Dave Davies from Watersend Nursery, near Dover. Before I knew it, we were sitting on fold-up canvas chairs beside their campervan, laughing and chatting over cups of tea like old friends.

'You're welcome to park your van in our garden at Dover. The drive is just past the George and Dragon pub.'

I misheard it as the 'Georgian Dragon'.

On London Road, we found the turn off. We were amazed at their home, a huge flint coaching house, three hundred years old, a resting place for travellers, and a change of horses. An enormous bath astonished us too. Long enough for a six-foot man like my husband to lie down. A 'Pilgrims Way' sign pointed towards the modern highway. Once a footpath, it led to Canterbury Cathedral and the shrine of St Thomas a' Becket, murdered in 1170.

Nancy said, 'No visit to Dover would be complete without the iconic White Cliffs. Julius Caesar, St Augustine and William the Conqueror all began their explorations of England from our town.'

She drove us to the best viewing point. Below, the eastern docks throbbed with activity. Lighthouse beams knifed through the fog, probing hidden dangers. Invisible ships boomed warnings. Gulls screamed.

She told us, 'On a clear day you can see Calais.'

A green and white SeaLink ferry appeared out of the gloom. Smoke belched from its funnels. Manoeuvred into a safe mooring, trucks groaned up from the depths of the hold, large and small. Delivery vans joined semi-trailers. Cars and campervans honked impatience. Juggernauts roared off with bulky cargo. Weaving among other vehicles, a gaggle of cycles. Even a couple of pushbikes took their lives in their hands.

Streams of tourists arrived on foot; the jeans-clad generation were interspersed with bright splashes of colour from oldies. They poured into waiting coaches, which spun onto the highway.

'My goodness. What a sight,' I said.

'It's like this all summer,' said Nancy.'

Neville shook his head. 'I didn't realise Dover was such an important port.'

'Oh yes, indeed. It remains a major shipping and ferry site,' Nancy said. 'Over the centuries, Sandwich, Hythe, Romney and Hastings have all silted up. Some are now miles from the sea.'

A green Townsend ferry smoke-signalled imminent departure. A long queue of vehicles waited to board, motors pulsing, red tail lights aglow.

Neville squeezed my hand. 'In a couple of days that'll be us. Off to Europe.'

An old man said, 'Good for you.' He recalled voyages on the steamer, strolling the decks in the briny air. 'Sipping cool drinks in the lounge, awaiting that first glimpse of Calais.'

Neville grinned. 'That's our style.'

At that moment, a deafening scream assailed our ears. A hint of burning kerosene drifted on the breeze. Like some machine from outer space, a hovercraft rose on its grey rubber skirt, propellers whirring .It slipped effortlessly off the concrete launching pad, vanishing into the fog.

'The ferry takes an hour and a half to make the crossing,' Nancy told us. 'A hovercraft does it in a third of the time.'

The old man spoke up. 'Huh! Hovercraft passengers might as well fly. They miss all the fun.'

A British flag fluttered at medieval Dover Castle, which overlooks the town.

Nancy told of driving a military vehicle during the war.

Neville said, 'Wow. Tell me more.'

'It was built to repel invasions from across the English Channel. In the 1940s, Hitler's guns blasted us, to answering volleys from British artillery. Extensive secret wartime tunnels stretch for miles. Our boys were stationed here. Vera Lynn's popular song 'Blue Birds over the White Cliffs' raised spirits in the darkest days of World War II.'

The stone bastions of Dover Castle bore few scars of battle. The city had not been so lucky. In the blackout, buzz bombs sizzled over the buildings.

'One never knew where the noise would cease, signalling a hit.'

Civilians found sanctuary in the limestone caves which meander for miles beneath the streets.

'The same caves now provide perfect conditions for bond store fine wines and brandy, said Nancy. 'Dover has withstood the ambitions of the most determined conquerors,' she continued. 'Ironically, the latest threat came from developers. Thanks to the National Trust, we have avoided ugly housing developments.'

Nancy took us to Roman ruins, near busy Dover shopping centre. 'Cellars of demolished houses extended right down to a Roman wall, black with dust. Storage for modern occupants' coal.'

The site bore evidence of Neolithic occupation back in 200 BC. Supervised by experienced archeologists, university students did much of the meticulous work.

'Clumsy picks and trowels were discarded in favour of an artist's brush or palette knife. Even a tiny piece of bone may tell a story.'

Interesting discoveries included a Saxon ring, pottery, and thirty different *Classis Britannicus* earthenware seals. A variety of styles and designs indicate different times. Huge stone 'doughnuts' were used as loom weights in a Saxon weaving hut, destroyed by fire. We wondered, a raid by the Danes?

In preparation for our European visit, Nance lent us a Gaz lamp, blankets and folding chairs. Her card allowed us to buy cut-price supplies from a Dover grocery warehouse.

Farewell hugs.

Neville parked our Toyota van in the SeaLink ferry hold. Our shivers of excitement, Neville's wide grin. 'I'm pinching myself.'

I giggled. 'Same here.'

We made our way on deck. The breeze ruffled his hair.

'Just smell that briny tang.'

Sipping our G&Ts, we watched the waves roll past.

'To us.' The clink of glasses.

The very air of the crossing tingled with excitement.

Neville shook his head. 'I can't believe the number and variety of vessels on the channel.' His shout, 'You beauty! Calais.'

In moments, I'd be on French soil. 'Tell me I'm not dreaming.'

He laughed. 'Time to find our van.'

Neville drove our Toyota HiAce campervan. 'Who could fail to be enchanted by the French countryside?'

Abandoned stone farmhouses, mellow with moss. Historic villages, the spires of ancient churches. Forests of beech, elm, oak.

Trust him to spot the Eiffel Tower first. 'Wow! Just look at that.' Driving around the Périphérique ouest, he said, 'Keep your eyes peeled for our exit.' He not only found the right sign for the Bois du Boulogne campsite, but drove up just as the gates opened. He grinned. 'How's that for timing?'

A beautiful wooded site met our eyes, exactly as we'd imagined it.

A minibus took eager travellers to the Paris metro. Train services sped us to the *centre ville*. At the Louvre, we contemplated the *Mona Lisa* and other masterpieces. Back then, no queues slowed visitors' progress. I headed for the *Winged Victoire de Samothrace*, named as a must. She flew high above a flight of stairs, in all her magnificence. I let every image sear into my memory, fearing we might never pass that way again.

A fellow camper at the Bois de Boulogne, a dentist from Brisbane, needed sutures removed. 'Sun cancer surgery,' he told us. 'I dread waiting hours at some doctor's surgery.'

Neville grinned. 'My wife is an RN.'

I sterilised my suture scissors, wiped the site with meths. A few snips and pulls with my tweezers… 'There you are. Good as new.'

He laughed.

The train to Versailles had no vacant seats.

Our dentist friend said, 'A good sit's always better than a bad stand,' plonking himself on the carriage floor.'

Neville laughed and we followed suit.

An impressive avenue of plane trees beside the Grand Canal led us towards the Water Parterre and castle. Ornate designs, statues and fountains presented formal garden planning at its most impressive. In the wonderful Hall of Mirrors, we enjoyed the horizon perspective of the design, from the opposite direction.

When one group of visitors passed through, we had the hall entirely to ourselves.

Anything that didn't move in those royal rooms was covered in gold, sumptuous and extravagant. Marble columns, fine paintings and intricate embroideries met our amazed eyes.

We'd arranged a rendezvous with my French/Australian friend Maryse, a fellow graduate from RPAH. It was years since we'd met. She was now married with two little girls, and living on the provençale-Côte d'Azur, between Marseille and Toulon.

La Ciotat, her town, was dubbed 'the cradle of cinema'. Flags and pennants fluttered from yachts. Ropes were coiled just so, tactile and attractive. Delightful old maisons looked out over the bay.

Neville grinned. 'It's easy to see why filmmakers flock here.' He followed cars entering a certain street of the ancient town. 'I think it leads to the main drag.'

It was fine for smaller vehicles, which disappeared around a corner ahead. But with every turn of our Toyota wheels, house walls on either side edged closer. Neville set his jaw, determined to drive through.

I shouted, 'Stop! You can't go any further.'

A queue of vehicles had stopped behind us, horns blaring. Drivers craned from the windows of Deux-Chevaux, yelling in unintelligible French.

Neville gritted his teeth. 'I have to back up. Hop out and direct me.'

Cursing, I squeezed out of the van. Made frantic gestures to other drivers. Cries of what sounded like *'Nerde.'*

Our van turned back at last. We drove off to cheers and a chorus of horns.

I wiped my brow. 'Thank heaven that's over.'

'You should complain. I'm the one behind the wheel.'

Neville stopped to ask the way from a French realtor with florid face.

Monsieur's negligible grasp of English matched my French. 'Come.' He jumped into his Citroën and sped off at breakneck speed.

Our Toyota panted in his wake. He gave the thumbs up, right outside Maryse's apartment. Roared away.

Neville groaned. 'That was all I needed.'

Maryse welcomed us with hugs and the traditional bise, a peck on either cheek. 'You must tell me everything.'

Her two little girls, Christine and Patricia, giggled, hanging back. Shy, but utterly charming.

A much-needed pot of tea. She became almost hysterical on hearing of our being trapped in La Ciotat.

I giggled. 'A mad foreign woman and a campervan obstructed their progress. Shouting what sounded like *Nerde.'*

'*Merde?* Shit!' She fell about.

By then, even Neville saw the funny side.

The afternoon soared on wings of laughter. Probationer nursing woes, amusing in retrospect, shuffled into other adventures.

She wiped away mirth. 'You've arrived just in time. The girls and I leave to join Pierre in the Sudan next week.' She had tackled the burden of packing up their belongings. 'One move of many.'

The girls took a nap. Neville and I slipped away for a furtive dip.

On our return, Christine and Patricia eyed our wet costumes. '*La plage?*'

Everyone laughed.

Maryse shook her head. 'One can't get away with anything around here.'

2

Nothing had prepared us for the drama of the Italian autostrade. They spanned valleys, hundreds of feet below, followed by tunnels, cutting through hillsides. Windsock direction finders soared at each exit, enabling drivers to make corrections against the powerful cross-currents.

Viaducts resembled giant concrete sculptures, soaring high in the sky, above houses and apartments. We passed hills neatly terraced with vineyards. Crops changed to lettuce, cabbages… Acres of greenhouses met our surprised eyes. On dry and barren hills, quaint stone cottages clung to steep slopes.

Neville said, 'Wonder what's their source of income?'

Pleasant glimpses of the ocean and resorts gave way to a cluster of towns in smog-ridden valleys. Industrial chimneys belched smoke. Neglected apartments marked by peeling paint. Wheeled toys lay forlorn on balconies, far from play areas.

Some tunnels glared orange lights. Others were gloomy and dark.

Neville whistled. 'This one needs sonar to plot our course.'

Heavy trucks, cars and caravans diced for priority at a speed of 130k per hour.

At times, we breathed a delightful fragrance of pines. Mountains were clad in delicate shades of green. The land levelled out into a colourful patchwork of farms. Silver birch and other deciduous trees clustered along both sides of the road.

Late afternoon yawned into dusk. An out-of-kilter spire of welcome, the Leaning Tower of Pisa, appeared out of the gloom.

Neville parked our campervan. What a luxury to push up the roof, and be home.

He did some stretches. 'I'm aching in every muscle.'

'Me too.'

Hot showers sorted us out.

A cup of tea and a simple meal of pasta, thanks to Nancy's supplies.

A yawn. 'I'm ready for bed.'

He kissed me. 'Night, Clara.' We collapsed into our sleeping bags.

Behind my closed lids, tunnels and viaducts flashed past. I said, 'After the first half dozen, the novelty wore off. How many do you reckon we traversed? Fifty?'

'I've lost count. I do know we've travelled hundreds of kilometres and paid a small fortune in tolls.' Neville wriggled into a more comfortable position. 'Boy, am I going to sleep tonight.' He turned off the Gaz light.

We heard a whine.

'Ouch!' Neville slapped an unseen assailant.

A stinging sensation in my cheek. 'Oh, no!'

Neville switched on his torch. 'Eureka!' He grabbed a spray can, treating every likely entry point in the van. 'It'll burn the blighters in flight.'

'What…?'

He grinned. 'Deep Heat.'

A good nights sleep was had by all.

Next morning, we learnt that Pisa had once been notorious for mosquitoes.

Neville said, 'The scourge of every traveller in Italy. Largely eradicated…'

I laughed. 'A remnant attack last night?'

'You've guessed it.'

A queue of vehicles readied to cross the Austrian border. The Panthera ahead of us jerked to a stop, braked. Jerked forward.

Neville whistled. 'That's one helluva nervous driver.'

Officers waved the Panthera aside. They swarmed over the car.

'A full strip search,' My husband groaned. 'Our turn next.'

He wore a hand-made denim leisure suit I'd crafted for him. Sported a navy blue cap. The customs agent took Neville for a military officer. He gave a brisk salute, waving us through.

Neville returned the courtesy. He drove off with a chuckle. 'Thanks to your sewing skills, my dear, border control was a cinch.'

Jagged mountains recalled the wonders of Julie Andrews and Christopher Plummer singing in *The Sound of Music*. I'd enjoyed the movie, even if the actors later came to regard it as sickly sweet.

On icy Viennese nights. we blessed Nance and Dave for the extra blankets. 'Without them, we'd have frozen in this jolly campervan.'

Good news greeted my return to Wattle Grove. Matron had employed an extra AIN, assistant in nursing, universally called nurse.

I could hardly wait to tell Neville. 'It's marvellous. I can begin my RN duties immediately, no longer required to get residents up and make beds. A round to say hello and check on my residents. Then I can start medications and my dressings.'

'Excellent, sweetheart.'

Angela had left the morning shift to start a business. Menik was now the West Wing RN. She hailed from Sri Lanka, the teardrop of India. Her warm, gentle personality and nursing expertise made every shift a pleasure.

Neville's resumption of work proved less happy. In his absence, an erstwhile friend and colleague had all but edged him out of his position. Neville mounted a counter-attack.

It seemed the colleague had drinking problems. Missed days from work. Arrived late. The hierarchy reinstated Neville in a higher post with a salary increase.

'It's called the last laugh.'

I shared with Menik memories of my first shift. 'I took a break from nursing to birth my children. Naomi was five when I resumed. Cedric, three, came with me for Matron's interview.'

'Did you find it hard going back?'

'I had read widely on geriatric nursing. Matron employed an extra RN to work with me that first day, ensuring my skills were up to speed. A huge help. But I did feel nervous.'

She laughed. 'I can imagine.'

'Work brought me a sense of independence. Crisp notes in my pay-packet.'

Menik chuckled. 'I know the feeling.'

'I love my patients, too.' Adding, 'And renovations on our Californian bungalow won't come cheaply.'

We did bits and pieces of repairs in the next couple of years. A splash of paint here and there brightened things up. But one day Neville put down his brush, a faraway look in his eyes. 'Travel's more exciting than renovations. We could take Naomi and Cedric. The adventure of their lives. What do you think?'

'I think, fix the house later. When do we leave?'

People shook their heads. 'Travelling with two kids? You're bonkers.'

Another said, 'It's cruel to take youngsters on that sort of jaunt.'

I giggled. 'If only I could have had such cruelty as a kid.'

Others puzzled. 'What else is there to see? Australia is good enough for me.'

Our GP shook his head. 'You're brave.'

Backed by these glowing endorsements, we pushed ahead with our plans.

'A family-size Bedford campervan will make our travels a reality.' Neville leapt at an offer by Pan Am airlines. 'A stopover at Disneyland. Cream on my rice pudding.'

'Won't the theme park be crass and overdone?'

'I was raised on marvellous Disney animation cartoons like *Fantasia* and *Bambi*.' His eyes glowed. 'Believe me, it'll be worth every cent.'

Cedric, five, worried about the safety of flight.

We reassured him, 'If there's a problem, there'll be parachutes.'

The moment we were seated, Cedric's treble piped up. 'Okay. If there are parachutes, where are they?'

The plane rocked with laughter.

At the Honolulu luggage pick-up area, Neville simmered. 'Where is our luggage?'

Other passengers on our flight disappeared with theirs. Eventually, an airline official plucked us from the crowd.

A customs official directed us to a different carrousel. 'Are these your cases?'

Neville blinked. 'Oh, there they are. Thanks, mate.'

Outside the airport, palm trees undulated. We caressed the rough bark, tactile souvenir of another land. Sent postcards and small tokens of our visit winging back home.

On the next flight, we craned out of the jumbo windows, fascinated by dark peaks of the Hawaiian islands. Just twenty-four passengers, in an aircraft designed for hundreds.

Champagne flowed.

Neville grinned. 'No first-class passenger could enjoy a more comfortable journey.'

Armrests folded out of the way, we chose our row of seats. Stretched out full length, covered in red blankets. Glorious slumber.

On return from the loo, Neville mistook his row. Snatching up a blanket, his eyes met the startled ones of the legitimate occupant, a young woman.

Neville chuckled. 'Sorry. My mistake.' Reclaiming his spot further along.

Anaheim, Los Angeles. A dirigible floated outside our Holiday Inn window. We blinked. Could it be real?

Cedric rushed for a better view. 'Mum, Dad, look.'

Naomi cried, 'Wow.'

How could anyone sleep with such wonders before excited eyes?

Fantasyland's Small World. A catchy tune and happy lyrics brought miniature countries, towns and cities. Gentle and pleasing to the kids and me.

The Pirates of the Caribbean, a swashbuckling adventure on water for lads, dads or ladies, young and old. Whoops of delight, yips in semi-darkness. Bloodthirsty music, cries and sword fights. Everyone was on the edge of their seats. Screams and hoots of laughter brought the ride to an end.

A cup of tea and Cokes for the youngsters.

Neville bubbled excitement. 'Ready for the next one, kids? Tom Sawyer, a boy's adventure come true.'

A paddle-steamer loaded with exhilaration sailed on the Mississippi River.

I babbled, 'To think Mark Twain wrote the original story way back in 1876.'

Neville squeezed my hand. 'And just as much fun for both adults and children in 1975. What do you reckon, kids?'

Cheers.

I chuckled. 'The magic never stops unfolding.'

Neville laughed. 'What did I tell you?'

We watched the kids spin in cups of wonder and delight. They raced to see an Indian chief with feathered headdress.

'Nice to meet you, son. Where might you hail from?'

Cedric stood, wide-eyed. 'Australia.'

'Land of kangaroo and emu. Good for you.'

'Looks a good place for lunch,' Neville said. 'Dare we risk the turkey?'

'Maybe.'

Surprise in Neville's eyes. 'Why, it's excellent. Even the vegetables are well cooked.'

I drooled over another mouthful. 'Yet they cater for so many.'

The children's empty plates gave it their tick of approval.

My memories rushed back: the Royal Easter Show catering in Sydney. 'Those ghastly, Pancho Pups? Saveloys in batter. Yuk.'

He grinned. 'Disneyland is everything I expected, and more.'

A guide said, '*The Queen Mary*, folks. Grandest ship of the Cunard Line. Permanently in dry dock at Long Beach, California. In her day, she was lauded as 81,000 tons of fun. Won the Blue Riband of the Atlantic in 1936. Launched on 27 May of the same year.'

Neville shook his head. 'I was about seven when Rabbi Spiegel took me to see her in Sydney. World War II drab grey, carrying Aussie troops off to battle.'

We strolled the decks, admiring the luxurious cabins. I grinned. 'Indeed a fine lady. I love her glamorous red funnels.'

Back in London, Neville sported a trim beard. He glowed with health and well-being. Pollock's Toy museum. He had a blast enjoying it just as much as Naomi and Cedric.

He looked sombre at the Tower of London's bloodthirsty tales of Anne Boleyn. All of us were impressed by glinting coats of armour, especially King Henry VIII's giant one. Ravens on patrol contrasted with the splendour of the Beefeaters in their red and gold embroidered outfits.

We collected our Bedford campervan from GB Rent-a-Car, Sunbury. 'Another adventure, kids.' We sang, 'Rolling, rolling rolling, Rawhide.'

The song took us through the English countryside. Castles, waterfalls and ancient remnants of Roman buildings met eager eyes.

Naomi strode Hadrian's Wall as if she owned it. Posed for photos on an old, leaning tree at Burton-on-the-Water. It perfectly framed the picture, and drew the eye to a blue-patterned vase in a house window, rendered in black and white.

Evening drew down the veil of sunset.

'Time for spot-a-camping, kids!'

Cedric loved playing the game. A chocolate, or some other small prize, was given to the one who found that night's stop.

The famous Roman ruins drew us to Bath. Neville scanned streets for a likely place to park. Uniformed traffic wardens manned every block, struggling to sort out the congestion. No Parking signs abounded.

Neville groaned. 'No places for any vehicle, let alone a large one like ours. He spotted one. 'Aha! At last.'

He made to enter the parking station. It had been designed for small cars. Our campervan risked becoming a permanent fixture, wedged between two pillars.

My husband muttered, 'I hate this.'

Other drivers obeyed my frantic signals to back up. We drove off at last.

Never a man to suffer in silence, Neville's tirade gained volume. 'I hate this. It's not worth driving around for hours to see some boring ruin.'

Long experience had taught me the best remedy was silence.

'Eureka!' I'd spied a disused railway station, converted into parking space. 'It's for large vehicles.'

We stepped twenty feet below the chaos of modern Bath traffic, and two thousand years back in time.

The Roman baths complex made Neville's eyes bulge. 'Wow. This is really something.'

For centuries, Aquae Sulis, dedicated to the goddess of hot springs, had been hidden by mud from flooding of the rive Avon. Rediscovered in 1880, excavation of the complex took twenty years. Discoveries and exploration were ongoing.

Neville said, 'Imagine. Over a hundred million gallons of steaming water pour out of the ground each year.'

Goodbye Mr Grumpy.

'It is impressive.'

In Roman times, the healing properties of the greenish water, laden with minerals, brought arthritic sufferers flocking to seek treatment. Ropes stretched across a small pool, allowing incapacitated sufferers extra freedom of movement. Metal rings were donated by grateful clients to secure the ropes. They bore inscriptions naming the dates and names of persons cured. More enfeebled patients sat on stone benches, immersed in water up to their waists.

'My back aches. If only I could slip into that water.'

Neville grinned. 'Go for it.'

A large pool catered for the fit. Once, a spectacular arched roof of hollow bricks soared above, to protect clients from the weather. A central fountain agitated the water to prevent surface deposits of unsightly chemicals.

Modern folk enjoy a sauna. The Romans loved their hot rooms. Central heating came from underfloor hypocaust channels. A cold plunge bath followed. They gossiped with friends, in alcoves surrounding the pool.

I said, 'Just think, kids: these paving-stones were worn down by Roman sandals.'

Naomi's eyes widened.

The healing waters brought relief to sufferers at a nearby arthritic hospital.

Neville said, 'Let's return when they open the public bathing pool.'

We traipsed upstairs to the pump room. Drank tea and ate Bath buns.

I gazed at potted palms, superb architecture and sparkling chandeliers. 'A perfect backdrop for this three-piece violin ensemble. It reminds me of scenes from *The Duchess of Duke Street*.' A giggle. 'Maybe these musicians played to jaded aristocrats back in the 1700s.'

Naomi groaned. 'Mum, don't be silly.'

Neville grinned. 'I can see why the complex is called the finest Roman remains in Britain.' He squeezed my hand. 'Sorry about earlier.'

Beside the small fountain, a sign invited us to sample a glass of Bath water. I thought it tasted okay.

Neville grimaced. 'I'll stick to gin.'

'In days gone by,' I told the youngsters, 'folk assembled daily to drink three glasses of this mineral water.'

The kids cried, 'Yuk.'

Cedric plucked at my sleeve. 'Can't we go now, Mum? We've eaten the Bath buns and drunk the Bath water.' He wondered why we laughed.

Bristol introduced us to the SS *Great Britain*, now a museum.

Our guide said, 'Designed by Isambard Kingdom Brunel for the Great Western Steamship Company. One of the great engineers. She plied the transatlantic service between Bristol and New York City. In the 1850s, she carried passengers from Liverpool to Melbourne. Advanced for her time, she was the longest passenger liner in the world.'

Neville said, 'Just think, kids. She carried six hundred passengers. Up there with a jumbo jet.'

I sniggered. 'Daddy doesn't mean it flew.'

They giggled.

3

Stonehenge, the famous prehistoric monument in Wiltshire, brought further excitement. Back then, children could climb over the fallen stones. A sign told us, 'It is regarded as the most sophisticated prehistoric stone circles in the world. The ring of large standing sarsen stones are each around thirteen feet high. This structure has helped scientists to understand Neolithic and Bronze Age ceremonial and mortuary practices.'

Naomi wondered, 'How did they put up those huge stones?'

Neville grinned. 'Good question. It may be five thousand years old, but it's almost certain that pulleys and ropes were used. Imagine, it was built before written language, before metal tools and before the invention of the wheel.'

Onlookers shook their heads.

Naomi took out her pencil, making sketches for a project book.

A ride on the Romney, Hythe and Dymchurch light railway, in Kent, was a must for Neville. A whistle wailed and we were off. It swarmed with middle-aged train enthusiasts. The kids enjoyed it just as much, judging by the shrieks and laughter.

Next stop Dover to visit our old friends, Nance and Dave Davies. They'd retired from their nursery business. Moved from the three hundred-year-old coaching house, built from flint, to modest Sunset Bungalow.

Nance said, 'This cottage is exactly what we needed.'

Dave, in his nineties, proudly drove his ride-on mower.

Nancy said, 'Your letters make me feel I already know your children.' Adding, 'It would be wise to buy Naomi and Cedric wellies for the camping.'

Whenever mud entered the scene, we felt thankful for her advice.

Wellington boots kept trousers reasonably clean in sodden children's play areas.

Extra blanket, folding chairs and a Gaz lamp added the comforts campers needed. International Camping Carnets at the ready, we crossed the channel by a SeaLink ferry, our kids wide-eyed from excitement.

Neville grinned. 'It's even more fun the second time around, thanks to these guys.'

Arrival at Bois Boulogne Camping in France felt like going home. In Paris, everything from the Louvre to the Arc de Triomphe thrilled our youngsters.

Neville shook his head. 'And why not? So much for all the naysayers back home, predicting disaster. This city never fails to amaze and delight.'

In the Metro, Naomi rushed to board a train. The doors closed. She glided off, leaving the rest of her family in shock, stranded on the platform.

Neville mouthed, 'Get off at the next stop.'

Cedric, five, howled, 'Now we've really lost her.'

We found Naomi nervous but unscathed at the following station. Cedric hugged her, as if he'd never again let her out of his sight. The last time she rushed to board a train.

A cruise on the Seine in the Bateaux Mouche, was a relaxed way for a family to enjoy the sights from some distance. The youngsters couldn't wait to see the Eiffel Tower up close. The towering size impressed them. Out of breath upstairs, they rushed around every level, gazing at the Seine and city buildings, far, far below. Afterwards we enjoyed ice creams.

I chuckled. 'I think Cedric finds these just as exciting as the last hour in the sky.'

At Chamonix, a resort area near the junction of France, Switzerland and Italy, Neville rubbed his hands. 'Mont Blanc is the highest summit in the Alps. Anyone for a closer look?'

Cedric rushed closer. 'Let's go, Daddy.'

We took our places in the téléphérique cable car. It glided to the Aiguille du Midi, high in space, valleys far below.

The kids yipped. 'Look, Mummy, Daddy, snow.' They grabbed handfuls of it.

Neville warned, 'No throwing. I mean it,'

We stood on the viewing platform. 'You couldn't get a more breathtaking vista of the French, Swiss and Italian alps.'

They youngsters giggled and charged off.

I shivered in the bitter wind. 'They're not old enough to appreciate it.' Adding, 'Come along, you guys.'

We piled back into the van.

'Mt Blanc tunnel leads to the Aosta valley, Italy. Amazing technological feat,' said Neville. 'Almost twelve kilometres in length.'

The lamplit darkness went on for ages.

Cedric piped up, 'Daddy, is it night now?'

We all laughed.

'Could be, son. We'll have to wait and see.'

Blinking, we emerged into brilliant sunshine. Flags of every colour and nation fluttered in the crisp breeze.

In Rome, a guard unlocked a padlock to let Cedric through, fascinated to see a little boy with blond locks. We were permitted to follow, inspecting an antique bath. The locks clicked shut behind us. The crowd outside must have wondered what special privilege had allowed us to enter.

Campings all over Europe offered play areas for the young.

Neville grinned. 'A break they need from museums.'

Children squealed, yelped and laughed. They climbed trees, ran, built cubby houses and shared tales of their adventures. Lack of a common tongue never presented any problem; the language of childhood was international.

At Florence, Naomi sketched Michelangelo's *David*. Seeing her busy with pencil, nearby adults exchanged patronising glances.

Expecting a childish sketch, a young man stepped up for a closer look. Unable to hide his astonishment, 'Why, it's good.'

Naomi played the fool at our camping one day, to Neville's exasperation. 'Stop horsing around, will you?'

She whinnied.

An American woman nearby said, 'Who is that wonderful, terrible child?'

We all laughed.

One day, Naomi took a fall at our camping. A young Italian heart-throb, all of eleven, carried her back to our campervan. Naomi suffered a few grazes. He later sent her a postcard of the balcony scene from *Romeo and Juliet*: 'It is the east, and Juliet is the sun. Arise, fair sun, and kill the envious moon...'

An Italian visitor at Wattle Grove had told me of the Villa D'Este. 'It's not to be missed. A sixteenth-century villa in Tivoli, near Rome, it's listed as a UNESCO World Heritage Site.'

Enchanted by all the fountains, we wandered the famous terraced hillside Renaissance garden.

'Isn't it a marvel?' I said.

A little girl clad in white posed for her first communion photo against a curtain of falling water. It poured from the largest fountain. Naomi and Cedric took great delight in wandering behind it, a unique view of the cypress trees and the gardens.

I spent a memorable time chatting to a monk about mortality and the meaning of life. Our conclusions were left open.

On the terrace, a scent of cypress. We lunched on delicious chicken, mushroom and mayonnaise sandwiches. A scream of swallows dive-bombed us, shrieking in unison.

'Go away! Protecting hidden nests,' I told the kids.

A short bus ride away, Hadrian's villa welcomed us with water features, arched columns and headless statues. The impressive ruins included the remains of a large villa. I read, 'Built at Tivoli about AD 120 by the Roman emperor.'

Neville gazed at the complex with wonder. 'A glimpse of past glory. Hinting at the scope of Hadrian's architectural accomplishments.'

Pompeii took us by surprise. We hadn't expected so many tangible remains. Huge frescoes and wonderful terrazzo floors indicated the luxury of life in those villas by the sea. Details included grooved Corinthian columns. Cobblestones streets bore the marks of metal carriage wheels.

Plaster casts of humans and animals brought us poignant reminders of that terrible catastrophe.

Naomi wiped her eyes. 'Look at that poor little dog.'

His suffering was just as evident as it must have been the day he died.

Long after returning to our campervan that evening, we discussed how, in AD 79, Mt Vesuvius had spewed out clouds of ash.

Neville said, 'Women and children took shelter in their houses. Men probably left to find escape routes. Hopes of a brief seclusion were dashed. For eighteen hours, lapilli rained down.'

Pyroclastic flows of lava finally doomed everyone.

'A whole society was buried alive, to be rediscovered by archeologists centuries later. It's a time capsule of Roman civilisation. We're fortunate to have this wealth of evidence available.'

Amsterdam.

By sheer good fortune, a Dutch man who had lived in Australia gave us a guided tour of the Rijks Museum. 'The wonderful items on display give you some idea why it's the most visited in the Netherlands.'

We marvelled at the *Night Watch*, a 1642 painting by Rembrandt van Rijn.

Neville gazed in delight. 'It's always been among my favourites.'

A pilgrimage to Anne Frank's house left us all sombre. The museum paid tribute to the Frank family, and especially to Anne. Built in 1635, this long, narrow house had an annexe, where the Frank family hid during World War II. Anti-Semitism marched with jackboots throughout Europe. Otto Frank, her father, had made plans. The family and other friends took shelter when Hitler attacked France on the 10 May 1940. Who would not be profoundly moved by reading *The Diary of Anne Frank*? Every word a silent witness to the humour and courage of a young girl, trapped in extraordinary times. Otto published it after her death. He was the only member of their family to survive the Holocaust.

We stepped behind a bookcase into rooms where the families took refuge. The very air seemed heavy with sorrow. Anne's favourite pictures, cut from magazines, adorned the walls. Naomi wiped her eyes, touched by the treasures of an innocent young girl. The family were betrayed, shortly before the war ended.

'Imagine!' I raved, 'This brave young girl was one of the last victims of Auschwitz.'

We all wept. The senseless loss summed up the futility of armed conflict, the horror of prejudice.

Neville's love of the *Ring Cycle* took us to Schloss Neuschwanstein, in Bavaria. 'It's universally known as Mad Ludwig's Castle.' He wondered, had Ludwig built it to compensate for a miserable childhood?

Becoming king, he began an extravagant stint of castle building.

'Neuschwanstein was begun in 1569 on top of this mountain,' the guide told us, 'on the site of an earlier castle.'

Two items made the castle unique: a throne room without a throne. Gold inlay, and elaborate columns, introduced us to the second. '

'This, folks, is the king's Moorish banqueting room. He never hosted a banquet.'

A ripple of laughter.

'Ludwig was a creature of the night, travelling in a sled or coach, covered in gilt figures. He rescued his friend Richard Wagner from debtors. Established him in a villa. Staged his elaborate opera, the *Ring Cycle*.'

Extravagant building works emptied King Ludwig's capacious funds.

'He appealed for loans from the Shah of Persia, the Austrian king and the king of Norway. Rejected, he hatched a scheme to have men break into banks. Arrested as mad, and stripped of his rank, he died in mysterious circumstances. Luckily for visitors, we ignored Ludwig's desire to have the castles destroyed upon his death.'

Our group reached the top floor. A dark layer of clouds hung low over the mountaintop. Wild winds battered the castle. Cedric shivered, clinging to my trousers. Flashes of lightning one moment, assailed by a deafening boom of thunder the next. Every light in the room failed. The building shook. So did we.

An American voice wailed, 'I quit.'

Nobody laughed.

At last the storm abated. Lights blazed.

Neville asked, 'Why does lightning precede thunder?'

I shrugged.

Naomi grinned. 'That's easy. Light travels faster than sound.'

He patted her shoulder. 'Good girl. You're right.'

At Dover, Nancy and Dave laughed over our adventures. Hugs in farewell.

'Tell your Aussie friends there's always a place to park their vans in our field.'

Over the years, many of Neville's Film Australia colleagues would take up their offer.

Our return to Aussie shores.

Neville grinned. 'Our children's lives and understanding of other cultures will be forever enriched. It feels good.'

4

I stilled my misgivings about resuming weekend work. Like other staff, I'd miss time with my family. 'I'm never there when my kids are home from school, or Neville is off work.'

Sharing travel tales helped me settle. The oldies made my shifts a pleasure, too, with their wisdom and stories from long ago.

Colleagues like Elsie and Merle knew my dilemma. They said, 'Penalty rates do make the sacrifice worthwhile.'

I laughed. 'You'd see the back of me without them.'

On the occasional free weekend at home, I felt like a spare piece in a jigsaw puzzle.

Only the strongest marriages survived. Elsie's didn't.

Few of us would have lasted the distance without the support of Ninette, our matron. Everyone appreciated her incisive advice.

She praised weekend staff. 'Thanks to you, I can sleep nights.'

In the fifties, Blackfriars Correspondence School had lacked the technology to teach kids French. I'd longed to learn it since the age of ten.

I began my studies at L'Alliance Française de Sydney in 1980, aged forty. Raoul, our professor, conducted classes entirely in French, avoiding the tedium of constant translation into English. Verb forms were an imperative place to start. Most of the other students had studied the language at their alma mater. I worked twice as hard to grasp the basics. Raoul's patient approach helped.

Not that I received top marks. My workbook dripped red ink. On the way home after the class, I would sit on a bench outside Bankstown railway station, processing disappointment, failure and guilt. I told myself, mistakes are inevitable. You'll need patience, girl, to reach the dizzy heights of your dreams.

I played the happy, relaxed student for Neville, not wanting him to ask uncomfortable questions.

Well-liked and skilled in technology, Neville was a gentle, loving man. Exuberant and full of fun. His occasional outbursts had never been a problem. Plagued by persistent indigestion, he flew into rages on a daily basis, and over the most trivial problem – a lost road directory, missing keys. Previously a careful and considerate driver, he was booked for driving at 150 kilometres an hour in a fifty-K zone.

His declarations of love began to feel hollow. I resented the strain his tantrums put on the marriage and our family.

Shaking, I said, 'Go see your doctor.'

'Don't nag me. I've no time for doctors.' At Film Australia, he worked on one documentary or another.

I thought of leaving him. Often. Being a non-driver was a major barrier to flight.

Merle and I swapped memories of our probationer years. She had graduated in the group ahead of mine at RPA. A vital and funny woman, she brought laughter to every shift at Wattle Grove. She was dedicated to her patients, and well-versed in their care. Yet Menik and I weren't so fond of her darker side.

I said, 'Anyone who crossed her as a young nurse copped a handful of thorns.'

Merle laughed about her exploits. A certain sister gave her a dressing-down, the offence long forgotten. 'The poor woman owned a prized cactus collection. One by one, they died. I poured boiling water over each pot in turn.'

Later, Menik shook her head. 'That's going too far.'

My husband's tantrums gained pace. 'Please, please, see your doctor,' I begged. 'There must be a reason for your indigestion and burping.'

'Stop right there.' His eyes bulged. 'After the next film, I might think about it.' He stormed out to his workshop. Skipped dinner, refused breakfast. Drove off to work, burping. Pale, but determined to keep going.

French became my passion and lifesaver. Learning had always been among my greatest joys, but now it took on a crucial importance. Small phrases provided inspiration for poems. I wrote them in French on the train. Raoul encouraged my efforts. I moved through the preliminary study levels.

Merle complained of severe headaches. She carried analgesics in her uniform pocket, was plagued by dizzy spells. Panadol could no longer control her pain.

I worried. 'You must see your doctor.'

She shrugged. 'I'm sure it's nothing.'

Usually, I thought, it's men who are reluctant to see their doctor.

She was chilled, but not surprised, by her diagnosis. An inoperable brain tumour. Over the phone she told us, 'I've months, if not weeks, to live.'

We pondered the courage of her calm acceptance. Made a staff collection. Could bows and ribbons help to show how much she'd be missed? I felt honoured to bring her gift to the hospital, a Royal Albert plate.

Stoic and tranquil to the last, she died in her early forties, leaving a young family.

I told Neville, 'Fine china might help to show Merle's husband how much we've valued her caring role. Her daughter will inherit the treasure.'

Neville had shared a friendly chat at every meeting. 'I enjoyed Merle's company. Such a shame.'

Her loss brought reminders of our own mortality.

A private funeral gave me a sensation of unreality. Exclusion of all but the closest family puzzled Greek staff. They have mourning rituals down to a fine art.

Our one solace came from shared grief between colleagues.

Adam Lindsay Gordon, an Australian poet who lost his only child in infancy, put our feelings succinctly:

Life is mostly froth and bubble, but one thing stands like stone,
Kindness in another's troubles, courage in your own.

I'd given up begging Neville to seek help. Finally, he listened to his symptoms. Terribly ill, he sought GP advice. Underwent scans.

'You need a cholecystectomy. Whip out your gall bladder and you'll be a new man.'

'Will I need a special diet?'

'Nah. You'll be able to eat what you like.'

The GP never knew that what Neville liked were packets of sweet biscuits and processed meats, high in nitrates. He rejected salads as rabbit food.

In days before laparoscopic surgery, cholecystectomy was a major operation. An incision stretched from one side of his abdomen to the other.

Given six weeks sick leave, Neville figured he'd spend the first one recuperating. 'Then I'll potter in my workshop with model trains. Five weeks of bliss.'

Pallid and weak, Neville showed no signs of improvement. One week stretched into three. He could scarcely raise the energy to leave his bed. The tender suture line kept him awake nights.

It puzzled me why he was taking so long to recover. Then it clicked. Prolonged eating difficulties, missing the majority of his meals. 'Your body must be low in vitamins.' I gave him a course of Multi B Forte and vitamin C.

His smile returned. Energy levels surged. 'Thanks to you, sweetie, I feel amazing.' Unfortunately, his leave was over. He returned to work, fit for the first time in ages.

I felt enormous relief at having my husband back. Best of all, his rages seemed a thing of the past.

We'd had our share of troubled employees at Wattle Grove, funny only in retrospect.

One lass had kept seeking compassionate leave for this illness, then that.

Elsie wiped her eyes. 'Deaths…funerals… You name it. All for supposed relatives who never existed.'

'Matron felt sorry for her. It took a while to ferret out the truth.' I shook my head. 'Then there was that nurse with a thirteen-month pregnancy.'

Elsie's dark eyes sparkled. 'Large g-u-t. Matron kept giving her time off.'

Nurse Rose questioned the time her baby was taking.

'Oh,' the young woman declared, 'my doctor has pushed the birth back.

Elsie said, 'It bugs me when I recall club nurses who've picked quarrels. "I can't work with that girl," they whine. "It's too hard."'

My chuckle. 'I glared one youth down. "Stop right there. Life is hard. I spent four years working in difficult situations. Treated like shite. If you can't manage the hard stuff for one day, what's wrong with you? Get back to work."'

Elsie laughed. 'I'm sure she got the message.'

One cold, wet Saturday, I groaned. 'Neville's on location in WA for a few weeks. I'm taking the train.' Our vehicle sat unused in the garage.

'I'd never manage without my car.' Doone brushed back her grey coif, neat with a natural wave. 'You've never thought of driving?'

I told of my sole driving lesson, decades earlier. 'It ended in a shouting match. Neville reckons it's safest with him doing all the driving.'

'Men.' She raised her eyebrows. 'Try a driving instructor.'

'It's only a short walk at either end.' Was I trying to convince myself?

That afternoon, I stalked off, guessing that Doone was right.

It seemed no time before Neville's tantrums stormed back. His burping and indigestion were worse than ever. He glared. 'There's no problem, I tell you.'

Why's he in denial? 'Nonsense. Having indigestion all the time isn't normal.'

He raged on. I tuned out his tirade. Lived on tenterhooks, expecting news of his collapse.

I sought solace in French classes, which raised other possibilities. I'd acquiesced too easily in regard to driving.

Druce gave me an initial lesson in his fifties Valiant.

'Thanks, bro.' I moved on to an instructor.

Much as he prized his motoring skills, Neville seemed a nervous driver. He'd say, 'Suppose you had an accident? What would happen to me?'

'It isn't all about you.'

Neville groaned. 'Where would you go if you could drive?'

I laughed. 'Everywhere.'

He blinked.

Months passed. Neville's indigestion and rages thundered on. He groaned over the cost of my driving lessons. 'That bloke's sure getting his money's worth out of you.'

Gritted teeth. 'I don't care how long it takes, or what it costs. I'll continue until I'm a safe driver.'

Late in 1989, I had the opportunity to sit a French examination, from L'Alliance Française de Paris.

I hesitated. 'Am I good enough?'

Neville grinned. 'Go for it. What have you to lose?'

I managed to control my nerves during the written and oral tests.

Afterwards, my husband asked, 'How did you go?'

'It seemed okay. Still.'

'Until you receive that piece of paper?' He gave me a hug. 'Sweetie, I'm sure you'll do well.'

Staff faces went back decades, family in all but blood. Lambrini and Tina, the Greek cook and assistant, were regulars. Thanks to them, residents enjoyed tasty meals. Cleaning staff, like Voula, were equally prized, ensuring the shine to rooms and corridors.

Our standard of nursing care was envied by less meticulous institutions. Relatives gave glowing praise. Letters of commendation spurred us on.

We cherished the camaraderie, sought the luxury of second opinions, crucial in resident assessment. A 'don't know' led to 'find out', ensuring that the best medical treatment was available.

Each weekend afternoon, I honed my speaking skills. Elsie gave the handover in fluent French. I responded in kind.

I'd been newly elevated to a higher class at L'Alliance. In January 1990, I took my seat.

Moments later, Monsieur le Directeur strode into the room. A wide smile. 'The results are in from the International School of Language and Civilisation in Paris.' He gestured my way. 'Clara has received the Diploma from L'Alliance Française of 1989.'

The professor, 'Felicitations, Clara.' He shook my hand.

Loud applause.

In shock, aglow from head to toe, I savoured every moment. Too often, fate had denied me the acclamation such occasions warranted. Lost documents or missing family members meant they became non-events.

The professor escorted me towards the higher group, a conversation class.

One of the other students chuckled. 'That's the quickest promotion I've ever seen.'

Neville received my news with a huge hug. 'Congratulations, Sweetie. I'm so proud of you.'

Naomi and Cedrick added their 'Well done, Mum.'

Champers bubbled at Stacey Street. Glasses clinked. A roast chicken wafted its aroma, along with that of baking potatoes and pumpkin. Laughter. Conversation babble. It seemed almost like old times.

Matron had recently gained a new title, the Director of Nursing, or DON. Old-fashioned or not, most staff liked to call her Matron. Senior sisters used her christian name, Ninette.

She told me, 'I acquired my driving licence later in life.' She offered valuable advice. 'Don't tell Neville until you pass the test. I made that mistake. My husband drove me mad.'

A laugh. 'Thanks. I'll keep that in mind.'

I moved to the WEA (Workers' Education Association), a French group in the city. It saved a few dollars on fees and brought baskets of laughs from our Professor Gabriel, or Gabe. A bunch of us moved to his private class at Jannali.

Hailing from New Caledonia, Gabe had undeniable charisma. Dark hair, bronze skin. Warm eyes. '*Chansons d'amour*', love songs, augmented our knowledge of the French language and idioms. Enough to melt the hardest female heart.

Nerida was what the French call a woman of a certain age. *Une femme d'un certain age*. She clanked with enough gold jewellery to start another rush. She'd left the tag on her latest chain, wanting us to know the price she'd paid.

We giggled afterwards. 'She fancies herself his favourite.'

Wednesdays in the Rainbow Room, the highlight of our week. Crystals at the window turned sunshine into every colour of the spectrum.

Gabe's tales of a troubled childhood and boarding college distress touched us all. 'One Christmas, my parents refused to take me home. Forced to remain incarcerated for my holidays.'

Exchanged glances. What misdemeanour had occasioned such punishment? Did he become the victim of predator priests?

Nerida blinked back tears. 'Poor you.' She had dubbed him 'a chocolate sweet of a man with a soft centre'.

I planned an advanced driving lesson, the instructor at my side. A test was in the offing.

I whispered to Cedric, 'Not a word to Dad.'

We woke to a downpour.

Neville paced. 'It's dangerous on wet roads. I don't like you driving in this weather.'

I stamped my foot. 'Stop, will you? I'm nervous enough already.'

Knuckles white, I gripped the wheel, calling forth all the angels I could muster. Thankful for a safe arrival.

In the Rainbow Room, Gabe's compliments on a smart dress, new hairdo or pretty scarf brought a frisson of delight to the lucky recipient.

I felt smugly superior to those foolish, middle-aged women, infatuated with a much younger man. Until I too, fell under his spell. Who could resist that long, slow smile?

Nerida confided, 'I've always fancied a French lover.'

I laughed. 'Haven't we all?'

Students plied Gabe with treats. A slice of apple pie? Linda's gastronomic delicacy became the flavour of the day.

He grinned. '*Superbe!*'

Nerida seethed.

The day of my driving test. One final lesson. Or so I thought. I made one mistake after another. Needing encouragement, a white lie might have done the trick.

My instructor frowned. 'You'll never pass if you drive like that.'

Hopes dashed, I took my place beside the RTA testing officer, clocking up every error in the book.

Humiliated by failure. Determined to do better next time.

What an effort it took to hide my feelings that night. I confided my shame to Cedric.

He hugged me. 'Don't take it to heart, Mum. You're bound to do better next time.'

Another Wednesday morning. Diamonds on the grass. Flowers of a hue never seen before or since. A magpie carolled in a gum tree.

Chez Gabe, Edith Piaf songs soared on a cloud of music. The wild rock of Johnny Halliday. Gentle harmonies of Jacques Brel. We harvested useful phrases from singers like Adamo, Brassens and many more.

At home, Neville puzzled, 'What is it about this guy that makes you old birds so crazy about him?'

'Actually, the attraction is purely spiritual.'

'Tell me another.' Neville figured that anyone who made his wife look and act fifteen years younger must be up to no good.

I giggled. 'You should send Gabe a thank you card, for making your wife more attractive.'

He had the grace to laugh.

Weeks later, my second driving test. Every drop of moisture disappeared from my mouth. Grimly determined to do well, I clung to the driving wheel like a lifesaver. Convinced I'd botched things again.

A kindly testing officer, the warmth of his smile. 'I could see you were a bundle of nerves. Practise in a parking lot. You'll be fine.'

I arrived home in triumph, waving my licence. 'I've passed!'

Neville's face fell. 'Congratulations.'

My husband finally saw his GP, hoping the tests and scans would discover the source of his distress.

Grim-faced, he showed up at the surgery for the results.

His GP beamed. 'Reflux and an ulcer are your problems. A daily tablet and you won't know yourself.'

Neville bounced home, overjoyed. 'It's only ulcers.'

I had a terrible feeling the diagnosis might be wrong. Sadly, the tablets increased his distress.

I said, 'You need a second opinion.'

The specialist took a long look. 'With an ulcer, there wouldn't be that shadow.' His secretary made an appointment for an endoscopy in September 1990.

It was open house Chez Gabe from nine thirty a.m. In the Rainbow Room, I seized the opportunity to practise French with, Kay. That day, Gabe gave Nerida a cursory greeting, engrossed in conversation with one of the others.

Nerida rattled her bag. Sighed. Mirror at the ready, she reapplied lipstick.

Kay chuckled later. 'Her ruse might have seemed sexy at twenty.'

'But at seventy?' I laughed. 'She's a double for Blanche in the *Golden Girls*. Imagines she looks forty.'

Kay nodded. 'Proud of her firm boobs. Never had children.'

September 1990. The last sleep before Neville's endoscopy. My husband paced.

Distraught, I said, 'For goodness sake, come to bed. We need a good night's sleep.'

He lay rigidly beside me. 'The last few years have been the happiest of my life. You. Our family. I'm afraid something terrible is about to happen. Taking it all away.'

His words amazed me. How had he plucked happiness from the ruins of our marriage? 'Darling, stop expecting disaster.'

He groaned. 'It'll take twice the anaesthetic to knock me out.'

'Don't be silly.' I wished the GP had ordered sleeping tablets. 'I'll bring you a mug of warm milk and Panadol. That'll help.'

We endured fitful sleep.

The following morning, dismal skies matched our mood.

I told Neville, 'I'll drive to Royal Prince Alfred Hospital this afternoon to pick you up.'

Panic in his eyes. 'No, go by train. We'll take a taxi home.'

Cedric drove his father to RPAH for the endoscopy, on his way to university. Trembling, I waved them off.

5

That afternoon I took the train under lowering skies. Tricked onto public transport by Neville's fears – and mine. A change of lines and trains. Sighs of frustration.

Newtown Station loomed, grey and gloomy. A walk away from RPA.

A juggle of multicoloured umbrellas ascended the stairs. Drizzle speckled the steps. A sudden thought: what will my reaction be if the news is bad?

I fell to my knees.

The endoscopy clinic. Moans issued from behind a green screen. All the other patients had been discharged. Neville was hunched forward on the narrow gurney, face grey. He had aged years since the morning. Seventy, instead of fifty-five. 'It's grim. Cancer. I want to see my doctor.'

I blinked. Clinging to the thought that Neville tended to exaggerate. Probably it would be less serious than it sounded.

Loud moans. He coughed and spat up. It embarrassed me.

A grey-haired gentleman strode our way. Pinstripe suit, blue bow-tie. 'I'm your husband's surgeon.'

'Clara, Neville's wife.'

He gave me a long look. 'How come a wife so quiet and gentle, and her husband so loud?' He sniggered. 'It's a wonder you didn't hear Neville shouting at Bankstown. He told us we needed different lenses. All our equipment was wrong.'

I loathed the doctor's jokey tone, his lack of empathy. My husband sat slumped over. Beaten.

The surgeon blundered on. 'Took twice the normal amount of anaesthetic to knock Neville out.'

I froze, recalling my husband's words.

He added, 'The dose was enough to kill a horse.'

He made me feel like shouting, 'Shut up. Neville isn't deaf.'

The doctor's cheerful tone. 'It's a large tumour. Won't be long before Neville's oesophagus closes off completely.'

His words struck me, a blow in the gut. On the verge of fainting, I pushed things aside. Collapsed onto a chair.

He turned to Neville. 'You'll be better off at home, old chap.' Ever cheerful, he sauntered away.

My teeth chittered.

Neville moaned. 'I need something for the pain.'

'Keep still, darling. You'll fall over the bed rails.'

My head pounded. I'm a nursing sister, I thought, meant to handle any situation. But…how will I manage Neville at home, in this noisy, restless state?

Staff kept busy, packing his medications. Their weekend break beckoned.

I fronted the desk. 'I'm an RN. My husband's in pain. I need the resident doctor to order something. I could give him injections.'

The nurse shrugged. 'He's off duty. See your GP in the morning. If it's necessary.'

I thought, can't she hear me? 'Neville couldn't walk to the car. Not in his state.'

'We'll fetch a wheelchair.'

My head spun. She wasn't listening.

Neville sat bolt upright. The tenor of his voice left nobody in doubt. 'I'm staying right here. In hospital. And don't lose my dentures.'

By some miracle, a resident doctor appeared. A bed was made available.

Outside, lightning flashed. Thunder rumbled. Water lashed the ward windows. How would I get home? A sudden thought, Cedric was doing an electronic experiment at Sydney University.

At one remove from reality, I thumbed a tattered directory. Found the number. Stammered out my problem. 'I need my son, Cedric, to drive me...'

She promised to let him know.

I thanked the Lord for Cedric's second-hand Mazda. It had taken a lot of talking to overcome Neville's objections to our son becoming a driver.

Shaking, I put down the phone. Tomorrow at seven, I was meant to be on duty at Wattle Grove. Their new number eluded me. Another search through torn pages. A spaced-out message. 'My husband...seriously ill... Can't work my weekend shifts.'

Deputy, Liz, seemed uninterested in Neville's condition, the reason for my absence. 'I'll find a replacement.'

Cedric arrived. I faltered out his father's diagnosis. He didn't equate tumour with carcinoma. Shocked to see a once strong man curled up in the foetal position.

On Monday, I telephoned Wattle Grove. Liz hadn't bothered to pass on my message.

DON immediately granted me compassionate leave. 'Take off as long as you need.'

I'd be forever grateful for her empathy and kindness.

Cedric and I visited RPA, expecting to bring my husband home. Joined by Druce, and our sister, here from overseas.

Doctors told us, 'Neville moved during the endoscopy. It caused an oesophageal ulcer, now infected. He's having antibiotics.'

Each day, we arrived expecting to take Neville home. Each day, he remained pale and ill. Doctors conferred, puzzled over why my husband showed no sign of improvement.

Our third visit to RPAH. Distressed by Neville's pallid appearance, I had a flash of insight. Lifesaving information, no less. I rushed to share it with staff. 'My husband's barely eaten for months. He must be nutritionally compromised. Needs extra vitamins.'

Doctor's exchanged glances, scorn in their eyes. Convinced that extra vitamins played no part in a patient's recovery. How dare this mad woman try to interfere in Neville's treatment? They continued to ignore my pleas.

By then, I didn't give a damn about medicos' approval. Vitamins had worked following the cholecystectomy. Why not now? I sneaked Neville Multi B Forte capsules, and orange juice laced with vVitamin C. His dramatic improvement astonished doctors. Twenty-four hours later, they discharged him, none the wiser.

Neville pottered in his workshop. I attended the French group. Wednesday's rainbows shimmered with sorrow. Shocked faces. Gabe and the others were in disbelief, devastated by Neville's terminal diagnosis. I cherished their support.

For hours at a time, I put aside my grief. The respite was just what I needed to carry my burden.

I shared the group's dining out experience with Neville. 'Gabe waited politely until the ladies were seated. Nerida hung back, in order to gain the last place beside him.'

Neville chuckled. 'Why am I not surprised?' He declared us all foolish women. 'Your guru doesn't give a fig for you old birds. His attention is just a ploy to keep you all coming back.'

I laughed. 'You're probably right.'

My caring role left little space for grief. One day, Neville's hopes of a full recovery took wing. Then I reassured him that miracles did occur. The next, his expectations were shattered like Icarus on the jagged rocks of reality. So I supported him in his sorrow. I lost two dress sizes, dropping to a ten.

Neville began to accept that the end might be near. 'I've had a good life.' Doctors had given him four months. Sixteen weeks. A death sentence, shivering with the air of unreality.

The French group came on frequent cheer-up missions. Neville loved their visits. I felt touched by their support. He chatted to them in the twilight garden. A purple rain of jacaranda bells drifted down. He felt happy.

I worried about Neville's tender right leg. A clot? One side effect of the disease.

The GP said, 'He couldn't possibly have a thrombosis, given his high dose of Warfarin – blood thinners.' The doctor suggested hospitalisation the following day. 'Your husband will be more comfortable in his own bed.'

Neville spent a night of agony. I gave him morphine injections at midnight and dawn. In the gloom, I checked the correct dosage, yawning back to bed. My husband was transferred to St George hospital the following afternoon. By then, half his foot had turned gangrenous.

I cursed myself for not following my gut feeling. Why hadn't I insisted he leave immediately? Early treatment might have avoided the calamity.

Neville told me of a dream. 'I ran free, fit and healthy.'

I surreptitiously wiped my eyes.

One day he said, 'When I drive after they cut off my foot, I'll stuff a sock into the front of my shoe.'

I gulped. 'Of course you can.'

I warned members of my French group in advance. They pretended not to notice his black foot. Nerida, bless her, laughed and joked and flirted with Neville. He responded in kind. The hours of laughter and fun did wonders for his flagging spirits.

Daily pilgrimages to St George hospital began to take their toll on me. I dreaded the four changes of train, heavily laden.

One blazing December day, I gathered lambswool rugs, vitamin drinks, grapes, the *Herald*… I sagged under the mountain of stuff to carry on public transport. Our red Camry cast scornful glances my way. I could almost hear it saying, 'Dammit, girl, you have your licence.'

Edging out into heavy traffic, my heart thumped. P plates shouted inexperience. Glad of them, I let my vehicle crawl along King George's Road. Grateful for taxi rides which had taught me all the correct turns. I emerged at the hospital car park, jubilant over my achievement. I couldn't have been happier had I safely landed a fully laden 747 on the Hume Highway, in peak-hour traffic.

Staff directed me to my husband's latest ward. I found Neville hunched forward on a rigid mattress.

IV fluid dripped into his left arm. His pallid face crumpled into a smile. 'There you are, Sweetie.'

We had to raise our voices above the clang and clatter of building extensions outside. One hard pillow, I noted, his spine pressed against metal rails. I should have brought him a feather-filled one.

I called a nurse. 'Would you be so kind to bring my husband an extra pillow.'

She shot him a cursory glance. Nodded, and sped on her way.

It wasn't the moment to be exultant, but I couldn't help sharing my news. 'I drove here.'

He beamed. 'Well done, Sweetheart. Good for you.'

I held Neville's hand, stifling yawns. My energy levels hovered around zero. I struggled to appear cheerful and upbeat.

Neville shot me a long look. 'You look worn out, Sweetie. Go home and get some rest.'

I fought tears. 'Are…are you sure?' He's so gaunt and grey, I thought, guilty at the prospect of leaving him.

He insisted. 'You go, Sweetheart. I'll be fine.'

The extra pillow still hadn't arrived. I lacked the energy to ask staff a second time.

Bless Elsie: she arrived at his ward later that evening. Noticing my husband's discomfort, she said to staff, 'Look, I'm a nurse too. I know you're busy. Neville needs another pillow. If you can just show me where they are.'

I pictured her, tenderly putting it in place, adjusting it to his comfort. Why hadn't I thought of that?

Neville took one tiny, final breath, on 29 January 1991. My eyes brimmed. Grateful to see him go peacefully. Struggling to accept that I'd never see my friend and lover again. Not in this life.

Film Australia expressed shock. A highly respected colleague, husband, father and friend had died at only fifty-five, 'After a short illness'. My ironic smile. Little did they know of his challenging final years. Somehow, he'd maintained a healthy façade at work until the last days before his leave. Bounding along the corridors, as if overflowing with energy. What effort it must have taken, I thought.

A fake widow participated in the funeral rites. Reality just out of my reach. Unable to shed a tear. Welcoming guests at the wake, I offered sandwiches and tea, the perfect hostess. Protected by a surreal sense of role-playing. Touched by the fragrant floral tributes, the dozens of letters, the cards, colleagues and family eulogies.

The following day, sick to the stomach, I wondered, 'What's wrong with me?'

Cedric told me, 'You need a good cry.'

Naomi and I hugged. Sharing the luxury of tears.

Only months after Neville's demise, my mother also died, of motor neuron disease. Poppy, a cousin-by-marriage, and very dear family friend, was taken by heart failure. Both passed on 29 July.

I felt the world disintegrating around me.

I was grateful to everyone for their empathy in my transition from wife to widow. At Wattle Grove, Doone, and her husband, John, helped me to arrange my financial affairs. They advised me on investment options.

Elsie said, 'Don't try to mourn all your sadness at once. Approach each sorrow gently, one by one. Then you'll gradually be able to accept them.'

Her words helped me greatly. Yet grief would creep up without warning. A favourite piece of music my husband and I had shared, the memory of happier days. Only those who'd suffered a significant loss understood my vulnerability.

Before Neville's death, I'd never noticed how many couples wandered the community. Alone, I glimpsed them everywhere. Holding hands, chuckling over private jokes. I wished them well in their happiness. But half of me was missing.

Gabe's French class ceased. Would my losses ever stop?

In February 1991, I returned to L'Alliance Française, Sydney, an advanced speaking group.

Anthony joined us. His lively sense of humour spiked my laughter. 'I'm from Bristol. Lived in Sydney for years.' British as the Avon Gorge, he told of a trip to Montpellier, in France, enjoyed the previous year. 'How long have you been studying it?'

'I made my debut the year I turned forty. My daughter, Naomi, began learning French in Year Seven. I plucked up the courage to follow suit.'

'Good for you.'

It emerged that he was divorced. Not embittered, though he did refer to his ex as 'that bloody woman.' His main gripe was financial. Poor advice from his solicitor had resulted in a low property settlement.

'House prices weren't expected to change much. They skyrocketed.'

'So your ex hit the jackpot?'

'Exactly. She could pay $500,000 for a unit, and still have plenty over for travel and extras.' He made do with the aged pension, boosted by teaching French and English to adult students. He grinned. 'It's a hard life but someone has to do it.'

I forgave him for taking me to a fish restaurant on our first date, his treat. Little did he know that I thought life was too short to eat fish. With three exceptions: trout, salmon and barramundi.

'To think that my passion-filled eyes met yours over a book of French verbs,' Anthony joked. 'A toast to us.'

Crystal glasses clinked.

We shared an interest in current events, politics and, of course, French. Fifteen years my senior, his mature English charm melted the gap. It was great to share movies and a love of travel. We laughed over everything from the mundane to the monumental. Enjoyed dinners and concerts. Vivaldi was high on our list. My favourite was *The Four Seasons*. He broadened my repertoire.

I began calling him Antoine.

Told of my role as a registered nurse, he grinned. 'I've always liked nurses. Strong, practical and intelligent women.'

Elsie was keen to hear all about Antoine. 'What's he do?'

'Retired sea captain. Master mariner. Speaks French perfectly.'

'That's fantastic.'

'He's spent a year studying French with friends in Montpellier. Hopes to return. I'm thinking about having a month at ELFCA, a French language academy at Hyères, on the Côte d'Azur. Boarding with a French family.'

She clapped her hands. 'Go for it.'

'I'll keep you posted.'

Young people introduce their dates to parents. I took Antoine to meet my kids. Cedric didn't oppose our friendship, understandably cautious. It emerged later that he Naomi feared we'd rush into marriage. It made me laugh. 'I haven't yet lost my senses.'

I was working one day when Antoine decided to lop branches from my liquidambar tree.

Luckily, Naomi saw the shears, rushing to intervene. 'Stop! Mum wouldn't want this tree touched.' How right she was.

At times, I griped about my weekend losses. 'I spent too little time with Neville. I see that now. Should have enjoyed leisurely family meals with him and the kids. Seldom saw their sport.'

Elsie nodded. 'Time missed with children can never be regained.'

'Well, I'm about to make amends. Dad's down from the farm. I've taken leave this Sunday for Cedric's cricket match.'

'Anthony will be along?' Elsie smiled. 'Good for you.'

I couldn't hide my excitement. 'We're having a picnic after the game.'

I drove to Kogarah ground, on the lookout for Nelda and Cedric. Chuckling, 'My early arrival ensures an excellent view.'

Antoine grinned. 'And a good parking spot. Well done, Pet.'

We left Dad in the car, walking around the ground. Not one cricket bat, player or spectator.

My heart sank. 'What's going on?'

Antoine soothed, 'The players are bound to turn up soon, Pet.'

No players. No crowd. No Cedric and Nelda. In days before mobile phones, there was no means of making contact.

My eyes brimmed. 'I can't believe it.'

He patted my shoulder. 'There, there, pet. What can I say?'

My sandwiches tasted of loss.

Later, I learnt that the field extended for miles. Who'd have guessed that Cedric's team was playing at the far end?

'It symbolises all the matches I've missed during my son's senior years at Caedmon Grammar.'

'I know, Pet.'

Afterwards, Cedric had the last word. 'Shite happens, Mum.'

'Travelling alone will be a first for me.' I tried not to feel scared. 'A friend at 'L'Alliance Française suggested a hotel in Paris. I've written to book.'

'The city of light.' Elsie's eyes shone. 'Lucky you. I'm saving to go again.'

I shared my plans with Antoine. 'I've booked into a private hotel in Paris, the Prince Albert. It's on the Rue Saint-Hyacinthe.'

Antoine nodded.' Know the area well. Central location, between the Opera, the Louvre and the Metro Tuileries. Near big department stores.'

'I'll spend a day enjoying Paris. Then I'm taking the fast train, Le TGV, to Toulon. Hyères is nearby. Mireille, my hostess, will pick me up from the station.'

'The fast train? Good, good.'

A moment's hesitation. 'Wish I had the courage to travel further afield.'

Antoine's eyes gleamed. 'That's where I might come in.'

I laughed. 'Really? That would be wonderful. Join me in Hyères. After my French classes finish. We could go to Paris. Maybe a trip to Italy. I adore Florence.'

He looked thoughtful. 'It would mean cashing in a term deposit. Still. Life's for living. I'd need to include Montpellier, to see the Odiers.'

'Your French friends? Great idea.'

Like Neville, Antoine had suffered from the absence of a father. In his case, following his parents' divorce. 'A last image, my father, on the doorstep. An armful of toys for us at Christmas. Mother screamed at him, "Never darken the doorway again," or some such.' We'd torn the wrapping from our gifts. Mother grabbed them, throwing them out into the street.' His eyes clouded. 'Late that night, after everybody was asleep, I crept outside. A little boy, going to retrieve his toy train. It was broken. I hugged it to my chest.' Loss of a beloved father still raw, in his sixties.

'Never saw my dad again.' Antoine shook his head. 'Mother would never let us speak of him.'

Our holiday plans took shape: dates, venues. Antoine and I consulted a French travel agent. Arrangements were booked. A seven-day Eurail Flexipass cost us $350 each, well worth the money, we thought.

A month later, I took a closer look at our receipt. 'Yikes. The figure on the right isn't the final one. Look at the left: They've diddled us $1,000.'

He whistled. 'You're right.'

I led a charge into the French travel office. 'We've paid too much.'

Monsieur didn't look in the least surprised, let alone repentant. Or glance at our file. 'Yes, madame, it would seem so.'

Antoine shook his head. 'We must double-check invoices in the future.'

I made holiday arrangements at Wattle Grove.

The director of nursing said, 'Nurses aren't entitled to penalty rates for holidays.'

I checked our award. 'It states that it's either penalty rates, or the lesser figure of a 17½% loading.'

Elsie said, 'Doubtless, Ninette has her orders. I read that at one nursing home alone, the company has underpaid staff by $400,000.'

'Is that so? No wonder the boss is a multimillionaire. What cheek him calling other people bludgers.'

I kept a sharp eye on payslip figures. For once, mine seemed accurate.

Elsie wanted to know the latest.

'I'll visit Vivi in Canada. Then attend the language academy at Hyères. Afterwards, Antoine and I will visit Pisa, Florence and Paris. Then catch up with his friends in Montpellier. Oh, and I'll see my French penfriend, Andrée, at Cholet, in the Loire. I'm so excited.'

Her eyes widened. *Formidable!*'

I waved farewell to my colleagues. Made a round of my lovely patients. I hugged Molly, a lady of ninety, feisty and special to me.

'I'll miss you, sister. I feel safe when you're here.'

'Thank you.'

She smiled. 'I asked God to take me, but, as you can see, he hasn't.'

'Well, Molly, I'm jolly glad you're still around.' I patted her shoulder 'See you after Europe.'

On the Monday, I bade Antoine *adieu*, and flew off into the endless night.

6

I landed at Vancouver, British Columbia. Vivi and my brother-in-law Nate welcomed me at the airport. Hugs, flowers and floating balloons.

The air sparkled, with a hint of chill. A fragrance of spring blossoms wafted on very breeze.

Later that afternoon, Vivi took me on a drive. She talked non-stop. 'Just look at the spring blossoms. Mum would be delighted with the daffodils, jonquils and lilac.'

I gazed at carpets of tiny white daisies in parks. 'They remind me of snow.' Yellow buttercups faced the sun. I looked around. 'This city deserves better than glittering waterways. Framed by snow-capped peaks.'

Vivi laughed.

She drove like a fiend one minute. Slowed to a crawl the next.

I seized the hand grip. Praying. At that moment becoming a believer.

'Vancouver loves hedges. Gardeners use various types of cypress as topiary.' She pointed out the amazing variety of deciduous trees. 'Elm, oak, chestnut, birch, beech. And that sequoia isn't called giant for nothing.'

It was indeed an amazing size.

The Anthropological Museum at the University of British Columbia. Fascinating exhibits of world arts and cultures drew me on and on. I gazed at a timber sculpture by Bill Reid.

Vivi said, 'The legend of creation by the Haida people. An indigenous Indian nation of the Pacific north-west. A raven discovers humans in a clamshell on the beach at Rose Spit, Queen Ella, BC. Persuades them to join this world. Isn't it wonderful?'

'Myth, parable and legend. The same as those of Christianity and Judaism.'

At five p.m. we arrived home. Guests were expected for dinner in an hour. The house was in chaos. Vivi raced around throwing stuff into cupboards. I tackled the sink, overflowing with dirty dishes. Then vacuumed carpets, while she rustled up a meal. A chicken went into the oven. Potatoes peeled, beans topped and tailed. Corn ready to boil. Hot rolls made ready.

Somehow, it was all cooked perfectly, and on time. Smart as a daisy, she giggled and hugged her friends, as if she'd spent a relaxed afternoon. She'd rustled up a special sweet, too: dessert cheese, liqueur and flaked almonds. An evening of fine wine and fun.

Nate chided her at times in his gentle Canadian drawl. 'You don't have to tell us every thought that comes into your head, Vivi.'

I appreciated Vivi's efforts to entertain me. A Latino dance? She and Nate surged around the floor tapping toes with those half their age. Him a bounce of ponytail, Vivi bubbling with laughter. I watched from the sidelines, glad to take a break.

Whistler welcomed us to its snowy peaks. A grove of stunted cypress on a bare patch of ground made a perfect cloakroom. Skiers there for the day, hung red, black blue and brown backpacks, high on broken branches. Others rested on bare earth.

The Harrison hot springs made a steamy contrast. I wallowed in the soothing water, leaving Vivi and her Nate to their own devices for an hour. Envious of their intimacy.

Another day, time to fly on. Touchdown at Charles de Gaulle airport, Paris. My heart raced. Would anyone understand my French? The bus driver from Les Invalides had no problem with my less-than-perfect accent. Pleasantly surprised, I chatted to my taxi driver on the way to the Prince Albert hotel.

'Good luck…' He left me with a Gallic grin.

Key in hand, I entered my comfortable room. Hmm. A safe for valuables. Suppose the combination didn't work and I lost access to my funds? I slept on my money belt.

Venturing out alone at night wasn't an option. I dined early in a small bistro, watching the Parisian world stroll by. Relaxed and happy.

Two violinists and a cello player offered a musical feast at the Gare de Lyon Parisian railway line for the TGV sud est. I boarded the fast train, heading south-east, the orange TGV. Its elegant nose sniffed the morning air. Speeding off at exactly at 10.41 a.m., and meant to reach Toulon at 15.55 p.m.

We travelled at about 300 kilometres an hour, the fastest I'd ever moved on land. Trees and houses whipped by. A blurred but excellent way to cover a lot of countryside in a short time.

I stumbled out of the carriage onto the Toulon platform. Acutely aware of being alone in a foreign country. Outside, I expected to see Mireille, my hostess. Dismayed. Suppose she didn't turn up? Never had I felt further from home. Time ticked by. Twenty minutes. Half an hour. Soon I'd have to do something.

Mireille breezed up with neither apology nor explanation. Confirmed my identity. 'Allo, Clara. *Enchantée.*'

Her little girl, Elodie, tagged along, wide-eyed.

'Let's go.'

We drove off in her Renault. A barrage of information. Mealtimes. Breakfast arrangements. Dinner hour. 'My son, Romain, is having first Communion in two weeks.' She repeated the date, several times.

'*Formidable.*' Her kindness reassured me. I felt honoured to be included in such a special family celebration. A caring woman, after all.

We drew up outside their home. A double-storey villa, of a type which seemed popular with the middle class of Hyères. A wide natural stone balcony, white-railed, with decorative concrete balusters. Flanked by huge cypress trees, in the garden. Glimpses of red and pink geraniums.

'This is your room.'

I guessed it belonged to Elodie. Transparent voile curtains blew in the breeze. A little girl danced in a picture above my bed. Puffed-sleeve dress, floating skirt held aloft, black dancing pumps stepping out.

I clutched my student identity card. ELFCA welcomed students from all over the world. I read the spiel. 'An intensive course in the French language and civilisation for four weeks from 25 May 1992.'

A few European students expressed surprise that someone from far-away Australia would choose to study French.

I laughed. 'It's been my lifelong passion.' Being the oldest student among the group made me a parent figure to those twenty and thirty somethings.

Classes were conducted entirely in French, and were of the highest standard. We enjoyed morning tea in the courtyard. Europeans basked in the sun. Aussies, aware of the damaging rays, took shelter under the white umbrellas. We tucked into a delicious hot lunch too, the main meal of the day in France. Superb desserts introduced me to the wonders of crème fraiche.

Classes over for the day, I trod the winding, narrow streets of Hyères, an ancient Provençal town. I adored those mellow stone buildings and the French atmosphere. Seizing snatches of conversation for later use. Signs added to the wonderful foreign flavour: *C'est interdit de marcher sur la pelouse*. It's forbidden to walk on the grass. *Boulangerie*. Baker.

I practised French with anybody and everybody. Sipping coffee in a popular local restaurant brought the perfect opportunity to people-watch. A wedding party passed by in full bridal regalia. Musicians carried violins. A dog walked his owner, pulling at the leash.

I made friends with Anne-Marie, a student from Denmark. A married woman in her thirties, she studied French for work. We set out to climb to the top of a nearby peak, the Colline du Castéou, site of the old town. We puffed our way up the long slope, steeper than at first sight. Hot and perspiring at the summit, we gasped for breath, laughing. The countryside stretched out for miles in every direction.

She exclaimed, 'Wow! What a view. It's worth every aching step.'

'The perfect defensive spot, too.'

The brochure told us that a medieval castle had once occupied the site, now a few crumbling walls.

'The missing stones must have created maisons all round the village.'

'It's the championship of France, the football final,' said Hans. 'Like to join Ingrid and me at Toulon to see the fun?' German students, they roomed at chez Mireille, too.

I felt pleased the young couple had asked me. 'Why not?'

We took the bus. Elation and excitement laughed up and down every rue. Multicoloured flags jerked and fixings clanged from the gusts. Pennant-decorated yachts rocked to and fro in the bay. Red T-shirts cheered and shrieked. Shouts of exuberance roamed.

Ingrid giggled. 'Just look at that a tan and black pooch.'

Decked-out in red team colours, it yipped as we passed.

One weekend, I took a bus to St Tropez. It's a peninsula, or tidal island. I prefer the French words, *presqu'île* – almost an island. I wandered narrow, cobbled streets. My photo of the town showed a riot of red poppies dancing against the a radiant blue sky and Mediterranean sea. A white cruise ship rocked at anchor in the bay. International flags of every hue and design fluttered in the breeze. Umbrella palms fronds undulating over red tiled roofs.

Chic window displays made me drool. Their colour coordination, the attention to detail, the pizazz. Yes: I'm biased. A Francophile like me sees nothing but the wonders of this culture. One vitrine, in particular, caught my eye. The back view of a visitor seemed crucial to the exhibit. A colourful shirt, one half floral reds, the other striped red and white, with matching shorts. Her outfit made a perfect foil to other quirky details.

Here, a green and cream ceramic owl chatted to a black metal whippet. There, a yellow ceramic duck quacked beside the young woman's legs. Enraptured by trinkets within *la vitrine*, she would never know of being part of the show. My camera captured the wonderful image for posterity.

Romaine's big day. In pristine white gown, almost to the ground, he strolled off with the family for the official church ceremony, his first communion. That afternoon, our usually mild hostess seemed enraged.

Mireille never said as much, but it was suddenly clear to us that she'd expected Ingrid, Hans and me to absent ourselves from the family home that Sunday. What we'd all taken to be an invitation was her warning to piss off.

Tant pis! Too bad. We'd paid board and lodging for the duration of our course. If she'd been straightforward, or offered to reimburse us for the monies paid in advance, we'd have made other arrangements.

Our hostess flounced around the villa, smoke curling from her ears.

By dinner, Mireille had accepted the inevitable. Three extra places appeared at the table. Speeches brought laughter. *Chansons* and congratulations flowed with glasses of the best French red. Spaghetti and sauce jumped onto plates. Salad and buttered French rolls joined the feast. A choice of strawberry tart with fresh cream and an apple tart with crème fraiche – or both – followed. Yum.

A classic case of the viewer participant; the evening felt surreal. It gave me added insight into French family life, culture and religious practices. I doubted that our presence had made a whit of difference to their pleasure.

ELFCA classes drew to a close. We received our certificates. Mine in the *troisième niveau*. Only in third level. Still, another achievement.

Students moved back to jobs and lives.

I left small gifts for my hostess family. Mireille was absent when I left. She'd made no offer to drive me to L'Hotel des Orangers, where I'd booked a room for Antoine's two-day visit. Departing on foot, I cursed my large and small suitcases, bumping along. Silly me – why hadn't I booked a taxi?

I was meant to meet Antoine at Toulon station that afternoon. But my camera had developed problems with the shutter mechanism. I rushed it to a nearby camera shop, hoping to have it repaired before Antoine's arrival. 'I need this fixed urgently.'

It took longer than expected. My watch told me the worst. Antoine's TGV must have arrived without me.

I wriggled impatience, picturing his dismay and frustration.

At last, they handed the Minolta back. 'In perfect order, Madame.'

'*Merci*, monsieur.'

I rushed to meet Antoine. 'I'm so sorry.'

He glared. 'I've travelled thousands of miles and you weren't here.'

'Sorry I didn't make it on time. Camera issues. Needed it for our European jaunt.'

He scowled.

'How about a G&T before we go to Hyères?'

'That's the best idea I've heard all day.'

I recounted some of my tales. Did I detect a mellowing?

He grinned. 'I can see it couldn't be helped, pet. All is forgiven.'

We caught the Hyères bus. At our hotel, a riot of red and pink geraniums celebrated our arrival.

I took Antoine to my favourite bistro. 'My shout. To make up for this afternoon.'

I introduced him to a couple of my German friends. We practised our French, laughing uproariously.

The 20th of June, my fifty-second birthday. A short ferry ride took us across a bay to the Porquerolles, one of the Golden Isles.

I told Antoine, 'Underwater shipwrecks abound in the area.'

He chuckled. 'I fear my diving days are long gone.'

'Alas! So are mine.'

I took my first bicycle ride: I'd longed for one as a child. A spin around on level ground and we were off. 'Gosh. I hadn't expected it to be so easy,' I giggled. 'A dream realised.'

'At long last, pet.'

We spent a memorable day exploring the island.

The Forte Saint Agathe Exposition brought splendid historical photos of shipwrecks. Roman amphora, retrieved from the ocean depths, came heavily encrusted with shells, barnacles, calcium carbonate.

Antoine shook his head. 'Once they carried wine.'

We lacked time to visit the salt marshes, a haven for waterbirds.

That night, my regretful farewell to Hyères. 'It's been delightful. I loved this village.'

We moved to the Hotel Terminus, at Toulon, a short walk from the station.

Antoine said, 'A good choice, pet. Perfect for our six a.m. departure.'

In the glare of early morning light, we found the numbered carriage of our train. I hefted my large suitcase up into storage, cursing the weight and size. What had possessed me to bring such a monster? My smaller case set me thinking. We sat down, headed for Italy.

Brilliant rays streamed through the train windows.

A young woman and her baby occupied my booked seat. I figured it would all sort itself out before day's end. So I sat in Antoine's place, and he plopped down beside me.

Later that morning, we crossed the Italian border. A guard entered the carriage. He spoke to the young woman in voluble Italian, gesturing towards the empty seats.

I puzzled over the woman's smug expression.

After he'd gone, she smiled at us. 'Most of the seats are booked from here on. You're in the wrong ones. You'll have to go through the train to find others.'

Thankful for my earlier Italian studies, I gave her a withering look. Flashed our tickets. 'No,' I told her in Italian. 'You are in the wrong seat. You are sitting in mine, and this one belongs to my friend. You'll have to look for another place.'

Astonished at my grasp of her native tongue, she left.

'What a cheek.' Antoine shook his head. 'I wonder how often she fails to book?'

'Then tricks tourists into giving up their seats? My suitcase is too heavy to fall for that game.'

We settled back to enjoy the countryside.

An American family occupied the remaining seats. At lunchtime, they stood up, spreading out a small red-checked tablecloth. From a cooler bag emerged cheeses and sliced salami, German sausage, biscuits.

A tall stranger grinned, all grey-speckled hair and teeth. 'You're welcome to join us.'

We contributed tomatoes, cold chicken, cucumbers, bread, tomatoes and butter.

The carriage erupted into laughter. Stories of their adventures jostled with ours. They hailed from Texas.

'We're from Sydney.'

It was one of the best picnics we'd ever enjoyed.

We detrained at Pisa, saying farewell to our new friends.

Antoine sat on a concrete bollard, gazing at the leaning tower. 'Isn't that something? Amazing how it stays upright.'

'Lots of work has stopped it collapsing,' I said. 'But they couldn't afford to make it too straight.'

He chuckled. 'You're right.'

I told of Neville having dragged my son Cedric from the edge, way back in 1975. 'Just grabbed him in time.'

He whistled. 'It's no place for kids.'

Antoine's Gladesville travel agent had booked us L'Hotel California.

The shower water rose almost up to my knees. 'It's a bath, too.'

Antoine blinked awake from a nap. 'Is that so? Could be worse, I guess.' He rubbed his back. 'Don't expect to sleep tonight, though. This mattress is harder than rocks.'

To cap it all, an Israeli and an Arab shared a taxi with us to the Piano Bar Restaurant. Hotly debating the Middle East situation.

Antoine chuckled afterwards. 'I thought another war was about to erupt. What a pair.' He bought our tickets for Florence.

The following day, I shamefacedly admitted, 'I can't find them.'

Antoine frowned. 'Women.' He sought replacements. 'I'll take charge of this lot.'

I dragged my large suitcase along the narrow train corridor. Cursing as I hefted it into high storage.

'You should have let me lift it, pet.' Antoine massaged my painful shoulder muscles.

'No way: you're my senior.'

Something needed to be done. What, was not yet clear to me.

Florence railway station. A long queue surged with youthful travellers, seeking accommodation.

Antoine shot me a smug glance. 'Ours was organised in advance.'

Outside, he consulted a bus driver. 'We need a bus to this farm stay.'

The driver glanced at the address. A frown. 'You'll need two buses.' He gestured towards the distant hills.

Antoine spluttered. 'Two buses? My travel agent has stuffed up again.'

There are moments to keep silent. I never had thought the farm stay was a great idea.

Antoine set his jaw. 'I've made an executive decision.'

Cutting our losses, we walked two blocks.

He spied a sign, 'Rooms available.' Well-maintained, and close to the centre of town, the Hotel il Noveletto was replete with antique furniture. A generous Continental breakfast set us up every day.

Antoine grinned. 'It's reasonably priced and close to restaurants.'

I grinned. 'You've done us proud.'

The beauty of Florence brought joy to my soul. We climbed Brunelleschi's famous Dome. Innovative architectural techniques had reduced the weight of the massive structure. I gazed at marvellous views of the city.

Antoine said, 'You can see why Giotto's bell tower is regarded as a wonder of geometric symmetry. And classical beauty.'

Outside, we studied Ghiberti's renowned doors. A flowing silver moustache assured us it represented a return to spatial realism in Italian art.

My knowing smile. 'Indeed.'

We watched a splendid parade, preceding the medieval football match. A moving spectacle of music colour and superb costumes.

Antoine said, 'The Italians are unmatched in these skill.'

It would have taken months to create costumes – and all perfect. Some men were clad in red and white striped bloomers, red stockings and shoes. A wide pink ribbon crossed the white top under a leather gherkin. Their metal helmets were decorated with golden feathers.

Drummers were clad in yellow and blue striped bloomers with yellow stockings and shoes, along with plain yellow tops and blue undershirts. Drums, edged in red and white, bore a large central red cross on one side, the fleur de lis on the other. Dum de dum…

A staid gentleman carried a white proclamation with yellow lettering: 'Societa di San Giovanna Battista'. Blue bloomers and top, his black hat with pink feathers.

Other young men marched in white and red costume. One, clad all in red, carried a flag. It depicted the fleur de lis and blossoms.

A lady in a long black gown bore important papers. Clerics in cerise vestments with white lace aprons moved in their ceremonial roles.

Antoine said, 'The symbolism is elusive, but against the backdrop of Florentine architecture, carvings and decorations, they're a powerful image.'

We took our places for the historical Florentine football match. It originated in sixteenth-century Italy, and was probably first played in the Piazza Santa Croche.

Antoine's eyes bulged. 'It's unlike any football match I've ever seen. Not that I'm an expert.'

I giggled. 'Football always puzzles me.'

A ritual of blue and red flag-waving preceded the match. Again and again, participants threw their blue or red cross decorated flags into the air, deftly catching them by the flagpoles.

A haze of sapphire smoke clouded the scene. Spectators in the stands wore the red and blue colours of their teams. Bemused visitors like us stood out in our plain attire.

The rituals over, players appeared. Striped bloomers, plain tops. One side in red, the opponents blue. Pugilistic stances.

Antoine shook his head. 'More like boxers than footballers.'

Vanquished players landed on the ground. The winners sat on them. I stifled giggles. Standing players tossed a ball back and forth. Blue-clad fans in the stands leapt up and down with excitement.

Antoine muttered, 'Some people are getting their money's worth.'

I laughed. 'Just enjoy the spectacle.'

He squeezed my hand. 'Doing my best.'

Further pugilistic stances. Ball throwing. All-in-tussles… Fans shook their fists. The score ½ to zero.

Antoine shot me a bewildered glance. 'Can you believe this?'

Cheers from the crowd. Blood on one player's forehead. Warning whistle. Defeated players were sat upon. Applause. Yells. Score 1 to zero.

We shook our heads.

Ecstatic cheers. Flag-waving from the blue side. Score 2–2.

'A draw?' Antoine chuckled, 'What was that all about?'

I laughed. 'Let's call it an experience.'

Canvas-topped market stalls displayed a tantalising variety of goods, from trinkets to treasures. Wine and leather goods. Clothing, handbags. Prints, statues of Michelangelo's *David*. Superb quality masks were arranged against a red background.

One stall-holder glanced at Antoine, then at me, saying, 'She's far too young for you.'

Mock-offended, Antoine later grinned. 'Darned cheek!'

A photo taken of me at the time shows a woman still youthful enough to look good in shorts. She knew nothing of the ravages that time would play on once shapely legs.

Antoine read the pamphlet. 'Venice city of history and mystery.' We found St Mark's Square inundated by tidal water. People took to walkways.

After an excellent continental breakfast at Villa Pannonia, our hotel on the Lido, we boarded the vaporetto (water bus), which stopped nearby and was the perfect way to move around. A cruise took us to the Palazzo Venier du Leoni, on the Grand Canal, former home of Peggy Guggenheim. A guide told us, 'After Peggy's death in 1980, an international group assembled to oversee and preserve her personal collection. The palace is one of the most important museums of European and American art of the twentieth century.'

I loved the Jackson Pollock works, the Impressionist and Post-Impressionist paintings.

Antoine felt less comfortable with some of the modern and contemporary oeuvres. 'But it's an impressive collection, worth millions, no doubt.'

Each day at Villa Pannonia, we greeted one fellow guest, a woman travelling alone. Painted nails, immaculate coiffed hair. Sad eyes. In the gloom of night her sobs haunted thin walls. What sorrows had followed her to Venice? I longed to ease her pain. But how could a stranger invade her privacy? Antoine and I went out of our way to be friendly. Helpless to still her grief.

In the busy harbour, boats of every type sailed crowded waterways. One carried bags of produce, ready for delivery. A white cruise ship lay at anchor. We enjoyed a ride in one of black gondolas. Antoine admired it all. Canal reflections, the multiple bridges, antique architecture.

We explored the famed Bridge of Sighs, Italian Ponte Dei Sospiri. Built about 1600 by the architect Antonio Contino, the enclosed passageway echoed to the sighs of convicted prisoners who passed over a narrow canal, the Rio di Palazzo. It connects to the Doge's palace and old prison.

I shivered. 'The interrogators were notorious for their cruelty.'

We looked forward to a concert of music by the red priest, Vivaldi.

Antoine groaned. 'Would you believe it? All of them are booked out during our visit.' By sheer happenstance, he spied a flyer abandoned on the grass, not far from the Venetian Basilica. 'Eureka! It's for a Vivaldi concert rehearsal.' Antoine shouted in glee. 'Here. This very afternoon. And for free.'

'Shh! Tone it down a bit. People are looking.' I laughed. 'What luck. Buy a lottery ticket.'

He chuckled. 'I will.'

We joined a small audience. Enthusiastic applause for his Sonata No. 6 in E Flat for cello, his Concerto No. 5 in E flat major, *La tempesta di mare* (*The Storm at Sea* or *The Sea Storm*) And much more.

Shop windows brought a treasure trove of Venetian masks.

Antoine said, 'In demand for coming festivals or balls, no doubt.'

Rushing to leave our vaporetto, I left my folding red hat on my seat. 'How will I manage in this heat?'

My Italian language guide, and a smattering of Italian, enabled me to navigate my way to the lost property office. *'Eccoli!* There it is.'

Another find was La Biennale di Venezia (the Vienna Biennale). We wandered through the garden setting, amazed by the dozens of national pavilions.

I said, 'Named for a variety of countries, including Australia.'

Antoine's passion was an architecture exhibition. 'Present and future innovations. Fantastic.'

Impressive paintings and sculptures took my vote.

Deciduous trees wore the fresh green leaves of spring in the Via Giuseppe Garibaldi. They included palms, yews and cypress.

Antoine asked, 'Did you know that the number of gardens in Venice exceeds the four hundred and three bridges?'

My giggle. 'I've never counted them.'

'A lot are hidden behind the walls of palazzos.'

'I can believe that.'

Antoine and I flew on a small plane to visit his friends, the Odiers. On

1 July 1992, we arrived late at the Hotel Noailles, in the Ville de Montpellier.

Antoine frowned back from the check-in. 'Would you believe it? They can't even provide a sandwich for two weary travellers.'

'Can't or won't?'

Tired and ravenous, we trod almost-deserted streets, happy to settle for a pizza.

Back in our room, I sighed. 'Threadbare quilt. Dodgy chest of drawers.' I towelled myself dry. 'The shower's only a dribble of lukewarm water.'

His grin. 'Apart from all that, a five-star hotel.'

That night, Antoine confided, 'It took months for a response to my letter announcing our visit. Marcel wrote, "We'll do our best to see you."'

I chuckled. 'Such enthusiasm.'

'Years of friendship in Queensland. Learning French from Arnyes. It did disappoint me.' His voice trailed away.

'And you her star mature-age student.'

He laughed. 'I enjoyed my time at Montpellier last year. Marcel seemed overjoyed to be home in France, saying, "I'll never again set foot in that cultural desert called Australia."' Antoine added, 'Solenne's their *enfant unique*. Bright girl, full of fun.' His eyes shone. 'Modest.'

'I like her already.'

He mused, 'Three buses to get to their Montpellier maison. Funnily enough, Arnyes never once asked me to stay overnight. I'd have appreciated it, now and then.'

'What do they say? A cynic expects nothing and is never disappointed.'

'Don't be like that.' He chuckled. 'Mind you, she's friendly enough. Teaches German in addition to French. Oh, and she's a cordon bleu cook.'

'Yippee. We've a treat in store.'

7

Ten a.m. The temperature had hit thirty and was on the rise. Hot and sticky, I donned a light cotton dress.

Antoine slipped off his tie. 'That's better.' Adding, 'Did I warn you? Marcel can be over the top.'

'Surely he'll make our tour brief, given this sizzle?'

He laughed. 'I wouldn't count on it, pet.'

Antoine made the introductions.

Marcel tall and dark. Wide grin, gloom in his eyes. Solenne hardly said a word. We'd expected a smiling and vivacious teenager.

Antoine shot me a puzzled glance.

Marcel took the wheel of the Renault. 'Les Matelles is a medieval village. *La crème de la crème* of local attractions. We 'ave to walk when we get there. No cars allowed.'

Heat flared from windows and stone houses. I squinted in the glare. Oh, for my missing sunglasses.

Marcel gestured towards the tiles on a mellow stone building. '*Typique de la region*. Essential for the restoration. Arnyes and I 'ave considered buying this maison.'

Antoine mopped his brow. 'You decided on your bigger place?'

'*Oui*. For Solenne.' He put a protective arm around his daughter's thin shoulders.

The mirage of a smile.

Marcel went on, 'This village dates back to Neolithic times. Evidence of Palaeolithic settlement.' He pointed out *un pharmacie*, a baker

The Pic St Loup restaurant. I longed to step inside the shadowed interior. Hold a tall, frosted glass. Tonic, floating with ice. Lemon and a smidgen of gin.

'This will interest you, Antoine, being a master mariner: the latitude

75

and longitude of Les Matelles are 43.73 degrees north, and 3.809 degrees east. Languedoc-Roussillon region. The Lirou river only flows after heavy rain.'

Antoine gasped to his side. 'Any…any idea of the population?'

Perspiration tickled my breasts. I thought, don't encourage him.

'*Oui, oui. C'est dans la région de 1,000 personnes.*'

On a cooler day, I would have adored those shuttered windows. The lace curtains. A black and white cat licking her paws, enigmatic as a dream.

Marcel led us on and on. His voice loud, insistent. Bullets of historical information ricocheted from stone walls.

Hot and breathless, I struggled up steep streets.

Now and then, Solenne just appeared beside us, in a conspiracy of silence with the cobblestones.

I wiped my damp brow. When would this *cauchemar* end?

Blaze of sun. Not a breath of air.

Marcel indicated a prickle of dried Chardon on one of the doors. 'How do you say it in *Anglais*?'

Antoine peered closer. 'Thistles?'

'Ah, *oui*. Thistles. Middle Age custom. Wards off evil spirits.' His odd laugh. 'Now, if you go back…'

Oh for the sanctuary of the Odier maison, I thought The air con on maximum. Tucking into Arnyes's superb lunch.

A small chapel.

'Designed and made by local artisans.' Marcel gave the stone and mortar details.

Antoine nodded, flushed and breathing hard.

Scarlet and gold glass patterned the polished floor. I swayed in the aroma of incense, savouring a small respite. The others moved on. I rushed to catch up.

Marcel glanced at the village clock '*Mon dieu!* It's after midday. Arnyes will be waiting.' He loomed above us. 'You 'ave liked the village?'

Antoine mopped his dripping brow. '*Charmant.*'

Revived by the Renault's cool air, I asked Solenne, 'Was it hard settling into your Lycée Française ater Queensland schools?'

Solenne opened her mouth.

Marcel's voice boomed into the space where she might have spoken. 'Look to your right. See the beauty of le Pic St Loup? The peak of the wolf.' A haze of blue. 'Notice the contrast with the yellow of those sunflowers. Magnificent, aren't they?'

In the glare, they seemed vulgar and overdone.

Antoine said, 'You must be happy being back in La Belle France, Marcel?'

'Appy? *En Australie* one lives. Here? Ouf.'

'You should have stayed in Brisbane, old boy.'

'If it hadn't been for the education of Solenne. Her baccalaureate.'

Guilt flitted across his daughter's pale face.

Without warning, his Renault swerved, aimed straight for a van.

'Watch out,' shouted Antoine.

I gripped the back seat, mouth parched. Seconds, stretched into hours. Expecting a crumple of metal, the spinning out of control.

At the last moment, Marcel jerked the wheel. The van whizzed past, blasting a protest.

Hairs stood up on the back of my neck.

Solenne trembled, white as her top.

Marcel's silly laugh. 'That Frog should learn to drive.'

I shivered. Why was he acting as if he's not French? And it wasn't the other guy's fault.

A wide entrance drive swept towards a low-set villa. Weeping cypress. The scent of red roses. Lavender abuzz with bees.

'Clara, we meet at last. *Enchantée.'* Arnyes offered her pinched little face, for the traditional peck on either cheek.

Shaken, I found myself enunciating every word. 'Lovely…to… meet…you…Arnyes.'

She waved me to a big leather sofa. I admired a sixteenth-century gilded mirror.

Her tight little smile. 'From Venice. Quite rare.'

Marcel chose a piano concerto. '*La Naufrage.*'

The shipwreck. A shiver ran up my spine.

She pursed her lips. 'Lately, Marcel plays little else.'

Antoine turned to Marcel. 'I hear you're on a roll with your computer business?'

A moment's hesitation. '*Oui.*'

Antoine whistled. 'Lucky you.'

Marcel opened the gilt-decorated cocktail cabinet. 'Whisky, Antoine?'

I sipped a G&T. Solenne, silent as ever, offered olives and savoury biscuits.

Arnyes showed me family photos. 'Our wanderings in the Pacific and Americas.'

'My, you've been everywhere.'

Happy pics. A world away from the anxiety that prickled around me.

Marcel drummed his fingers on the table. 'How's the employment situation in Australia?'

Antoine nursed his whisky and dry. 'Grim. Lots of jobs are gone for good.'

Arnyes bit her lip. 'But, surely, if someone tried…'

'Much of our manufacturing industry has gone to China. Even tourism is in trouble with this recession.'

Arnyes said, 'The college here cut my German teaching hours by a third. I feel like quitting.'

'Stay put until you find something better.' Antoine chuckled. 'Of course, unemployment is unlikely to trouble you.'

They shared a troubled glance.

She rose. 'We're dining on the terrace.'

Was Arnyes kidding? But, no, Antoine made to follow.

I lingered in the cool. A movement made me look up. Surprised to see Solenne, hesitating, near me. I had the feeling she was about to ask – or tell me – something. 'What is it, dear?'

Marcel appeared, bringing the wine. 'Come along, Solenne. Your mother needs help.'

Solenne's cheeks flamed.

Marcel waved us into the broiling sun.

Gleaming silver and glassware winked in the brazen light. A gold cloth sighed with matching napkins. Forget-me-nots sagged in a crystal vase. I puzzled. What had driven Solenne to approach a stranger? And Marcel's peremptory interruption seemed odd.

In the throb and the glare, our host poured the Sauvignon blanc. 'It's the dry white you enjoyed so much last year.'

Antoine forced a smile. 'Excellent.' He turned to me. 'Marcel's a wine expert.'

Perspiration trickled. 'Lucky us.'

A mousse wobbled on its dish, sweating drops of moisture.

Arnyes cut me a large slice. 'Start before it melts. *Bon appetit.*'

I forced myself to eat it. Gagging over the claggy taste and snippets of vegetables. Oh, for freshly steamed broccoli and carrots.

Solenne looked desolate. No wonder, I thought, surrounded by oldies, A pity her parents hadn't invited a school chum.

Antoine leant towards her. 'I expect you're involved in all sorts of activities with your school pals?'

Marcel butted in. 'Sol has little time for friends. Too much study.'

I blinked. 'What a pity.'

'Top of *la première* class.' Arnyes beamed.

'Congratulations, Solenne.' We said. 'Well done.'

That fleeting smile.

The second course: a salmon the size of the *Queen Mary*. A few wilting morsels of lettuce and halved cherry tomatoes, decorations.

Antoine's eyes bulged. 'What a delicacy.'

I liked salmon. But not in that frizzle. Not without vegetables. Or a decent salad. A few drops of lemon juice might help? None.

Marcel cut each of us an enormous portion.

Arnyes's sauce was bound to be superb. I poured myself some. The bitter taste took me by surprise. A mini French Revolution began between my stomach and the food. A second glass of Marcel's superb wine might do the trick. One empty bottle. No offer of another.

Marcel leant back in his chair. 'We want Solenne to attend an American university. Maybe Yale.'

'But first *vendre la maison*.' Arnyes twisted her wedding ring.

Antoine struggled to finish his slice of salmon. 'You're selling this lovely home?'

Marcel shrugged. 'Solenne's university studies. We must go to America with her.'

I chuckled, 'Surely your daughter would prefer to tackle tertiary education on her own?'

The warmth of Solenne's real smile.

Arnyes gasped. 'Impossible. We do everything as a family.'

I longed to shout, 'Children grow up, leave home. You can't keep her bound to you forever.'

'And now for the *pièce de resistance*,' said Marcel. 'Arnyes's famous peach pie.'

The lightest of pastry might have helped. A heavy, undercooked slice. My digestive system roiled. Coffee added an extra nuance to my distress.

Thank the Lord, lunch was over. I tottered to the sofa, stifling burps. Antoine covered a yawn.

Marcel grinned. 'You'll want to see the vineyards. A walk will do us all good.'

Antoine shoved on his hat. A sweltering white road. One minute, Marcel extolled the virtues of the region. The next, lamented the stupidity of some French custom. You'd have thought he was separate from the Gallic race.

Grapevines wilted in the heat. I dragged one foot after another.

Solenne walked in some space of her own. Overlapping all of us. Or so it seemed to me on that surreal afternoon.

'It's great to see Antoine again,' said Arnyes. 'He seems years younger since you've met.' She glanced around, as if making sure not to be over-heard. 'I often asked him to come and stay when he was in France last year. He never would.'

I gaped. Her lie shimmered on the oppressive air.

Arnyes added, 'You were lucky to find someone when your husband died. I'd be lost if anything happened to Marcel.'

The cliché, life goes on, was the best I could offer. 'Uh… Have you made many friends?'

'Friends?' Her voice was edged with bitterness. 'When you've trav-elled as much as we have…'

'Locals aren't interested?'

'Huh! They're jealous.'

Back at the villa, I slumped onto the sofa, accepting a glass of pep-permint cordial. Not the best idea. Somewhere a kitten wailed.

Solenne made to rise.

Marcel snapped, 'No, leave it.' His eyes glittered. 'Antoine, I need books from London.' He dictated a long list. Obscure existential works in English. Journeys out of the body. Texts on near death experiences, NDEs, life after death.

Arnyes bit her nails. 'I do think you have enough.'

Marcel said, 'Get paperbacks, Antoine. Nothing over $12.50.'

The kitten's wails went on and on. Her father's attention diverted, Solenne crept from the room. A door creaked. Her furtive return. Feline silence.

Arnyes muttered, 'Marcel's always wasting money on those sorts of things. I don't understand most of them.' She stopped. 'It's kind of An-toine to buy them.'

Antoine cleared his throat, about to raise a delicate matter. 'How do you mean to pay?'

Marcel blinked. 'I…uh…have we the cash?'

Flecks of anger flashed in Arnyes's small eyes. 'No.'

They settled on a credit card number.

Never had I heard a lovelier sound than the clack of seat belts.

Marcel said, 'If only you'd been staying three or four days. We could have climbed the Pic St Loup.' He extolled picnics we might have enjoyed. Visits to monuments. 'There's so much to see and do around here.'

Outside our hotel, I groaned. The Renault disappeared. 'Thank God.'

Antoine chuckled. 'I was on the verge of offering to stay.'

'Don't even think of it. I'm in agony. That ghastly meal.'

'Nothing adds up.' A shake of his head. 'Solenne's silence.'

'She tried to tell me something.'

'Let me guess: Marcel interrupted.'

'They barely let her utter a word. What's going on?'

'Teenage issues? Marriage woes?' He shrugged. 'I can give you advice about real estate and the stock market. Don't ask me about relationships.'

I laughed. 'So you've told me.'

We took the train to La Séguinière, Cholet, a commune in the Maine-et-Loire department of western France.

'We've been penfriends for years.' I reminded Antoine. 'Andrée's a pharmacist. I can't wait for us to meet.'

Her husband Louis lived up to his splendid moustache: friendly and welcoming. The three girls, Anne, Céline and Thérèse were sweet and charming – *mignonne,* as the French say.

We were greeted like long-lost family, their hospitality nothing short of amazing. Whisky and the finest French wines appeared at breakfast, lunch and supper. Along with salads, chicken or slow-cooked beef. Potatoes au gratin, a classic dish. Quiche… A tarte tartin. Oh, those superb meals.

Photos of Antoine and me with a backdrop of a weeping conifer show us at our smiling best.

'It's lovely to see this family so relaxed and happy,' he said to me later. 'After the Odiers.'

I shivered. 'Something's terribly wrong there.'

He groaned. 'I can't figure it out.'

We toured historical Cholet. Amazed that old buildings still bore the scars of the French Revolution.

Our friends told us, 'You'll enjoy a wonderful historical show of this region tonight.'

Antoine grinned. 'Bring it on.'

At Le Puy de Fou theme park, tourist coaches from Britain and other European countries massed, row upon row, along with private vehicles. The car park was crammed to the very last space. Crowds poured into the stands.

Andrée told us, 'This sound and light spectacular is the most amazing re-creation of times past.' She smiled. 'The creator, Phillipe de Villiers, calls it an artistic, cultural and spiritual adventure.'

Louis nodded. 'A heartfelt accord of a people with antiquity.'

The glitter of stars hid behind a grumble of clouds. The *brume* failed to dampen our enthusiasm.

Louis told us, 'Just fifteen hectares, Antoine. Host to hundreds of actors, a brace of cavaliers and thousands of locals in costume.' Adding, 'The epic begins in the Middle Ages. Told through the eyes of elder members of the Maupillier family, century through century. The oldest son is always called Jacques.'

A hush of anticipation. Firelight flickers on Jacques's face. He shares the tales passed down to him by his ancestors. Memories shared with his son of the same name. 'Listen, little one, listen…' Images form in the child's mind, mixed and melded in ours.

Music, movement and colour. Watchers gasp as one scene unfolds into another. Heads turn this way and that. Gasps. Knights gallop on horses clad in caparisons, embroidered with the owners coat of arms. A haystack becomes the retreat for lovers. Giggles and laughter ripple across the stands. The wonder of a carrousel, spinning on a lake. Geese wobble by, wagging tail feathers.

In 1793, a revolt begins. Jarring music. Peasants rush from town to town to garner support. Soldiers join the fray. Insurrection ignites. Hand-to-hand fighting from St-Fulgent all the way to Cholet. Explosions and screams rent the air. Smoke and gunfire. In a scene of Cinemascope proportions, the Puy du Fou Chateau takes its final breath. Engulfed by flames.

One fine day, peace, joy and life returns. A merry accompaniment from the musicians, explodes into colour and crackles. Fireworks light the night sky.

'Formidable!' Antoine spoke for both of us. 'An unforgettable evening.'

Next day, we hugged our French family farewell at Cholet Railway station.

We travelled through the delights of forest and town of the French countryside. By Paris, we had convinced ourselves.

'Solenne's silence is an adolescent stage she's going through.'

I hefted my monster suitcase down from overhead storage. Mutters of discontent. 'One of us has to go. I've had enough of this…this…'

'Bête noire?' Antoine laughed. 'Let's air freight your black beast home.'

In Paris, I transferred a selection of clothing into my smaller case. 'More than adequate to see me back to Stacey Street.'

A last ride for the monster suitcase. Wheels rattled over cobblestones. The promised airport bus took ages to arrive. We shifted from one foot to the other. Checked our watches.

Antoine groaned, 'Where is that jolly bus? You have to laugh or…'

'You cry.' To my consternation, I burst into tears.

Antoine patted me. 'There, there, pet.

Two knights of the road, *camion* drivers, stepped forward. 'May we help?' Chivalrous to a fault, they offered to drive us to the airport in their truck.

Antoine's widest smile. 'That's very kind of you.'

We could scarcely believe our luck. Friendly and fun, they chatted all the way to the Charles de Gaulle airport, Paris main freight CDG Air.

Les hommes departed with a wave and 'Good luck.'

We talked our way to the appropriate office. An official named a price. My French francs were at the ready. They proved insufficient. I brought forth funds from my travelling bank: two calico pouches, fastened to my bra. Blouse lifted, I peeled off notes. The bald clerk didn't blink an eye.

At last, a sufficient number of francs lay on his desk. His fingers made a rapid check. Wrote out my receipt.

Outside the building, Antoine did the sums, and whistled. 'Five hundred dollars.'

I shot him a rueful glance. 'Why didn't I give my clothes away, suitcase and all?'

'Never mind, pet. We're sharing expenses.'

Roads led off in every direction.

Antoine clutched his head. 'Where's a bus or taxi to the railway station and Paris?'

In a nearby car park, he spotted a lady in a Citroën Deux Chevaux. She had the motor running, about to leave. He explained our problem.

Madame offered to drive us to the station.

I smiled. '*Merci*, madame. That's very kind of you.'

Dropped off, I felt a marvellous lightness of being.

Antoine watched Madame drive away. 'Great little car. Air-cooled front-engine. Front-wheel drive. The French call it a TPV…*très petite voiture*, very small car.'

I was only half-listening. A monster was on the way home. Too bad that it had gulped so many of my French francs.

The Louvre was on our list. Arguably, most famous for da Vinci's *Mona Lisa* and the splendid *Victoire de Samothrace*, the *Winged Victory of Samothrace*. I couldn't resist a second look.

'Also known as the Greek goddess of victory,' Antoine said. 'Incredible to think that this beautiful work dates back to the second century BC.'

I blinked. 'Are you making that up?'

'No, no. I read it in my *Short History of Paris*.

Hand in hand, we wandered on.

Bastille Day, the fourteenth of July.

The roar of French air force jets. I jumped out of bed, just in time to see them zoom past our makeshift clotheslines, at the window. Glimpsed between my knickers and Antoine's under-daks.

Antoine had his head in his book.

'Let's hurry to breakfast. Watch the parade.'

We took the metro for the centre of Paris, and the Avenue des Champs-Élysées. I pictured hoof beats. *La Marseillaise*, the French national anthem. A gleam of sunlight blinked from metal helmets. Immaculate soldiers' uniforms.

We arrived to piles of horse manure, steaming in the crisp morning air.

Antoine chuckled. 'Do you get the feeling we've missed it?'

I laughed. 'Did you bring your spade? This would be fine for my garden.'

On a quay by the Seine, we saw a lithe Parisian woman dancing. Long titian hair, lovely face. There may have been other dancers, but we saw only one.

In a small bistro that evening, we clinked glasses of Sauvignon blanc. 'Here's to plans gone astray.' Laughing until the tears ran down our cheeks.

In the Bois de Boulogne gardens, we explored the lake.

'Oh, look,' I said. 'One can hire rowing-boats.'

Horse riders trotted by on the winding trails.

Antoine pointed out oak, cedar, beech and plane trees. 'Aha! Here's a perfect picnic spot, under this elm tree.'

We devoured chicken and mayonnaise sandwiches.

Antoine surprised me. 'The Bois de Boulogne was formerly part of the forest of Rouvray. Named for the type of oak trees once found here, the *quercus robur*. It surrounded the Gallo-Roman city of Lutece. Used to be a monks' hunting grounds.'

'Wow! You've been reading history again,' I laughed. 'You're a virtual encyclopaedia.'

He shrugged. 'I like to know these things.'

A blonde woman of a certain age caught my eye. 'Tanned like a suitcase. Don't look now.'

He looked.

The lady cavorted with her decades younger boyfriend. Gold glittered at her wrists and throat. He massaged sunscreen onto her back and arms. Brought her drinks and treats. Serenaded her with his guitar. She relaxed with the contented air of a Siamese cat.

Lounging in the shade, Antoine suppressed chuckles. 'A perfectly trained toy boy.'

I giggled. 'Where do I find one?'

A grin. 'You'll have to make do with me.'

8

We celebrated Antoine's sixty-seventh birthday at the Renault Restaurant in the Avenue des Champs Élysées. I shared memories of a former visit. 'Neville dined with me here way back in 1973. A lifetime ago.' I wiped my eyes.

'There, there, pet.'

He praised the courteous and attentive staff. Our dinner, coq au vin, chicken with mushrooms in a red wine sauce, was perfect. Coffee crème brûlée proved a winner, too. We splurged on huge glasses of a delicious cocktail, laced with Cointreau.

Thus ended a special day, and our time in France.

A stop-off at Dover to visit my old friends, Nancy and Dave Davies. Their splendid black cat looked at us with haughty eyes, as if to say, 'What are you doing here?'

Dave grinned. 'Heckle is a superior sort of feline, not one to stroke without prior invitation.'

We laughed.

Nancy said, 'I called him Atticus, from *To Kill A Mockingbird*. But he yowled and miaowed for food so often as a kitten, Dave dubbed him Heckle. It stuck.'

They'd retired from their nursery business. Demolished that wonderful three-hundred-year-old coaching house built from flint.

Dave grinned. 'The wreckers discovered a long-unused well under the kitchen floor.'

Modest Sunset Bungalow had welcomed them home.

Nancy said, 'This cottage is exactly what we needed.'

Dave, in his nineties, proudly drove his ride-on mower.

Around the patio danced a riot of peonies, daffodils, freesias. Elm trees stretched limbs towards the skies. Cypresses lined the drive.

'Your garden is really something.'

'I'm pleased the way it's grown. 'Nancy smiled, adding, 'and, by the way, I'm glad you and Antoine are an item.'

We chuckled at Dave's tale of being bitten by a wasp. 'They don't bite once like a bee. Keep right on stinging.'

His remarkable capacity for understatement amused us.

'Felt so bad I had to sit down.'

Heckle eventually descended from his throne to rub against my legs. I ran a hand down his shiny fur. 'You know I like cats.'

Nancy drove us to Canterbury. 'It's regarded as one of the most beautiful and historic cities in England.' The cathedral dated to AD 597. 'It's been a European pilgrimage site since the assassination of Archbishop Thomas à Becket in 1170.'

We eyed the magnificent stained glass and antique stonework. For a Brit like Antoine, it was a treat to revisit this ancient site.

I said, 'My son Cedric was blessed over the tomb of Thomas à Becket, way back in 1973. He's since become a Christian.'

Antoine looked thoughtful. 'Wonder if the two are linked? Not that I'm a believer.'

London brought us a special treat. Dinner with my Royal Prince Alfred Hospital fellow graduate, Barbara. Our previous meeting had been the graduation, back in 1962. That final, heady day rushed back.

She said, 'Four long years slog as probationer nurses. The culmination, a group of veiled graduates, ready for presentation of certificates. Oh, the speeches and excitement that day.'

I nodded. 'Parents and friends travelled from far away. Some from interstate and overseas.' We'd never forget the aroma of roses, lavender, jasmine and other blossoms from fine bouquets. I told Antoine, 'They tantalised the nostrils in the seniors' corridor at Queen Mary Nurses' Home.'

'I'll bet. All you lovely young things on the cusp of your nursing careers.'

Eyes shone anew, dining in Barbara's sleek Wimpole Street apartment. Hugs and giggles made years of separation crumble and vanish. I'd always admired Barbara for her *joie de vivre* and charm.

Antoine, too, fell under her spell.

We admired Barbara's paintings by old masters. Reminisced about training days. Laughed over the ups and downs of our European adventures.

Sipping the finest white wine, we enjoyed a superb meal of veal saltimbocca and steamed vegetables.

Antoine, all mature charm, grinned. 'My dear, your veal was perfection. It jumped in my mouth.'

Barbara giggled. 'I'm glad to hear it.'

After midnight, we reached our Knightsbridge serviced apartments, mellow and happy. 'A perfect evening.'

One final European treat: Daniel Lloyd Webber's *The Phantom of the Opera*, at Her Majesty's Theatre. An unforgettable spectacle. I especially liked that haunting 'Music of the Night,' sung by the incredible Sarah Brightman, a voice I cherished in the original performance and in memory. The theme of the musical, a difference between appearance and reality, revealed many different layers of human interaction. Did Christine really love the Phantom?

Later, in Sydney, someone happened to mention *The Phantom*.

'Yes, we saw that in London,' I said, little realising it would be taken as showing off.

The flight home, with a stopover at Singapore. The underground train impressed us with its spacious width and glass safety doors at stations. Tropical flowers had me in ecstasies. Pleased that Antoine made a point of taking me to the lovely orchid gardens at Raffles Hotel.

Famous for its Singapore sling, staff told us, 'Our cocktail was developed in 1913 by Ngiam Tong Boo, a bartender here at the time.' He added, 'There was an earlier version in 1897. It predates the Raffles recipe by twenty years.'

We tried the Ngiam Tong Boo recipe. It contains gin, Benedictine, cherry brandy and fresh pineapple juice. There's one word for it. Wow!

Back at Wattle Grove, I shared stories of my adventures with old friends, staff and residents.

One of the oldies said, 'Few of my generation could afford to leave Australia. It wasn't easy before jet travel.'

My tales of foreign lands fascinated them. The age of flight and the 747 had widened horizons for so many, including our cleaner and the cook.

I mourned patients who had died in my absence. They included my favourite, Molly.

Elsie said, 'She was ready to go. Feisty until the end.'

'That's what I liked most about her. A lovely lady.'

Elsie asked me about Bastille Day.

I decided, best keep it simple. 'There was a flypast of French jets.'

Her eyes sparkled. '*Oui.*'

'A troop of horses paraded down l'Avenue des Champs Élysées.'

'*Oui, oui.*'

'Drums, hoof beats. *La Marseillaise.*' I laughed. 'Dancing on the quays. You get the picture, Elsie.'

Her gaze stretched wider than Paris skies. 'If only I'd been there.'

I fancy further explanation might have spoilt the story.

We resumed French classes. Friends chuckled over our stories, and reminisced over their own travelling adventures.

Months passed.

Now and then our thoughts strayed to the family at Montpellier.

Antoine groaned. 'I'll never forget that heat. Marcel bombarding us with details of les Matelles.'

'Me at death's door from that dreadful lunch. Solenne's silence.'

'The way Marcel wouldn't let her speak.'

I shivered. 'What's he got to hide?'

'We'll never know, pet.'

In 1993, Antoine joined me on a trip to West Australia. Our thirty-first RPAH reunion. Friends from the Class of '62 planned to gather at the Royal Perth Yacht club.

He grinned. 'Sounds good to me.'

My jittery drive to the airport. I parked in a side street. 'Wish I'd learnt earlier.'

Antoine said, 'What would Neville have done if you'd insisted?'

I shrugged. 'Life is seldom cut and dried, Antoine. His doubts danced with my fears.' A sigh. 'Will I ever feel relaxed behind the wheel?'

Antoine grinned, indicating the TGV number plate. 'Soon you'll be driving your red car like a Toyota Grande Vitesse.'

'The super-fast French train?' A giggle. 'Maybe not.'

We both laughed.

A taxi deposited us at the domestic terminal. My pal Bella, a fellow RPAH graduate, joined us.

On the flight to Perth, we had crossed the rich, wooded countryside of Victoria, then the Great Australian Bight.

Bella said, 'A marked contrast to dry vistas of Western Australia. And the rolling hills of Adelaide.'

We had traversed the archipelago of Esperance.

'Named for a French ship which had taken shelter from a storm,' I said.

Bella spoke for all of us. 'So many hours. Still in the same continent.'

Antoine grinned. 'Makes one appreciate Australia's size.'

The Chateau Commodore Hotel. 'Three stars,' I said, 'and three minutes on foot from the centre of town.'

Antoine nodded. 'You've chosen well, pet.'

I loved the way Perth's glass skyscrapers reflected and distorted images. 'Like part of some art installation. It mixes and melds light with shadows.'

Bella smiled. 'I'm intrigued by the contrast between old brick buildings and modern ones.'

A ferry took us to Rottnest Island. Indigenous people called it Wadjemup. We admired the spectacular views of sea and sky. Glitter danced on every wavelet, bringing a palette of blue and green. Morton Bay fig tree shadows dappled the walls of attractive houses. Transforming them into moving images.

Our guide pointed out their yellowish beige hue. It made a pleasing contrast with the deep blue sky. 'Originally, they were painted white,' he said. 'People found the glare unbearable, hence the colour we see today.'

Narrow strips of lath, alternating with equal gaps, were screwed between veranda posts.

The guide told us, 'The design welcomes every breeze. But helps prevent intruder access.'

Recent and rather ugly houses occupied a grid pattern.

'Built for tourism,' the guide explained. 'Luckier guests are billeted in that octagonal building.'

A fine structure, it was enhanced by a narrow veranda, around a central courtyard.

'In May 2018, it would become a memorial to all the Indigenous men who fought to defend their homeland.'

Tourists roamed the island on hired bicycles. I suspect few of them knew of the island's terrible history. It had left me with mixed feelings about making the visit.

Aboriginal prisoners were kept in wretched little cubicles. The only light, from a grating in the door. Fed a poor diet: horses fared better, given vegetables.

'The first white settlers sailed up the Swan river in 1829.' Noongar people thought they were Aboriginal ancestors, bleached from being under the sea. 'Within three years of the invaders' arrival, indigenous people were pushed off their land.' Fences were built; springs blocked. Animals were driven from hunting grounds. 'Land grabs affected most Aboriginal settlements. The Noongar fought back, but were no match for muskets. Their culture taught them that animals belonged to the land, available for the taking. Facing starvation from lack of wildlife, Noongar men speared sheep, cattle and pigs. Outraged owners demanded action. The prison on Rottnest Island was meant to address the problem of tribal men, charged with these crimes.'

In 1838, about a dozen Noongar men became prisoners at Wadjemup. They were free to hunt, clear the bush and garden. But Henry Vincent, the new superintendent, changed all that.

'He beat men to death with the cat-o'-nine-tails. Shot them at will. Hanged prisoners, letting them swing in the howling winds, to warn others. Chained inmates at night. And, all the while, the Noongar men laboured, building their own prison.'

Visitors shivered at these shocking tales.

'Whites gathered the men with no thought of tribe, religion, language or culture. Chained by the neck, hands and feet. Up to ten prisoners were jammed into tiny cells, with no toilets. Beds were the damp dirt floor. Disease was rife.'

Antoine frowned. 'Small wonder prisoners burnt down their lock-up.'

'Authorities wanted the governor to construct a series of humpies as replacement. But Vincent had his slave labourers build the octagonal building which you see before us. Hundreds of prisoners died in the old hospital turned morgue. The deaths-in-custody burial site was first a camping ground. Later, a road was built over former prisoners bones.'

I shuddered, recalling one Indigenous leader's words from a recent documentary, 'Unrespected. Unsuspected. Under the white man's road,'

Scooping a handful of sand, I let it float away on the briny air. Hoping that this Indigenous custom might release souls of the dead.

The guide told of one visitor's nightmare: 'Blood ran down the walls of her room.'

I shivered.

Antoine spoke for all of us. 'The Noongar people were right. Wadjemup is a sad place.'

Among redeeming features were quokka, small marsupials.

Our guide told us, 'They're lovable, but rarely seen elsewhere. In old age, they resemble huge rats. Hence the island's name.'

Another positive, Wadjemup is a sanctuary for birdlife. Black and white seagulls and marauding crows caught my eye. Twitchers told us they had spotted wedge-tailed shearwaters, eastern osprey, curlew sandpipers, red-capped dotterel. Cameras clicked. Good pairs of binoculars are essential. They scribbled in their notebooks. We left twitchers to an exciting afternoon's bird watching, and rushed for our boat.

Back in Perth, Miss Maude's Swedish restaurant helped us to put aside raw memories of Rottnest. A superb smorgasbord breakfast included every type of cereal, fruit juices, bacon, eggs, sausages, scrambled egg, breads, cake.

'And all at $12.50.' Antoine grinned. 'Tuck in. It's a steal.'

Bella, a keen gardener, admired the city's street plantings. Kangaroo paw whispered to casuarina. Everlasting daisies swayed beside eucalypts and grass trees.

'You're right,' I said, 'Native species give Perth a unique Australian identity, lacking in Sydney.'

Trinity Church provided a bring your own food café, a fund-raising undertaking. A sign invited us to give as little or as much as you wished. One only paid for drinks.

Antoine and I brought cut lunches. Strawberries, blue cheese, bananas… The bearded man at an adjoining table gazed at our repast, drinking a single cup of tea.

Antoine grinned. 'Care to join us, mate?'

'Are… Are you sure?'

'Of course. We've more than enough.'

Down on his luck, lonely. We left him laughing.

'That was kind of you, Antoine.'

'I'm glad I asked him. Poor beggar.'

The following day, we gathered at the Royal Perth Yacht Club, Pelican Point. Husbands and partners brought a masculine dimension to our RPA reunion.

I giggled. 'Commander A.M. Christie, retired sea captain, don't you know?'

Someone gushed, 'Don't we all look good? A few extra kilos here. Grey hair there. Deeper lines are to be expected.'

Antoine grinned. 'An elegant bunch, the lot of you. And full of fun.'

Over a superb luncheon we sipped fine wines. Laughed, sharing reminiscences of life as probationer nurses.

Bella said, 'We shared the darkest moments of our patients' lives, and our own. Endured the humiliation of harsh reprimands by sisters and senior nurses.'

Someone added, 'Workplace bullying was the norm. Many of the sisters were unmarried, losing boyfriends and fiancés in World War II.'

In retrospect, even our worst experiences brought hoots of laughter.

Antoine and I rose early for an eight a.m. start.

Bella grinned. 'Margaret River, here we come.'

He chuckled. 'I can't wait to savour some of its famous wines.'

Jokes and laughter sped us on our journey.

The racist humour of our coach driver, Craig, brought frowns. Jibes directed at Aboriginals made me boil. Likewise, his traffic-light game soon palled. 'Think green, green, green…'

Margaret River township was dubbed Margaret Rivs by locals.

Craig vaguely pointed. 'Possible lunch venues.'

I groaned. Well-organised companies radioed or phoned ahead.

Soup? Sandwiches? A tasty meal would be ready on arrival, with no waste of precious time.

We gulped down a hasty snack. Made a lightning tour of a great little gallery, in lieu of a more relaxed visit. Took our seats on the bus. Craig indicated the outside of an amazing mud-brick church. Cameras whirred.

Antoine shook his head. 'It warrants more than a quick click through the coach window.'

We reached the chosen vineyard.

Antoine grabbed his bag. 'Boy, I've been looking forward to this.' He sipped several reds. Grimaced. 'I could have bought better, and cheaper, at our local.'

The day sagged into night. Nine thirty p.m. yawned on the long, winding road back to our hotel.

Craig stopped at some anonymous little town. 'There's the place for a cuppa, folks.'

The garish and glitzy exterior put us off.

Antoine said, 'A fast-service cup of tea won't do it for me.'

Revived by a G&T from the local pub, we chuckled our way back to the bus.

One of the other passengers complained about Craig's advice. 'My tea was stone-cold.'

Bella giggled. 'Poor you.'

Antoine described the pool at our hotel. 'It's so small you have to put in one leg at a time.'

Everyone laughed. Suddenly, even the weakest joke became funny. Good, bad or indifferent, we chuckled.

The company's lack of organisation on the Margaret Rivs jaunt made us reconsider Craig's tour to Wave Rock the following day.

Antoine teased. 'Don't be rash, girls. Remember, there's a dog cemetery.'

I picked up another brochure. 'This one sounds more our style. A wildflower viewing and visit to a Benedictine monastery. Leaving tomorrow morning. What do you say, guys?'

We joined our eighteen-person coach heading for New Norcia, the only monastic town in Australia.

On the way out of Perth, I spied a block of flats called Decima Court. 'Wow!' I cried. 'It honours Decima Norman, MBE.'

Bella giggled. 'Who might she be?'

'An Olympian. The only woman to win five gold medals for athletics at the British Empire Games in 1938.' Her stature had surprised me. 'She barely topped five foot two.'

Antoine chuckled. 'What do they say about good things and small packages?'

An elderly lady said, 'Melbourne is amazingly clean,' The fine bones of her face indicated a youthful beauty. Hair scooped elegantly at the back of her head, navy-blue velvet bow.

'We haven't been to Melbourne,' said her husband.

'Oh! I meant Perth.'

At an intersection, we noticed squashed metal, near gardens of yellow everlasting daisies.

'A beer can. The first I've seen,' said the husband.

A derelict spied it at the same time. He unsteadily leant over and picked it up.

'That's remarkable,' said the husband. 'Even Perth derelicts take pride in their city.'

Scarcely had the words left his lips than the vagrant lifted the squashed can to his lips. An expression of bliss suffused his lined face.

Eighteen pairs of eyes watched in horrified fascination. Eighteen people held their breaths. What would he do with the can once he'd sucked those last few drops?

He flung it into the garden, of course.

The bus shook with mirth.

Sarah berated her grey-haired husband. 'You never take the right photographs. Always the wrong angles.'

'Here you are, m'dear. 'He handed her the camera. 'You take them.'

'Huh! Not with that old thing.'

Sarah told the bus, 'We always travel first class – or did. I can't fly now. Last time the pain in my ears hurt like an abscess. Four days, to cross the desert by train.'

More than a hundred-kilometre drive awaited. We relaxed for the duration.

9

New Norcia's Art Museum took everyone by surprise.

The velvet-bow lady said, 'I didn't expect European masterpieces in such an isolated location.'

Julieta, our guide, smiled. 'We're indeed lucky.' She added that a number of valuable paintings had recently been stolen. 'Cut from frames with Stanley knives and rolled up. They've been recovered, but in a sorry state.'

Antoine groaned. 'A big task for restorers?'

'Indeed. But our team are determined to get there.' She explained that the monastery was founded by monks from Spain in the 1800s.

We admired objects and photographs from the period. Those au fait with the tongue marvelled at the perfect Spanish in certain letters. 'Written by two Aboriginal boys educated in the Holy City.'

A delicious lunch of steak and salad at the hotel lifted my energy levels.

Bella savoured her tea. 'Gosh! I needed that.'

Antoine glanced around. 'The old building cries out for repair.'

Like many other jewels of European culture at New Norcia, I thought.

Thrilled to find Spanish-style architecture in the Australian wilderness, we admired the magnificent cupola.

Antoine said, 'Painted by a Spanish monk, on his back à la Michelangelo.'

Frescoes and elaborate altarpiece had been imported from Spain.

Julieta told us, 'St Gertrude's College, built in the Gothic Revival style, was once a girls boarding college. St Idephonsus's was the equivalent for boys. As you can see, the Byzantine era influenced the architecture.'

We gazed at a series of stunning buildings.

Antoine grinned. 'To think right now we might have been visiting a dog cemetery.'

Bella and I fell about with mirth.

Julieta said, 'Former students' names include Cusack, from Western Australian pastoral families.'

Each college had its own chapel. Each was splendidly decorated. In the years to come, the buildings would operate as group accommodation, offering a range of meeting and performance rooms, including retreat space.

The complex included an exquisite chapel, founded by Rosendo Salvado. His tomb lies within the Abbey Church of the Holy Trinity, built in the form of a long and narrow cross. It boasted a large German organ, built in 1922 by Albert Moser of Munich.

We counted ourselves lucky to arrive in time for a mini-recital by a visiting organist. Antoine felt the timber around the player gently vibrate from the sound.

Someone whispered, 'The queen of instruments.'

The group was entranced by pane-shaking low notes and ethereal highs. Too soon, those magic sounds faded.

Sarah who-could-no-longer-fly groaned. 'I've seen enough churches for a lifetime.'

Jaws dropped.

The last Spanish Benedictine monk of New Norcia would later die in 2010, aged ninety-nine. He had baked the monastery bread for over fifty years, and helped grind the flour. The bakery dated to 1886. They made bread, biscotti and nut cakes.

At the time of our visit, one monk, in his nineties, was in charge of a moderately large garden.

Julieta said, 'Others make olive oil for their own use. A little extra is kept for sale. Ditto with the small amounts of monastery wine. Notice the hives outside. They buzz with the finest honey.'

A monks' chapel enjoyed splendid views over their private garden.

Julieta drew our attention to the ceiling. 'Richly decorated in green and gold, between exposed beams. Latin inscriptions on prayer, meditation and right living adorn the walls.'

The town of New Norcia later became part of the National Estate. Many buildings dated back a hundred years. It wasn't surprising that they were in urgent need of repair. Refurbishment gained pace after the 1990s. Many New Norcia projects were destined to receive tax deductible status, with the assistance of the National Trust. This included conservation, restoration, storage. The most important aspects of this legacy were later preserved for posterity.

Back in 1993, the ravages of time failed to conceal the breathtaking beauty of New Norcia. Much later, we were shocked to learn of sexual abuse, leading into past darkness. Who could fail to feel empathy for those innocent children? Some Aboriginal, others orphans, suffered at the hands of predator priests. Others were abused as slave labour. This issue has since been addressed by a Royal Commission. The pain continues to resonate. Some victims chose suicide. It was a sobering to discover that beside great beauty lurked agony.

Our bus stopped at the roadside.

A farmer happened by. 'Wildflowers? I'll tell you where to see the best ones.'

Henry, the driver, took us to that spectacular natural garden. A paradise of kangaroo paws, everlasting daisies and other native plants. Cameras clicked.

Sarah said, 'Is this all?'

The coach tittered.

Bella spoke for all of us. 'It's a long while since I've had such a wonderful day.'

We later visited a historic town called York. A little church had lost its steeple in the recent Meckering earthquake. The walls outside showed cracking.

Bella said, 'Thank goodness the lovely stained glass is intact.'

Among many fabulous old buildings, former public accommodation bore a stern warning: 'We cater for respectable married couples.' A hearty laugh was had by all.

At a liquor store in town, Antoine made to replenish our supplies of Ssauvignon blanc. I shared warm-weather remarks with a friendly stranger, telling of our travels.

'You're from Bankstown?' He grinned. 'I know it well. Used to live there. What did I do? Top honcho of the De Havilland aircraft engineering section.'

I gaped. 'Never! That's where my late husband, Neville, began his apprenticeship. Way back in the fifties.'

A twenty-minute ride on a fast modern train took us to Fremantle.

Antoine told me, 'The main port of Perth. Once a seedy sailor's haunt.

'But look at it now.' I laughed. 'An America's Cup facelift has transformed it into the most cosmopolitan part of town.'

We gazed at open-air cafés, and splendid dining balconies along the main street. A less salubrious goal lay nearby. We stepped from the height of modernity into the gloom of old Fremantle jail. Rubbing shoulders with its uneasy past, I shuddered over tiny, dark cells.

Antoine imagined being locked away for years. 'The only company a stinking waste bucket. Hardly room to move, let alone breathe.'

Cells were ranged along thin oblong spaces, with even narrower balconies.

The guide told us, 'Wire netting prevented suicides, or the throwing of objects at those below.'

Prisoners' artworks brought a glimpse of humanity to certain cells.

Our guide, Elias, painted a picture of prison life. 'Prisoners were told when to get up. When to eat. When to go to the toilet. When to go outside. After years of having every aspect of their lives controlled, they lost the ability to function in normal society. Riots and fires led to its closure.'

I warmed to his friendly voice.

'A compassionate approach to incarceration includes responsibility for the activities of daily living. It's been proven to work elsewhere, including the US.'

We avoided staring at his hands. One, a twisted claw, seemed barely able to hold a bunch of keys. The other was a metal hook. Touched by his horrible facial scars, with hints of plastic surgery, I suppressed a shiver. His eyes met mine, those of a sincere and caring man. A warder during the riot? Burnt in the fire? Whatever his story, one soon forgot the extent of his injuries.

A punishment cell. My throat constricted. Choking at the terrible implications of that execution noose. A chair stood at the ready, should the prisoner's legs collapse under him. That movable floor dropped the culprit/victim into eternity.

Elias said, 'The last woman hanged here painted the throats of her stepchildren with poison. They died a slow and agonising death.'

Sympathy morphed into shock.

Antoine shared my dismay. 'Some criminals deserve their fate.'

Our conclusion trembled on dust motes of the oppressive air.

We fled the abominations of Fremantle gaol, and breathed fresh air again.

An old synagogue, transformed into a French restaurant, brought delicious aromas. Lingering over lunch, we savoured snippets of roasted chicken breast. The crisp salad included Lebanese cucumbers, roasted pumpkin and beetroot. For once, the tomatoes had fragrance and flavour, reminiscent of home-grown ones in childhood.

Antoine eyed the buxom serving wench. Short skirt. Tanned thighs. Lustrous dark hair.

'A tad young for you, darling.'

He chuckled. 'Candy for the mature man.'

The Maritime Museum included the forward section of the Dutch ship *Batavia*.

Antoine gazed at every detail. 'They've even rebuilt the enormous stone gate.' It had lain scattered over the ocean floor for centuries. 'Among ships' timbers, broken pottery, and other objects of ancient life.'

Oops! My Minolta hit the floor, giving a little bounce. I didn't know whether to laugh or cry.

Antoine grinned. ' Floor's some special substance. Your camera should be OK.'

'Seems to be. Guess the case protected it, too.'

The Minolta continued to produce great pictures on the trip. In fact, Bella appointed me our group's official photographer.

Neville had often travelled to WA on location.

'He always liked Perth. Visited Fremantle, Busselton, the kauri forest. It feels strange seeing places where he stayed on location, decades ago.'

Antoine said, 'A shame you never got to see it with him.'

'Still, I couldn't ask for more delightful travelling companions.'

Antoine saluted. 'At your service, ma'am.'

Bella curtsied.

I laughed. 'Stop fooling around, you two.'

Our last day. We wandered Perth streets Carefree. Exultant. Silly for the fun of it.

'Stay right there, Bella. You too, Antoine. It's a good pic, against the distorted images of that building. Take one of me.'

I rode the escalators at Miss Maude's several times. 'That was just a rehearsal, guys. Hurrah! Just the right shot.'

Fun included cream tea.

'Nothing like quince jelly on fresh scones.'

We wandered into the Allan Green pyramid-shaped conservatory, built in 1979 for WA's 150th anniversary.

Bella exclaimed, 'Just look at all those tropical plants and rare palms. I'd love to grow some of those.'

Our adventures finished with a G and T at the Chateau Commodore bar.

The hotel bus whizzed us to the airport.

In those days before passengers were banned from taking fluids aboard, Antoine smuggled in a bottle of Sauvignon blanc. 'Domestic airlines don't offer wine in tourist class.'

A sour-faced fellow passenger rejected Antoine's offer of a drink.

Suppressing giggles, we toasted the success of our journey, tucking into our meal.

Antoine said, 'Why do people criticise aircraft food?'

The woman snapped, 'Because it's horrible,' pushing aside her chicken dish.

10

At Stacey Street, each lick of undercoat put me one step closer to my big move. I left Antoine scraping back paint remover from a window.

He grinned. 'Timber's solid. It'll come up a treat.'

I filled some nail holes. Glanced up. Roared, 'Stop right there.'

Antoine was walking the mess of old paint and remover onto the sitting room carpet.

'Clean your shoes immediately. Put that rubbish into the bin.' Reminding myself, he needs constant supervision.

By the 1990s, I'd clocked up a quarter of a century at Wattle Grove. Nurse education had moved to universities.

One Bachelor of Science nursing lass told us, 'It took me three to four years to gain the necessary confidence and expertise to carry out my nursing duties.'

I grinned. 'Ironically, the duration of our probationer nurse training to qualify as an RN.'

Elsie nodded. 'Everyone knows that theoretical knowledge must be supported by practical experience.'

Everyone knew that: except Tom. He had a brace of degrees, yet clashed with residents and visitors alike. Counselling seemed little help.

Doon sighed. 'Rumour has it that our DON is ready to pull out her hair. Tom may be well qualified, but he lacks common sense.'

Menik chuckled. 'Maybe common sense isn't so common.'

Doone added, 'At Tom's last employment, it was a question of resign or be sacked.'

I laughed. 'Surprise me.'

Weekday RNs had always envied weekend RNs their penalty rates. Doubtless, it was Tom who had put a match to other grievances. Unfair distribution of paperwork was the latest catch cry, ignoring our lack of back-up staff.

Resident care subsidies, or the RCS, represented the government's new funding tool. The variety of forms would have topped Mount Everest. Urine flow charts, bowel charts, behaviour charts, blood pressure charts, individual care plans. The list went on. All in addition to the progress notes, or daily report.

Encouraged to write our concerns in the Continual Improvement Log, we obliged. However, snide remarks greeted our input. Or the issues raised were not addressed.

Menik raised her eyebrows. 'It's best to write nothing.'

'Keep out of the firing line? That's my strategy from now on.'

Given our woes with Tom, it was a joy for me to work with one of the most humble individuals in the profession. A club casual, Troy RN, was an excellent practical nurse. He shared his knowledge and sought mine. Only later, did I learn that he was the deputy director of a large suburban hospital.

After our class at L'Alliance Française, we adjourned to a nearby café. Antoine bought the latest *Figaro*, dated 8 January 1993.

I sipped my coffee. 'Wasn't that an excellent class?'

Rustle of paper. An indrawn breath. 'Good Lord! It's them.'

'The Odiers!' Our anguished eyes met a headline, '*Suicide en Famille*. Family suicide. Autopsy results.'

Antoine gulped for air. 'Police suspected Solenne. But autopsy results showed that Marcel shot his wife, then his daughter.' He swallowed. 'Turned the gun on himself. Only, Solenne didn't die.'

A surge of hope. 'She's alive?'

Antoine slowly shook his head. 'Solenne regained consciousness. Paralysed on her right side.'

'A hemiplegic? Oh, Lord, no.'

His chin trembled. 'Solenne struggled to the ground floor. Injured, bleeding. Brought extra bullets upstairs. Loaded the gun with her left hand. Shot her parents a second time.'

I shuddered.

'Ejected each shell. Put the gun…'

My eyes blurred. 'To her own head?'

The preparation ritual was banal. 'They cleaned the car, house and refrigerator. Marcel sent a testament to a solicitor cousin at Toulon.' Antoine cleared his throat. 'Police received a note. Three signatures.'

'But…Solenne couldn't sign. Not at fifteen.'

He wiped his eyes. 'Marcel would've insisted. Making it seem…'

My fists clenched. 'As though she'd agreed?'

He went on. 'Teachers found Solenne preoccupied the last few weeks…before…before Marcel kept her home.' Antoine's voice broke. 'Marcel had no job. I fancy we arrived in the midst…'

'Of his planning?' I wiped a hot tear from my cheek. 'But Marcel's computer business?'

'Seems he hadn't worked since…since their return to France.'

For months afterwards, the calamity haunted Antoine and me. 'There's a lesson here somewhere.'

Antoine's groan. 'Yes. We should've listened to what they didn't say. If only I'd known he was jobless.'

'You'd have helped?' My teeth chittered. 'It's easy to be wise…'

'After the event? That's the tragedy of it.'

I stopped sharing the story. It was too painful.

Dad's hospitalisation took my mind of the Odier tragedy. A bowel re-section was not to be taken lightly. 'They got it all, thank the Lord.' Dad sat out of bed, his colour back to normal. 'And no colostomy.'

'Your insistence on scans paid off.'

Always up for a giggle, Dad drew my attention to one of the other patients. 'Young feller's a tile short of a roof. Spouts all sorts of rubbish.'

I glimpsed the young man, an unprepossessing sort of chap. Vacant expression. Straggly whiskers at the point of his chin.

Dad told me, 'One day we older blokes discussed the risks of marijuana. That young bloke piped up, "I've been smoking it for years. Never done me any harm."' Dad chuckled. 'The ward shook with laughter.'

Our deputy, Liz, feigned friendship one day, ignored us the next.

Elsie said, 'I'm sure Liz started the mantra of trained at the year dot.'

I laughed. 'Dismissing our years of experience. Liz must know we've handled all sorts of emergency situations.' I reminded her of a resident who'd suffered status epilepticus, a prolonged fit. 'We summoned urgent medical help.'

She nodded. 'Promptly given by his GP – also educated at the year dot.'

'Yes, a solid, dependable physician. He administered the appropriate dosage of IV Lorazepam before we sent our patient to hospital.

'He was fine. Thankfully, the DON knows she can rely on us.'

Dad had weathered his latest surgery. At eighty, he stood tall, fit and proud. His once abundant golden-red hair was thin and tipped with grey.

My brother Druce patted his shoulder. 'Where would you like to go, Dad?'

His eyes gleamed. 'I fancy a seven-day voyage on the Murray. Always planned to visit Echuca.'

Druce grinned. 'A holiday around Victoria? Sounds good.'

We set off on a golden spring day in October 1994. The freeway whirled through the Southern Tablelands. Undulating country, with outcrops of boulders, craving to be photographed. European cypress chatted with eucalypts. Liquidambars clung to the outmoded garments of yesteryear, faded to brown. I wondered why nature had failed to release the hormone, allowing autumn leaves to fall.

At Gundagai, we took photographs with the famed Dog on the Tuckerbox.

Dad's eyes dreamed into the distance. 'Came this way before, with

Mum. Back in the fifties. Must be thirty years ago. Fifty at the time. A man in his prime.'

Shadows lengthened. Our room at the Garden Motor Inn looked out over a peaceful valley. Spring blossoms graced the garden. Mauve primula, golden daffodils, jonquils in pink and white. A murmuration of starlings squabbled in the dense mass of a cypress tree.

Dad told us of a bad fall from a horse when he was fourteen. 'I lay unconscious for some time. Nursed at home by an auntie.' He was confined to bed for several months. 'In those days, people didn't worry about hospitals and doctors. My back was never the same afterwards. Sciatica gave me the gyp, even at eighteen.'

A lifetime of heavy manual labour had contributed to what he dubbed a weakness. He had carried heavy rabbit traps on his back. Juggled massive posts and forty-four-gallon drums of fuel. Not to forget bags of spuds. In his thirties, he suffered a number of debilitating attacks of sciatica. By his sixties, he had needed the first of four hip replacements.

Druce rose early. He tinkered with his old Valiant. 'Motor refuses to idle. Needs an electrical overhaul.'

'I fancy Druce carries out repairs in his sleep,' Dad groaned. 'It worries me. Will it see out our trip?'

I shrugged. 'That's the question.'

At long last, our driver appeared, wiping oil from his hands. 'I would've done more.' He washed and wiped his hands. 'Lacked a special tool.'

Dad shot me a 'Thank-God-for-that' glance.

We crossed the fast-flowing Murrumbidgee river.

Dad eyed the weeping willows. 'I've always liked them.'

Grey-green eucalypts, and flashes of golden wattle. Sheep reminded me of thistledown in distant pastures. Verdant green valleys. One lone farmhouse nestled into a hillside. Brown and fawn rust patterned the corrugated-iron roof. Smoky dreams drifted on the chill morning air.

'A black horse,' I said. 'Snug as a teapot in its winter rug.'

The Kookaburras Delight Coffee Lounge at Holbrook.

Druce pulled to a stop. 'Who's for lunch?'

Green checked tablecloths, a waitress clad in a crisp forest green. Notebook and pencil in hand, she smiled, noting our preferences.

Druce put down his briefcase. 'I'll be right back.'

A sideboard caught my eye, laden with local crafts, teddy bears, cushions. Home-made jams, jellies and chutney.

'Choose what you like, dear, I'll buy.'

I patted his arm. 'Thanks, Dad, but no. I'm resisting temptation.'

We laughed.

Druce returned, his smile wider than the room. 'Bought the tool I needed.' He waved a package.

Dad shot me a glance. More delays.

We tucked into home-made pies and mushroom sauce, served with chips and a crisp green salad. Exactly what we needed.

Dad drained the last of his tea, strong and sugar-laden. 'A simple but superb meal.'

Albury's houses of yesteryear boasted wide verandas, edged with iron lace.

Dad mused, 'Bull-nosed corrugated-iron roofs.'

An avenue of trees shivered in the chill air, feathered limbs bereft of leaves. A sign for Maxwell Carpets Advice Centre told us to get floored.

We laughed. 'Good one.'

Dad glimpsed the Boomerang Motor Inn. 'Don't suppose I'll ever be back.'

Masses of cumulus clouds, edged with gold. Mellow light.

Dad drew our attention to hive-dotted fields. 'It's a good season for the bees. Spring blossoms mean lots of nectar.'

A child's red, yellow and blue kite was trapped high in the branches of a gum tree. We chuckled at the way the beribboned tail lashed this way and that, struggling to be free.

Beechworth beckoned.

Dad dreamed into the past. 'A town famed for gold discoveries in the 1800s. Infamous for the prison where Ned Kelly languished, before his trial.'

The Victorian goldfields proved a treasure trove of memories for a man like our father. He'd spent a lifetime fossicking, augmenting activities as a grazier on his small farm in the mountains of Northern NSW.

His eyes gleamed. 'A saviour when funds were low. We'd have had to walk off the property in the fifties, had we not found that reef.'

It hadn't sold for a fortune, but enabled him to buy a bulldozer, farm equipment and get the electricity connected.

'My grandfather, also Joseph, arrived in Australia in the 1840s. Sought gold in these very fields.'

Over thirty buildings in Beechworth were classified by the National Trust.

Druce said, 'They reckon it's the best preserved colonial gold town in Australia.'

Dad's gnarled old hand caressed the sandstone. 'That's been here a while.'

We admired antique shopfronts.

Dad eyed the large, rounded gutters of the street, constructed of flat pavers. 'Don't see those in New South Wales.'

Afternoon tea at the Miners Crib Café. Whitewashed walls were adorned with attractive black and white photos of the diggings.

The owner informed us, 'Crib is a Welsh word meaning meal.

Artefacts of the period included a Chinese miner's pick, which had a wide rounded triangular digging piece.

Dad grinned. 'Ingenious device. Digs and scoops away the earth at the same time.' He took a closer look. 'The metal's not as thick or strong as a conventional pick, though. They probably broke easily.'

The Burke Museum was named after the early explorer. Historical objects cast light on the lifestyle of the 1800s.

Dad's eyes dreamed into the past. 'Tons of the precious metal were extracted here. Mines closed in the early part of the twentieth century.'

Rain drizzled down the motel windows.

Dad groaned. 'I thought we'd left winter behind. Doesn't give a fella much incentive to abandon the electric blanket.'

The Valiant didn't seem in the mood to start the day, either. Dad glanced my way, concern etched into his brow. Three cheers when the motor coughed into life.

The Ovens Highway sped past pine plantations, reminiscent of European landscapes. Vineyards unfolded. Golden moss clung to leafless trunks and limbs. Gardens danced with golden daffodils.

At Myrtleford, the sun peeped forth from behind dark clouds. I seized the brief reprieve, capturing photos of the Phoenix Tree. A sculpture by Hans Knorr, it symbolised new life, risen from the ashes. The trunk and roots of the toppled forest giant had been carved and smoothed, gaining a patina of power and beauty.

Rain stung exposed flesh.

Daddy shivered. 'Why didn't we choose Queensland?'

Neville's leather jacket hadn't been off my father's back since day one, except in bed. He was wrapped in my long, red, Mexican scarf.

I trembled, bitterly cold. 'Next time, it's the tropics.'

Dad's hands had turned blue. I rushed to buy him a pair of woollen gloves. His face lit up. I mused on the frailty demonstrated by those huge hands, a lump in my throat.

Carlos' Pizza and Pasta met hungry eyes. The shop walls were adorned with images of the leaning tower of Pisa, and Italian posters.

'I'm ravenous.' Dad chose their special.

We followed suit. The pizza melted in my mouth, rich with tomatoes, cheese, bacon, mushrooms, olives and capsicums.

Dad grinned. 'Anyone for seconds?'

We tucked into another round of those scrumptious treats.

I practised a few words of my rusty Italian. 'I love your beautiful homeland.'

Carlos gaped. 'You visited Italy? I come from Pisa.'

'So I've noticed. Your food is wonderful, by the way.'

His dark eyes shone. 'Don't forget to call if you pass this way again.'

Druce studied a map in our motel room. 'We're in the heart of Kelly country. The sign outside says only twenty kilometres to Glenrowan.'

Dad shrugged. 'Whatever you fellas decide.'

Unfortunately, some wag had removed a second nought. The distance proved to be more like 200.

We were greeted finally by the Kelly museum and a giant replica of Ned, an outlaw hanged in pioneer days.

'Larger-than-life, even in death,' said Dad. 'Imagine the work to make that iron suit of armour.'

I nodded. 'And the weight, when wearing it.' Fascinated by Ned's letters, and a debate with the judge who passed the death sentence. 'An intelligent man. Trapped by poverty? Unjustly condemned?'

'All of those,' Sally our guide said, ' A great many people signed appeals to save him.'

Posters, paintings and artefacts brought the era alive. We wandered around a replica of the family's bark hut.

'Small, but comfortable,' said Dad. 'Not unlike ones I built.'

Sally told us, 'I own land that was originally the Kelly family property. After Ned's death, his mother eked out a living as the district midwife. In fact, she delivered my father.'

The Hume freeway drizzled to Benalla.

'Hmm, Hides Bakery. Reckon it's the perfect spot for lunch,' Druce said.

Established in 1925 by a returned soldier and his pretty bride, bottle-green walls displayed family and historical photographs. They included one of Mrs Hide with the first bakery horse.

I told our waitress, ' Love the way your dark green slacks harmonise with the walls.'

A dimpled smile. 'Why, thank you.'

A small pine table. I breathed the aroma of freshly brewed coffee, the perfume of hot bread. We dined on delicious home-made pies and salad, with tasty wholemeal rolls.

The staff fussed over Dad. 'More tea perhaps? Another pie?'

Dad chuckled, delighted by the attention.

Downpours sped us along the Midland Highway. Wipers screeched, in a frenzy of windscreen-wiping. We traversed a large plateau through Shepparton. Lush green plains were edged with weeping willows and peppercorns, interspersed with eucalypts. An area of orchards, massed in pink and white blossoms.

Dad peered into the rain. 'Apples, I think, plums, peaches.'

At Echuca, Druce said, 'Hey, it's a sister city to Whitehorse, in the Yukon, Canada, no less.'

Dad shivered. 'It's cold enough to be the blooming Arctic. Let's find the motel before a man freezes to death.'

A reverse-cycle air con rattled, grumbled and groaned near my bed. 'Just hope the vibrations don't make the darned thing leap from its perch.'

Fake woodgrain wall. Tacky curtains. Reminding myself it was only for one night.

Dad basked in the warmth. 'My hands are starting to get the feeling back.'

'No Cooking,' warned a small sign near the power plug. I boiled the jug. The cups looked clean. Druce rinsed them over and over.

'You should ask for an autoclave.'

He shot me a pained look. 'Don't be funny, sis. Cleaners wipe cups out with soiled washers or whatever happens to be on hand.'

Dad nodded. 'It pays to be careful.' He savoured his cup of brew. 'Tea-making facilities are a boon.'

I said, 'Yes, we're lucky in Australia.'

Dad chose a bed nearest the loo. 'In case I need to get up at night.'

A generous bathroom made Druce happy. He headed for the shower, singing at the top of his lungs. Dad and I feared the hot water might run out. Ablutions over, he removed his towel from possible contamination.

In my cramped 'Privacy corner' a big panel separated my bed from the others. It reminded me of poor old Ned Kelly's cell in Beechworth prison. Mine had something his hadn't: a view of the television.

Druce suggested a stroll. 'We're in walking distance of the town centre.

'You fellas go.' Dad shivered. 'I'll stay here.'

'Dad, this is the spot you wanted to see.'

Rugged up, he shot a longing glance towards the bed and TV.

Wild duck swooped overhead, in reddish light, giving joyful cries to their mates.

Druce eyed the Murray. Brown water flowed between high banks. 'It isn't a pretty river.'

I laughed. 'That's an understatement, bro.'

Dad peered into the gloom. 'Look, the hulk of some old vessel. Came to grief long ago, no doubt.'

Cormorants called it home, diving from the wreck into the murky depths.

Later, Druce learnt that the boat had been partially submerged to preserve the timbers until restoration could commence.

Dad said, 'The Murray is the third largest navigable river in the world. Forms the border between NSW and Victoria. NSW owns the right river bank. Victorians pay us for the privilege of fishing or boat licences.'

Druce and I exchanged a glance.

'How do you know that?'

He grinned. 'A fella can read. The first ferry crossed the river in 1850.' Dad added, 'Echuca grew into the largest inland port in the southern hemisphere. An income equivalent to nine million dollars.'

I giggled. 'If you say so.'

Dad recalled days before road transport. 'Paddle steamers and barges carried wool and timber to the railhead. Brought back supplies on the return journey.'

Walking back to our motel, Dad mused what a vibrant place Echuca must once have been. 'Laughter and conversation. Boat whistles and splashing water. Passenger and working craft sailing to and fro.' He added, 'Hawkers sold their wares. The joy of weddings and sombre funerals in the portable churches on board.'

Bleak, overcast sky, in league with the freeze of morning winds.

I groaned. 'Teasing us with those warm and sunny tourist brochure.'

In Sydney, Druce had told me, 'I have plenty of leave.' That morning, he announced, 'I must be back home by the thirtieth. We'll need to scrap Swan Hill.'

My jaw dropped. I recalled his lack of input for the trip. A friend had brought maps and brochures. He'd made excuses not to take part.

He muttered, 'What you want to see?' And grumbled, 'You did all the planning.'

I gritted my teeth. 'And who left everything to me? This trip was meant to give Dad a good time.'

My brother looked guilty. 'But Dad isn't interested in what you're showing him. Didn't you tell me, Dad, that you'd seen it all before?'

Daddy looked uncomfortable. 'I'm just happy to be with you fellas.'

I didn't want to spoil Dad's holiday by bickering. He'd found it hard to enjoy life since Mum passed. But I wondered what we were doing there. I could have saved money, time and effort.

For the sake of peace, I let it rest. Later in the day, Druce tried to make amends for his boorish behaviour. Buying me a small gift, washing and drying my jeans.

I groaned, 'Echuca was meant to be the highlight of our trip.'

We fought our way through rain and biting wind. My sudden thought, I can't blame Dad for being reluctant to leave our warm room. Maybe at eighty, I'd feel the same. Still, I felt cheated.

We lunched at a café called Wisteria Cottage. Set in a red and white rose garden, a joy of spring blooms. The dancing flames of an open fire drew Dad to a nearby table. A delicious pumpkin soup and salad failed to lift my low spirits.

Dammit, I thought, we'll miss Swan Hill. But I'll not be deprived of a short cruise. 'Boys, I've bought tickets on the *Canberra*.

Long faces. Rain pelted down outside. The ships' whistles were muffled by fog. We sat indoors, Dad grim-faced, arms folded against the ordeal.

I drew his attention to different types of craft on the river. 'Houseboats. There's a fishing boat.'

Dad barely glanced up. 'It might be pleasant on a fine day. Imagine being trapped on their six-day cruise.'

Nobody laughed.

Grey and gusty winds drove us along the main street. Dad took a cursory glance around the museum of antique carriages. I guessed what would interest him: something that blazed and leapt at the Star Hotel.

Eyes gleaming, he sat on a chair near the red-gum fire. His big hands fanned wide to garner maximum heat. A broad-brimmed Akubra added a bush touch to the old-world atmosphere of ship posters, souvenirs, postcards and brass ships bells.

The hot fire drove Dad further and further back into the room.

Female hotel staff fussed around. 'Are you comfortable? Would you like a drink?'

Dad grinned. 'I'll stay here. You fellas go.'

We left him chatting to his fans.

Druce and I explored the cellars. Decades earlier, the Star Hotel had lost its liquor licence. It continued to serve alcohol. Frequent police raids led to illicit drinkers' evasive action. The twists and turns of secret passageways had allowed them to come and go with ease.

A guide showed us pictures. 'In the olden days, floodwaters overflowed the banks. Paddle steamers sailed down the main street.'

A chorus of 'Well, I never' and 'Imagine that.'

We adored the colourful names of the men who ran the vessels: river rats, inside sailors, freshwater seamen, mud pirates, river kings.

In the seventies, Film Australia had made a documentary of the paddle-steamers at Echuca. Wandering around the display of old steam engines and machinery, it was easy to see why Neville had been so keen to bring me for a visit. Alas, we'd never made it.

A huge red-gum wharf stood twelve metres high.

The guide said, 'Three landing platforms were necessary for the different water levels between winter and summer.'

Descending the many steps was like descending from the third-floor to ground level.

'It's time to leave, Dad.'

The girls were reluctant to see him go, a crucial part of the exhibit. He took a last, longing glance at those leaping flames.

Next morning a light fall of snow met Dad's weary eyes. 'That's all a man needed.'

At Bendigo, the setting sun's rays stretched from behind leaden clouds, illuminating the Sacred Heart Cathedral. It stands majestically on a hill. Built in 1895, using the Gothic Revival style, the huge structure was funded by money from the enormous quantities of gold reaped from the local region.

We drove into the drizzle of dusk. It gusted across the Valiant windscreen. Delighted to find a Budget motel.

The unsmiling owner. 'Here are your keys. We don't serve meals.'

Windscreen wipers whirred. We sought a takeaway. In the darkness, our headlights illuminated a red and gold sign twisting with dragons.

Dad peered into the gloom. 'Looks a pokey little place.'

I said, 'One can imagine what Chinese takeaway will be like in the middle of nowhere.'

Inside, we gaped. A magnificent restaurant, the decor of red and gold, splendid red lanterns, Buddha statues and crisp, starched tablecloths.

'Must be at least a hundred seats,' Druce whistled. 'Can't believe it.'

I chuckled, 'Let's find a table and dine in.'

Daddy added. 'Why not?'

I savoured a sauvignon blanc. The aroma of Asian spices teased our nostrils. Dad nursed a ginger beer, on the wagon long since. We drooled over superb crisp-fried beef with hoisin sauce, noodles, an aromatic fried rice, chicken with almonds.

Druce and Dad settled for fried ice cream dessert. I enjoyed lychees and cream.

'The cuisine is equal to anything I've tasted in Hong Kong or Singapore.'

Druce smirked. 'If you say so, sis.' My brother eyed the water-drenched landscape. 'Does it ever stop raining around here?'

Dad sighed. 'And there's not been a single rainbow.'

I giggled. 'Driving towards the rainbow, but never reaching it. That's life.'

Chuckles. 'Maybe you're right.'

Every farm dam – and there were many – shimmered, full to the brim.

The grass was greener than in any English field.

Dad peeked into the gloom. 'Hundreds of white headstones. Edging distant roads.'

Puzzled glances dissolved into helpless laughter.

Protective white plastic surrounded young trees.

Dad wiped his eyes. 'Splendid forests in the years to come.'

Dusk stole the landscape, downpours speckled with sleet. An anonymous motel. Awake at seven a.m., Dad took his shower. I'd forgotten to remove my undies from the bathroom. Dried overnight, drenched in seconds.

Druce tinkered with the fuel pump.

Dad groaned. 'Wish he'd save running repairs for Sydney.'

I chuckled. 'His pottering falls into the category of obsessive compulsive.'

In the low light of fog we set off.

Dad told of great-grandfather walking among tents and digging pits. 'The wild days of tents and drunken miners, site of the famous Eureka Stockade. More than thirty men died.'

Druce asked, 'Was your grandpa numbered among the fighters?'

Dad shrugged. 'God knows.'

<h1 style="text-align:center">11</h1>

Druce grinned. 'Surprise, surprise. Ballarat welcomes us with a cloud-burst.'

We burst out laughing.

A thriving city with attendant traffic problems, a demonstration shouted opposite the Peter Lalor Hotel. Fighting cuts to the health system.

I chuckled. 'The spirit of the Eureka Stockade lives on.'

Every business around Ballarat, from hotels to swimming pools, exploits the local legend. Our motel, Eureka Lodge, was no exception. Spruce, camellias and deciduous trees graced the garden. Daffodils danced with jonquils.

'The coldest day we've had yet.' Daddy snuggled into Neville's leather coat and my red scarf.

Druce checked supplies. 'A toaster with bread, butter and spreads. They've left us a cereal breakfast, and a big jug of milk.'

Dusk crept into night. The temperature plummeted. Our milk turned to ice crystals.

Rather than have it become solid overnight, Dad suggested a shelf in the bathroom. 'Will keep it cool enough but won't freeze.'

Priscilla's Cottage for lunch. 'A restored miner's dwelling,' the balding owner told Dad. 'Solid timber floors, a foot thick.'

Dad grinned. 'Your log fire makes a man happy.'

'Glad to hear it.'

Firelight shone on paintings and historical photographs of the region.

The owner regaled us with tales of the district and the gold-mining era.

Dad's eyes glittered. He shared stories of fossicking. 'My grandad worked hereabouts in Eureka days.'

'Is that so? You'll want to see the performance of *Blood On the Cross*.

He explained it was a sound and light spectacular. 'Excellent show. Not to be missed.'

We made bookings. Taking note of information on the main attractions of Sovereign Hill Village.

Yummy pumpkin soup was followed by a tasty individual quiche, jacket potato and salad.

Replete, I said, 'Just what was needed.'

Dad laughed. 'A lovely meal. A pleasant way for a man to relax and pass a couple of hours.' He finished his cup of strong, sweet tea.

I said, 'Pray for just one fine day. To enjoy outdoor activities.'

Someone up there heard us. Early clouds at Sovereign Hill gave way to brilliant sunshine. A wander through the reconstruction of a colonial mining village left me shaking my head. Cobb and Co. coaches. Splendid horses with whiskered hooves and flowing manes trotted by.

Students from the Ballarat Department of Mines and the Flamboyants' Theatre Company provided amusing skits and just the right music. Players in period costumes browsed the shops and roamed the streets, real folk in a genuine town. I felt an odd sensation. Had I swapped time zones?

Frontier-style shops welcomed customers. They sold quality locally made merchandise of a type that might have been manufactured at the time. Antique shops abounded. Before the advent of TV, the colonial newspaper office would have been a crucial part of any town.

The Gold Office sold small bags of soil.

Dad grinned. 'With luck, a man could find a nugget worth a hundred dollars.' He washed a dish in the creek. Like the other hopefuls, he reaped a few colours.

We joined the tour of a mine. Dioramas showed mining activity and reproductions of famous nuggets. The guide declared, 'No man over the height of about five feet four inches could work as an underground miner.'

Dad restrained his mirth, saying later, 'Where did he get that idea? My father, grandfather, friends and me, all went down the mines. All of us well over six feet.'

A ventilation shaft proved its efficacy. Freezing air turned Dad's poor old hands blue. His gloves had gone missing. On return to the surface, I rushed him replacements.

We felt more than ready for English cream scones, strawberry jam and tea. Dad dozed a while in the glorious sunshine, glad of a break.

We continued our explorations.

In the evening, we trooped outdoors into the freezing night. The sound and light spectacular, *Blood on the Cross*, played out on a huge screen. It presented the hardships imposed on penniless miners by the gold tax. 'Paid whether men had found the precious metal or not.'

Dad sat entranced, rugged up in leather coat, gloves and scarf. I fancy even he became oblivious to the temperature as the tale unfolded.

In the diggings, lanterns made elongated shadows of figures inside tents. Campfires sprang into life. Approaching hooves. Cries of alarm. Dogs barked, miners racing to hide. In the darkness, shouts from the men. Another police raid. Bitter clashes, arrests.

The finale took place aboard a train. It swayed to a clearing across the valley, an excellent commentary maintaining the mood. In the chill darkness, a huge moon, lopsided, hung low over the site. Stars glittered like nuggets in the dark sky.

The crisp September air stirred memories of long ago. Mists drifted over the goldfields. Campfires leapt. In the flickering light from lanterns, miners planned the uprising. Huge doors of the theatre swung open. A rough stockade became the setting for a bloody battle between the miners and police. Lives were lost on both sides, bringing a terrible toll of injuries. Peter Lalor lost his arm. He would have died if friends hadn't risked their lives to hide him.

Miners were arrested, taken to court, charged with treason. But no jury would convict them. A triumph of right over might. It changed the course of Australian history. Peter later became speaker of the legislative assembly.

Auntie Min, widow of Dad's eldest brother, was living at the Walmsley

Village Nursing Home. The hostels and units were set in a splendid garden, ablaze with spring flowers. A big black crow foraged for his supper among large shrubs and gum trees.

I pecked her cheek. 'I was twelve the last time we met, Auntie.'

'That would be right,' she chuckled. 'I'm ninety. And you, Joe?'

'Eighty, last time I looked.'

Auntie glanced my way. 'And you, dear?'

'I'm fifty-three.

'And you, Druce?'

He grinned. 'Forty-four.'

A chuckle. 'Why, you're only babies.' Wheelchair-bound, she added. 'I'm delighted to see you all.'

Druce asked, 'How did you and Uncle Arthur meet?'

'Geoff? Oh, yes, he's known as Arthur to his NSW rellies. God rest his soul.' A chuckle. 'We were buying tickets at the cinema. On turning to leave, his head collided with mine. We apologised, laughed, looked into each other's eyes.' Uncle Geoff/Arthur invited her for coffee. 'The rest is history. Six months later, we were married.'

At Phillip Island, spring blossoms were heavy with the fragrance of honey. That evening, we watched fairy penguins stream across the beach on their way home from fishing expeditions, an extraordinary spectacle.

Rich and tantalising aromas lured us inside Dutchie's Place. I admired the high wooden ceilings and huge white Chinese lanterns. Fresh flowers adorned each table. Stylish place mats bore the patron's initials in flowing script. Home-made pumpkin soup fulfilled every expectation.

Dad shared tales of long ago. 'I used to build my bark hut with a large fireplace at one end of the room, my bed nearby. I always felt warm.'

Druce asked, 'Did you ever sleep under the stars?'

'At times. Then I'd light two logs, one on either side. Kept me comfortable.'

Druce and I exchanged a glance. Shocked at the image of him lying between two burning logs.

Dad told us, 'Bushmen paid little heed to prowling insects. Everything from spiders to centipedes shared my hut. I left them in peace. When Mum arrived, she was horrified by those unwelcome guests.'

I laughed. Druce seemed less amused.

That night, howling winds and flurries of rain lashed our motel. On rising next morning, we found an invasion of ants. Druce washed plates and spoons at least three times.

Dad raised his eyebrows. 'Heaven help me if I'd worried about a few ants in my camping days.'

Druce frowned. 'I'll throw away that muesli.'

'Don't you dare.' I giggled. 'There's not a single ant-print.'

Dad and I continued to enjoy it, along with banana, apple, milk, nuts and yoghurt. Druce gave it a miss.

We set off to view Wilsons Promontory, shadowed by a scowl of clouds.

Druce said, 'It's the most southerly tip of Australia.'

Affectionately called 'The Prom' by locals, we expected a short drive. eighty kilometres stretched into a hundred, and counting. Mists alternated with heavy rain.

A winding road led through thick and unattractive scrub of the national park. Only one sign of wildlife, a lone kangaroo. The Darby River wended through marshland. Far, far in the distance loomed a mountain.

I'd had a fantasy of glimpsing jagged rocky headlands above a surging sea.

Druce checked his map.'The headland involves a trek through the bush of at least twenty kilometres.'

I laughed. 'Impossible for a man of eighty.'

Druce did a U-turn. 'Let's cut our losses.'

We spied the Yanaki Gallery and Tea Rooms. Along with his artificial hips, artificial knee and walking stick, Dad tottered towards lunch. He salivated at the prospect of freshly made scones and hot soup.

Druce reached the gallery. He gaped at the sign. 'Closed. Sounds a tad final.'

Luckily, we had the makings for sandwiches.

Darkness approached. Sleet and drizzle wept down the windscreen. Druce hunched forward over the wheel, peering into the gloom.

Dad asked a rhetorical question, 'Where are all the motels?'

We gave a miss to the promise of Golden Creek and Silver Creek. Passed Old Hat Creek and Poor Fellow Me Creek. I thought, what tales must lie hidden behind those titles.

A shout. 'There's one!' Dad had spied a motel at Foster, set amid tree-ferns and other native plants.

We brought in our pillows. Turned up the air conditioning, pulled out the clothesline. Found the ABC on our TV.

Dad grinned. 'A man's home.'

The restaurant owner had a friendly word. 'When Foster was founded in 1870, it was called Stockyard Creek. Once a gold-mining town, it's now the centre of a rich dairying region.' He chatted gold and cattle to Dad.

A superb meal of chicken breast with mango, new potatoes and salad, followed by orange caramel made my night. The others chose steak.

Druce hankered to see the Great Ocean Road. 'Spectacular scenery, I believe. What the heck if we're on the wrong side of Melbourne? We'll take the ferry from Sorrento and almost be there.'

A gorgeous drive through East Gippsland. Rolling hills, European cypress hedges. Here and there, a glimpse of golden wattle, reminding us we were still in Terra Australis.

Friesian cattle on tidy farms. Gardens ablaze with spring blossoms. A huge eagle, far above, outstretched wings adjusting to the thermals, eyes alert for prey. Grey ibis, curved beaks, pecked beside lakes.

'Oh, look.' I cried, 'A "Dollar" township sign. I'd no idea such a place existed in Australia.' I thought of my daughter, Naomi, on a teacher exchange in far-away Scotland, at a town of the same name.

'Darn. We've missed the Sorrento ferry.'

Druce did a route reset. We drove via the outskirts of Melbourne, through Werribee. Dusk crept over the landscape. The motel at Anglesea, nestled beside an attractive inlet. Diana's Place restaurant brought memories of a dazzling princess. Thick pumpkin soup, steaks cooked to perfection, succulent chicken breasts.

Druce rose at seven a.m.

I said to Dad, 'Is a quick departure on his agenda?' A short while later, I glanced through the window. Gaped. 'Oh, no.'

Dad hobbled over to look. 'Heaven help us.'

Parts of the Valiant were strewn along the concrete, outside our room. Druce crouched over them, happy as a trout in water.

Dad groaned. 'Why's he taken the carburettor apart? Everything was fine yesterday.'

Breakfast over, we packed our things. Eight thirty a.m. came and went. Nine. Ten…

Management threw us out of the motel room at eleven thirty. The 'repairs' were at a stage where Druce could replace things at speed.

We drove off, jollied along by thunder and lightning. Windscreen wipers in a frenzy. Visibility was almost at zero.

At that moment, the Valiant died.

My gasp. Dad ashen. The starter motor groaned, growled and grumbled. A splutter of life, the shaky rumble of an engine past its purr. We gave three cheers.

Druce grinned. 'Knew she would come good.'

We headed in the direction of the Great Ocean Road.

Intermittent showers put paid to a picnic. Cheese and tomato sandwiches in the car didn't taste the same.

Dad groaned. 'I'm dying for a cuppa.'

A small roadside café slaked our thirst.

The owner, a huge man built like a lumpy kapok mattress, shook his head. 'It's quite a-ways before reaching the best part of the coast.' An American, his tiny eyes glittered, from folds of grey of flesh. 'You all should have travelled down from Ballarat to Warrnambool.'

A tortuous route through rainforest, aptly named.

In the gloom, Dad warned again, 'Take it easy on the slippery surface, son.'

Drenched green valleys, criss-crossed with drains. It was no surprise to learn later that the area boasts the highest annual rainfall in Australia.

Dad said, 'It breaks my heart when I think of the dried-up rivers and starving cattle of NSW.'

At the coastline, we spied a rocky outcrop.

Druce yelped, 'The Twelve Apostles.'

It felt like spotting the Holy Grail.

Weak rays of light pierced the clouds.

'Come out of the car, Dad, for a proper look.'

He shivered in the gusty winds, stung by drops of rain.

I said, 'Spectacular in every way.'

A sudden deluge. He stumbled for shelter.

Devonshire tea at the Twelve Apostles Tea Room brought him welcome relief. He hogged the warmth of a heater. Thick and delicious local cream and home-made strawberry jam on scones.

He dabbed at his mouth with a napkin. 'Nothing is more delicious.'

A talented artist ran the place, judging by her paintings, drawings and photographs adorning the walls. She gave us a wealth of travel information, including a useful map.

We resumed our sightseeing. Dad sat it out in the Valiant.

In retrospect, I don't blame him. At times, our holiday treat must have seemed like a nightmare.

Dramatic outcrops of rocks were slowly being whittled away by the sculptural force of wind, rain and ocean waves. The sun emerged now and then, allowing photos. The Shipwreck Coast had seen the loss of many vessels. The *Loch Ard* clipper sank between Moonlight Head and Port Campbell in 1878, leaving only two survivors. A chasm of that name observes the loss, surging with turbulent waters.

Once, tourists had walked across an elongated rock formation, called the London Bridge. In 1991, the first span collapsed, luckily without loss of life.

Dusk stole away all certainty.

'Join us for the last spectacle, Dad: the Bay of Islands.'

He burrowed into his coat and scarf. I suspected his bad hips were hurting.

'You fellas go. I'll wait in the car.'

We dodged puddles, racing along the drenched path. A setting sun illuminated the beauty of multiple rock formations. A mass of black clouds, and rays of light danced a polka with falling rain.

Druce tackled the narrow bitumen road in fading light. Tyres splashed through pools of water. A hint of red and yellow markers indicated road edges. Valleys disappeared in the gloom. The welcoming motel sign at Cobden.

A delicious restaurant steak. Strong and sweet black tea. Dad's happiness was complete.

The following morning, Druce rose early, a known danger sign.

'You're not going to start fiddling with that darned car.'

'Just one a small thing. It has a flat spot.'

'You can't expect it to perform like a Maserati.'

'They're new parts. It should work perfectly.'

I laughed. 'No, bro. It's like Dad. New hips and a knee are fitted to an old frame.'

He resisted the temptation for a major overhaul. We breathed again.

Misty landscapes. Avenues of conifers made wind breaks for fields. Surrounded farmhouses. Trod beside the roads. Strode along horizons.

A parade of Friesians, black and white coats immaculate, marched in twos like school-children They followed their 'teacher', a farmer on his small tractor. A wire fence on one side, an electric one on the other, kept them to their designated path.

Dad said, 'On their way to milking.'

The Prince's Highway took us through Camperdown, the lakes and crater country. Flocks of sheep wore little green jackets. Essential after shearing, I supposed, in this climate.

We joined the Queenscliff car ferry. The twenty-odd vehicles on deck were under siege from torrents of rain. Raging winds and rolling waves, a giant rocking-horse ride. Up one minute, down the next –

rather fun. A dreadlocked youth braved the outer deck. Soon, he sheepishly sought shelter inside. Shivering, drenched and dripping salt water, joshed by his teenage friends. We could scarcely restrain our giggles at his disconsolate mien. Bursts of laughter inside the car.

Kilometres of low stone fences. Two donkeys, dappled by sunshine, chatted on the weather-bleached veranda of an abandoned cottage. A boy bent low over his red and orange roller-skate board, suspended, for all time, in that exhilarating moment of take-off. A team of road-workers, bright fluorescent yellow and orange aprons. One leant against his shovel, sunglass protected from afternoon glare. They waved us past.

The freeway for Melbourne.

Druce told us, 'I'm visiting my friend, Carmen. Divorced lady. Three children.'

We lost count of the number of direction changes. Perplexed, Druce consulted a hand-drawn map. He headed the wrong way at roundabouts. Missed street names, obscured by foliage.

Late in the afternoon, we finally met Carmen, a woman well under five feet tall. Almost a plump and cheerful dwarf. Clad entirely in black, with tiny, high-heeled boots and a friendly smile.

Dad and I exchanged stunned glances. If only Druce had warned us of her ultra-petite stature. May, her sister, was of normal height. Both women were in mourning for their mother.

We lingered over cups of tea and slices of currant cake.

Darkness. Dad and I worried. Would we reach Melbourne before midnight? Happily, May gave us clear directions. A tram forced us to turn right, and into the very street we needed.

At the Astoria, a shower dribbled lukewarm water. The iced-up refrigerator refused to accept Magic Bricks for our food cooler. Lost socks kicked about under the beds.

I complained, but it got me nowhere. 'The owner's a Basil Fawlty double.'

Druce laughed. 'Reckon he could go through a full wash cycle and still emerge with a logical excuse.'

A grateful farewell: our most expensive and least convenient motel.

We set off, headed for the Prince's highway. Or so Druce claimed. Frequent direction changes brought a sense of déjà vu. Surely, we were going round in circles? At last Druce stopped, at Cranbourne.

'Won't be a minute.' He darted inside the building.

Dad saw a Chrysler spares sign. 'Well, I'll be damned.'

A kookaburra laughed.

Druce crept back. Like an alcoholic hides his bottles of booze, newly acquired car parts were concealed inside his jacket.

12

Lakes Entrance and Eden, popular holiday resorts. A whiff of briny air made me feel good. And with a name like Eden, how could it fail to please?

Bleached and barren fields appeared around Bega, famous for its cheese. Their ad on TV showed cows wandering in lush green pastures.

Dad said, 'A pity we couldn't bring some of the rain from Victoria.'

We lingered at Mogo. Unique shops and a buzz of activity made us keen for a closer look. The diverse artistic community offered paintings and a wide range of handcrafts. Pottery, wooden ware, leather goods, gemstones, Aboriginal crafts, stained glass. A lovely little blue ceramic bowl caught my eye, while rose quartz for luck seemed a good buy.

Exquisite glass balls brought back a wonderful experience, my walk through the bush on the farm. Elated by the brilliance of sunny skies, purple toadstools and tree ferns, I noticed one fluffy cloud hovering above. Its sudden outpouring of its grief caught me by surprise. I scurried to shelter on a huge, moss-covered log. A hundred feet above, the sun sparkled on green and gold leaves, shone through each raindrop. Magnified by some trick of the light into enormous orbs, they drifted down slowly, one by one, floating spheres of crystal, magic in flight.

During the past weeks, Druce had driven four thousand kilometres. Fast-moving traffic. Ever-changing road conditions. Suffering the stress of careless drivers and poor visibility.

At Wollongong, he looked exhausted. 'My reflexes aren't up to going much further. A few hours break and I'll be fine.'

I hesitated. 'Shall I drive?'

Druce gave me a look, glancing back at his precious vehicle.

Half past five.

Dad said, 'We'll find a motel.'

A university function meant there was not one spare room.

I said, 'Let's have an early meal. Miss the peak hour traffic. Give Druce a break.'

Tantalising aromas lured us into a small café. Druce and Dad shared a pizza. I had veal schnitzel with salad. We enjoyed home-made ice cream and fruit for dessert. Pondered highlights of our trip. Laughed over low moments.

Dad picked up his walking stick. 'A snooze is just the ticket for frayed nerves.'

The car park swarmed with students. Motors revved. Shouts, shrieks of laughter.

Dad groaned. 'A man would have to be deaf and blind to kip here.'

Druce took a Panadol for his throbbing head.

A caution of red lights blinked at the edges of the dark freeway. Drunken youths played chicken with the passing traffic.

Dad said, 'Silly buggers. I saw one throw a rock.'

Kirrawee station loomed.

I said, 'Let's take the shorter Sutherland/Bankstown route across the Woronora River.'

The winding road led down to an old, low bridge, deep in the valley. A narrow and tortuous one climbed up the other side.

'Soon it becomes a faster route.'

At Stacey Street, I ached with exhaustion. 'It's great to be home. Thanks, Druce, for all that driving.'

Dad nodded. 'Great job, son. I've enjoyed my time with you fellas.'

Just before eleven p.m., I fell into bed, drifting off. Woken time and again by the rumble of passing traffic. Bridging the railway line had brought a direct link with the Hume Highway. Bumper-to-bumper traffic rumbled by at all hours, day and night. It was more than time to move. Only, would the selling price be enough to buy elsewhere?

At Wattle Grove, the powers-that-be extolled the virtues of cutting staff and of putting us on rosters. 'For greater efficiency, productivity and cost reductions.'

By its very nature, geriatric nursing is labour-intensive. Those with dementia take longer to attend and need additional staff.

'Huh!' Elsie said. 'It's all about profit.'

I sighed. 'Our dear leader never raises his eyes above the bottom line.'

Whispers reached us of ten-hour shifts.

Elsie frowned. 'I've no intention of working longer. My notice is ready and waiting.'

I laughed. 'Same here.'

A number of Greek-speaking patients informed my decision to attend an evening college class. Jim ran a community radio program in Greek, his native tongue. Classes improved interactions between a police woman and the public. Daughters-in-law learnt Greek to communicate with family members. My few phrases helped me to comfort residents from that far, and mythical land of the Argonauts.

I said to Elsie, 'A visit to Greece would be the perfect way to practise my skills.'

She laughed. 'Put selling your house on hold. This opportunity may not come again.'

I redirected mail. Paid bills. Packed my bags.

Antoine saw me off at the airport. 'Send me postcards, pet. Have a wonderful time.'

13

In May 1995, excitement zinged through my veins. Five weeks holiday on the agenda, and the opportunity to practise Greek. My 747 soared into the skies. Every care left behind, in drizzly, cheerless Sydney.

Lively Greek music sped us towards Athens. Glowing afternoon light, clouds a carpet of golden fleece. Turbulence. The wind tossed us around like a kite. A chorus of safety belt buckles clacked into place.

One row away, the cigarette brigade puffed and coughed. The stink of smoke swirled around me. Passengers from the non-smoking areas continually swapped seats for a fag.

One of the passengers wheezed. 'I've asthma.'

The hostess, cigarette in hand, snapped, 'We haven't enough seats for smokers. What are you complaining about?'

Lacking a mask, I grabbed my silk scarf. It protected my lungs from unbearable fumes. Sleep at last. Later, when I washed it out in the basin at my hotel, the water turned black.

Olympic Airport. A smooth landing: I'd slept right until we taxied to a stop. At seven a.m. Athens time, I stood on the aircraft steps. A chill morning breeze.

Ahead of me, a priest in long black robes. Luxuriant, curly silver beard, a cross on a gold chain around his neck. Grandmothers in the sombre garb of widows, chatted of villages and towns they had left thirty years before. Babies blinked in the harsh light.

I hailed a cab.

The driver had a face like a squashed soccer ball. 'Do you like Greece?'

I dared not voice my feelings. I'd thought that Aussies were the only ones to ask such crass questions on arrival. Amazed by my modest Greek, he shared a few myths and legends.

Ancient monuments welcomed me to Athens.

I parked my baggage with the hotel concierge, setting off to explore. Grateful for a last-minute decision to bring my green Gortex. The crusty aroma from barrows made me ravenous. Circlets of crisp bread with sesame seeds, kouloria, tasted even more crunchy and delicious than they smelt.

A glitter of white, green and red lights. The warm bar enticed me away from the chill air. My coffee cost four hundred drachmas. A small cup of inky liquid: it needed heaps of sugar to make it palatable. Sipping it, my jet-lagged brain began to thaw. I'd given the barista a thousand-drachma note. Change in my purse for five hundred. Minutes earlier, she had spoken fluent English. The moment I raised the discrepancy, she lost the language. I lacked enough Greek to persist.

A bank offered the solution. Split my drachmas into smaller denominations. A florist shop window bloomed with expensive arrangements of roses, lilies and hyacinths.

Steps away, a black-clad granny sat in the dust, crutches beside her. A sign in English: 'No home, no job. Please help.' Her situation touched me. A wizened smile at my small donation.

Panepistimiou Street roared and rumbled with head-to-tail traffic. It made Stacey Street resemble a country lane. Sirens wailed. A mad barp of horns. Swarms of mopeds diced with death in the chaos. A uniform booked every rider at a corner: heaven knows the infringement. One big tourist coach backed up.

A distraught woman jumped up and down, screaming, 'Change your approach our you'll crush my car.'

I dodged bike riders, invaders of the footpaths.

A pedestrian crossing brought me no confidence. Motors revved for a quick getaway, edging ever closer. A prayer of thanks: I'd safely made the other side. Cars were only permitted to drive on alternate days, meant to reduce the volume of traffic. Work sites and cranes greeted me on almost every corner. A hidden underground railway network inched forward, promising relief.

Caressed by sunshine at Omonia Square, I reclined on a seat. The whiff of cheap cologne edged closer.

A silver-haired Greek gentleman, smooth as an olive. 'Madame, I'd be delighted to show you around the city.' The waxed ends of his moustache twitched.

'Thank you, no.' I extracted useful information about transport and museums. Made my escape, map in hand.

I located a *taxidromeio* (post office). Letters and postcards winged on their way to Greek colleagues, friends and family.

Neo-Classical buildings which had survived storm and earthquake for centuries faced destruction from pollution. Surely that didn't include a magnificent library and university, adorned with frescoes?

Rainbows of dreams blossomed on pavements. Proprietors of these multicoloured ribbons of lucky numbers carried out their business with nothing more than stand and a chair.

A boot-black leant forward on his stool, vigorously polishing boots and shoes. Leather inserts protected customers' socks. Regulars stopped for a shine, greeting him by name.

Oriental music drew me to an organ-player, *sans* monkey. The instrument pictured an exotic beauty, surrounded with carmine roses. Strands of raven hair peeped beneath a richly decorated scarf. Voluptuous eyes promised boudoir pleasures which one daren't imagine. Red velvet, a saucer for coins. I tossed a few the lady's way.

Boutiques displayed the fine clothing and the gold jewellery for which Athens is famous. Bargain shops offered a variety of gaudy household goods. Periptero, kiosks, appeared, selling postcards, souvenirs and trinkets. Some sold fruit, nuts and kouloria. The name Periptero evoked the English, peripatic. Just one of the thirty per cent of words we've gained from Greek.

In every hotel, coffee bar and restaurant, Athens men chain-smoked. Cigarette in one hand, worry beads clutched in the other. They twisted, caressed and flung these komboli around, a compulsive ritual to calm frazzled nerves. Fascinated to discover that komboli date back to Byzantine times. Each colour has significance: gold and silver denote wealth and millionaires. Red for love. Yellow equals hate and dislike. Orange for prosperity. Green equals hope, blue evil, white purity. Black and brown, are for teachers and priests. Olive brings fertility.

Next day, our tour began. It would eventually depart from the Piraeus port. I thought it might be fun to photograph the area. Picturing a blaze of blossoms in gardens, highlighting the blue of sea and sky.

The old subway station at Omonia Square groaned of disrepair and despair. My nose wrinkled at the stink of stale urine. I rushed past drunks or druggies, half-dressed. Ragged children, with old-young faces, accosted me, hands outstretched. I hurried over broken Piraeus pavements, and through dimly lit station passages, glancing behind me.

A train sped me to the wharf. I shouldn't have been surprised to find nothing worth a shot. Stowing my camera, I dashed for a return train.

I grabbed a seat, grateful to be heading home. The next moment, two scruffy youths stopped beside me. A discord of piano accordion and a trumpet. The deafening din dragged on and on, reached a crescendo. Stopped. An acne-scarred face invaded my space. His left hand trembled, inches from my money sack.

Shouts of a feigned quarrel erupted between the invader and the pair behind me. In a flash, I recalled a similar strategy in the Paris Metro. That time, pickpockets had taken my purse.

Clamping my hands over the money belt, I turned my back. Moved further along the seat. Sweating. How many of them were in on this scam?

Guessing the game was up, the trio took off.

I fled the train. Rushed to escape Omonia station. Barely breathing until I reached the sanctuary of the Titania hotel. The foyer swarmed with smartly clad travellers, young and old. Coaches disgorged mountains of luggage.

I gained my room and wrote up my close call.

A continental breakfast offered everything from brioche to bread, biscuits and rolls. A compote of peaches on offer, cornflakes, scrambled eggs, ham and cheese.

The conspiratorial air of Italians sharing my table puzzled me. But then, never one to reject a good idea, I followed suit.

On every corner stood an ancient monument or temple. A statue appeared to Lord Byron, a fan of all things Greek. Eucalypts trees nestled up to fallen Greek stones. A Byzantine church brought hints of a distant past. The latest red Lamborghini seemed incongruous beside ancient marble columns.

That evening, I dressed for dinner. Black and white floral skirt, teamed with a black silk blouse, and wide, beaded belt, also in black. Set off by antique jet beads with matching earrings, inherited from Mum.

Spiros, the maître d' of the hotel restaurant, made it his mission to be friendly. In my limited Greek, I explained the reasons for my trip. Delighted to have a foreigner speaking his language, Spiros brought me a half-bottle of crisp white wine. It never appeared on my bill. A delicious souvlakia, rice and salad made up for my earlier troubles.

A very strange dream followed. I wore a beautiful gown and a 1920s Harley Davidson scarf with pastel-coloured ends in an Art Deco design. My daughter Naomi tried on slinky, jewelled evening dresses, fashionable in the era. A trunk revealed other treasures. Did Mum's antique beads carry some memory of times past? I fancy she acquired them second-hand, but I really don't know.

A taxi took me to the Grande Bretagne Hotel, ready for the tour. An imposing building, situated in Syntagma (Constitution) Square, next to the parliament buildings, it was once a private house. It stood beside the Tomb of the Unknown Soldier. His compatriots stood guard in national costume. Multicoloured flags of many nations fluttered in the breeze.

The get-to-know-you meeting would take place late that afternoon. I seized the opportunity to explore the Plaka, the oldest part of Athens. A place of souvenir shops and tavernas, it nestles at the foot of the great rock of the Acropolis. I strolled the narrow streets. Stone houses boasted tiny gardens. A white cat sunned itself on a windowsill. Seizing the opportunity to practise my Greek, I spoke to shop owners and locals. They seemed only too pleased to oblige. It amazed me how impressed they were to hear a foreigner attempting their language.

Hadrian is probably most famous for his wall across England. It surprised me how often his name and works appear in Athens, a city he adored. I learnt that the brilliant and witty emperor ruled the Roman empire for twenty-one years. In that time, he enhanced Athens with the Library of Hadrian and his amazing aqueduct. Adding the temple of Olympian Zeus, and the colossal bridge over Eleusinian Kephissos. Not to mention Hadrian's Arch, the Temple of Venus, and the Pantheon, regarded as one of the most important temples of ancient Greece.

Dark clouds gave way to a downpour. I'd left my umbrella back at the hotel, so I took shelter in a small tea room. Sharing a few phrases and remarks on the weather in Greek. The owner brought me a coffee for only four hundred drachmas. An American paid five hundred.

The sun burst forth. Exuberant, I bade my rainy-day friend goodbye. Striding along the glittering cobblestones, I mused, so what if I become lost? Soon, exhaustion overcame enthusiasm. Sleepless from excitement at four a.m., I'd packed my case well before breakfast.

I ordered a gold cartouche at a jewellery shop, with Egyptian symbols for my name. 'I'll collect it on my return from the cruise.' Athens gold has a special quality, very bright. A perfect birthday present for myself.

A glance at my watch. Yikes. Barely an hour before the meeting with our tour guide. I asked directions from an elderly barrow lady selling soft drinks.

'You're heading in the wrong direction.'

Street by street, I negotiated my way through the maze of stalls and twisting byways. Asking every passer-by in Greek, 'Excuse me, where is Syntagma Square?'

A poster caught my attention. Passed on my arrival earlier, the pieces had been glued in a malaligned position, giving an extra nose, and peculiar expression, to the female face. It was just across the way from my hotel. I relaxed in the warm sunshine of a park. Devouring my illicit ham roll.

Upstairs in the Grande Bretagne, my eyes widened. A de luxe, twin-share room with twenty-foot ceilings. Delightful view of the courtyard. Acres of marble in the bathroom, even a bidet. A telephone beside the loo brought giggles.

I decided it would be easy to become accustomed to someone switching on the bedside light each night. The fine cotton sheets turned back, a wrapped chocolate left on my pillow. My very own lady-in-waiting.

The charming representative from Siva Travel, an Englishwoman called Dilys, supplied information. 'During World War Two, the Grande Bretagne was occupied, in turn, by the Greek army, the Nazis and finally, Churchill. A bomb was discovered shortly before his arrival. One of the many unsuccessful attempts on his life during the conflict.'

She introduced us to an excellent self-service restaurant. 'It's called The Neon, and just across the square from the Grande Bretagne.'

It became a favourite of our group. On every visit, I drooled at the variety of salads, hot dishes such as rice and chicken souvlaki. Desserts included yummy cakes. Huge bowls of strawberries brought the tantalising aroma of real fruit, almost forgotten with the hard offerings from supermarkets. And I couldn't resist the luscious confections with cream and gelatine. Drinks included everything from wine, to iced water available on tap: Greeks love their Nero.

My bright pink blouse matched to perfection one of the shades of silk in my silver rainbow earrings, a gift from my daughter.

Outside the Neon, an attractive middle-aged Greek approached. 'A beautiful woman like you…alone… I just want to talk with someone.'

I suppressed laughter. No doubt, he made it his business to charm unaccompanied women of a certain age.

'Love your earrings… Like a bird's wing. What are they made of?'

'Silk.'

He flashed a brilliant smile. 'My car's at the garage, but that's no problem.' He indicated an enormous motor scooter. 'Let's go to the Plaka and have a good time.'

I could imagine my son and daughter's reaction. Silly old Mum roaring off on the back of some stranger's scooter. Risking travellers cheques, cash, credit cards, almost certainly virtue. Perhaps my life.

Long ago, I had learnt, never play the other man's game. I flashed a smile. 'What a shame. I'm leaving on tour.'

We parted with a handshake, gloom on his face. For some reason, the small interlude left me with a glow.

Dilys said, 'The Acropolis means city boundary.'

Built astride a huge volcanic rock, the ascent proved easy. I'd studied Doric and Ionic columns at Blackfriars' Correspondence School, thrilled to see them in ancient stone.

'Design details,' Dilys said, 'were by the architect Phidias. His work has never been equalled. The Parthenon or Virgin remained intact for centuries, surviving earthquakes and natural disasters. Badly damaged in the 1800s from explosives.'

An inexplicable storage site, I thought.

She added, 'The greatest modern threat comes from pollution.'

Later, 'Mount Sounion faces the Aegean Sea and the Cyclades islands,' Dilys said.

We strolled around remains of the temple of Poseidon. 'Dates to the fifth century BC. Keeps watch over the entrance to the Saronic Gulf. Sailors of ancient times prayed before facing the dangers of the open sea. Homer's Sacred Headland, it was a favourite of romantic writers such as Lord Byron and William Falconer, the sailor-poet.'

The ocean glittered.

'You'll see Glyfada, Vouliagmeni and Varkiza. Some of Athens most beautiful suburbs.'

The beaches of the Aegean lacked surf.

'Shingle replaces sand.'

Aussies muttered of sandy Australian Bondi.

At one spot, black backpacks hung from limbs of trees, reminding us of fruit bats.

'Barren hills, sparse vegetation and few natural resources make tourism a vital part of the economy.' Holiday villas abounded, painted white. 'Note the large number of partially completed concrete houses.' They perched on hillsides, with excellent ocean views. 'You might think it's caused by the exorbitant costs of imported iron, steel, concrete and timber. But no: a tax must be paid on completion. Canny Greeks ensure that some aspect of a building remains unfinished.'

The coach chuckled.

I chatted with an American academic from Oregon.

Toni taught Ancient Greek history at one of the universities. She sighed. 'It's my first visit. Wish I hadn't come.'

Her reaction surprised me. 'Why's that?'

'Reality's destroyed my romantic visions, I guess.'

Toni was also widowed. It pleased me to have a conversation about our single status. We debated whether to share dinner that night. Her not-so-subtle enquiry about my views on liberated sex put an end to that.

Next morning, a shuttle us sped us to the *Triton*, a smart white ship of the Epirotiki line.

Graham, a British expat, our tour leader, launched into the procedure for embarkation. 'Labels attached to the main baggage. Cabin numbers and red stickers wrapped around the handle of each suitcase.'

And so on. My head began to spin. How on earth was one expected to remember all that?

We proceeded en masse through security, passing metal detectors. An X-ray device scanned the hand luggage. It emerged for collection on a table at the other side. Our main baggage went off by itself, a worry. However, Graham seemed to have it all in hand.

Dilys collected travel documents. 'They'll be placed under your cabin doors later.'

I felt glad to leave all the organisation to experts.

We exited the bus.

Graham led the group towards the Triton. Stern exhortations to 'Stay in a group when boarding.'

Giggles. I stepped off the wobbly gangplank, frisked by an Israeli security guard.

Graham rushed our passports to the purser's office, to photocopy them. 'For use during the voyage.'

My twin-share cabin not only saved money. It also provided the luxury of a spare bed to stash my suitcase.

A million stairs took me to the cinema for Graham's next briefing. The room was in semi-darkness, a couple of dim lights at the rear.

Graham snapped. 'Where's an electrician?'

None arrived.

Graham's voice emerged from shadows, loud and clear. 'Mark your choices for shore excursions. I'll collect the cash and credit card orders, and distribute tickets.' His next news – 'You don't have to pay for drinks at the bar' – brought cheers. 'You must settle your accounts on Thursday.' Groans.

He boasted, 'I've an unbroken record: the first bus away on excursions. You must wait for disembarkation announcements, your doors open. Ignore the designation of the group, unless they're Asian. Whether it's French, German or Spanish, immediately join the first boat going ashore.'

The ten-minute briefing (funny how the opposite of that word is never longing) had extended to an hour. The group restive. Like me, they were ravenous. At last it ended. I collapsed on the bed in my cabin.

Throbbing motors announced we had left Piraeus. But preliminaries still had a way to go. We'd been told, 'Don your lifejackets. Proceed to designated stations for compulsory life boat drill.'

My spectacles enabled perusal of instructions on the back of my cabin door. I dragged on the bright yellow, padded life jacket, complete with whistle and light. Tied all the tapes. Losing my way a couple of times, despite the map. The safety drill left me wondering. How would I manage the real thing? Let alone have the courage to leap off the ship's side, seeking spare lifeboats.

'Occlude the nose,' the instructor advised us. 'Prevents the ingestion of too much water.'

We'd hoped our reception might be over.

But, no. A general briefing followed. Our cruise director, a glamorous young woman called Bianca de Jong, switched from Italian to French to English to German or Spanish without a second's hesitation. Who wouldn't be impressed? Her *Kaló taxídi* – have a good voyage, in Greek – was just one more branch on her language tree. Half-a-dozen assistants proved equally adept in Japanese, French, German.

'That's about everything you need to know. Have an interesting and pleasant holiday.'

If I could only remember half of it.

We fell upon a long-delayed lunch. Delicious salads, fruit, meats and treats, all well worth the wait. Americans, Don and his wife Barbara, a nursing supervisor, invited me to join them at dinner. Earlier, Don's scowl at the Grande Bretagne Hotel had caught my attention. But now he seemed pleasant enough.

I reclined in a white deckchair, nursing a gin and tonic. Joined by another American Bobby, a widow like myself, travelling with friends, Stu and Fiona. Sea eagles balanced on warm currents of air from the Triton motors, long wings outstretched. The sun smiled from a splendid blue sky. We enjoyed a long chat. Mysterious islands drifted past in a calm sea. I looked forward to every moment.

Table number 8 included me, Don and Barbara. Also, a middle-aged American called Jim. A contractor in the Middle East, I suspected his income flowed like oil, judging by the gold jewellery glittering on the wrists and throat of his much younger girlfriend, Hazel. Why not, I thought. An utterly charming and beautiful black woman, she made every other female on the cruise look plain.

Then there was Sarah, a gentle lady who used silence to cope with the barbed humour of her husband, Bernie. He didn't seem a bad sort of chap but he'd never learnt the moment to desist. On more than one occasion, his jokes brought tears to the long-suffering Sarah's eyes.

One night, Bernie confided he'd been cleaned out by a terrible auto accident involving his son. 'Cost me over a million bucks.'

The others drank a local red, too heavy for my taste. Barbara and I shared a very good bottle of white wine from Santorini. We only managed to drink half of it.

I asked the wine waiter, 'Could you please refrigerate the remainder for tomorrow night?'

He smiled. 'No problem.'

The table was amazed. A dozen choices every night for dinner made it hard to choose. Soup, salad and other entrees took away my appetite for the main. The steward noticed I wasn't eating, offering another dish. I refused that. He insisted I make another choice. I settled for the baked lamb.

Ah, the hardships of travel.

It excited me to lie in bed, the motors of the ship whirring. Outside my porthole, white caps raced by in the moonlight. My bed gently rocked to and fro. I couldn't stop thinking of that old nursery rhyme, 'Rock a Bye Baby'. It went back into the mists of time to Celts and Pictish folk. Rough water. The gentle motion became wild yawing of the vessel. I felt queasy. A couple of Travacalm tablets solved the problem.

In the pink light of dawn, I strolled around the wet decks. Watching the dark shapes of islands scud past in the mist: pure magic. We arrived at Santorini before six a.m. A violent volcanic eruption under the island, about 3500 BC, caused a major collapse. It created the circular harbour, anchorage for our ship. Black, jagged cliffs of the partly submerged crater rose hundreds of feet. Perched precariously on top, we could glimpse the little white village of Thira. Or so Dilys had told us. It later reminded me of white sugar cubes, overflowing the rim of a bowl.

We glided into the bay. A swirling fog hid all trace of those jagged ramparts. Disappointed, I made to put my camera away. At that moment, a young Japanese woman appeared at the rail of the ship. Flowing dark hair, big cream hat with a floppy bow, cream cardigan, long skirt and little white socks. I grabbed my Minolta. A perfect image against the misty background. Symbol of mystery and anticipation.

Santorini fascinated us.

'Ruins at Akritori are twice the age of Pompeii,' Dilys told us. 'Julius Caesar might have been a visitor. For centuries, this Minoan town was buried under hundreds of feet of volcanic ash. People thought Cyclops threw stones from the heavens. This legend was passed down from one generation to another. It had begun when huge basalt boulders from cooling lava rained down from the sky, falling up to eleven kilometres from the volcano.'

The *Triton* anchored. In the huge swell, a small caique boat rose and fell like a seesaw. Relieved to board it safely, I noticed that the landing spot, offered neither wharf nor planks. Helping hands saw most of us safely to dry land.

Until one obese lady lost her footing, helpless as a Christmas beetle. Frantic attempts to rescue her. Incoming wavelets sent the small craft forward, crunching near her legs. I held my breath. After several panicky attempts by the crew, she regained her feet. Struggling for air and trembling. Applause for a lucky escape. Her only injury, grazed knees.

'Certain archaeologists believe that Santorini and Crete once belonged to the same land mass,' Dilys said. 'Maybe Santorini was the legendary Atlantis.'

Some of the wall paintings of Santorini are similar to those at Knossos, on Cretes.

'Plato, historian and poet, told of a highly civilised people being engulfed by fire and water.'

Excavations by Marinatos commenced at Akritori in 1967, roofed over to protect wall paintings.

'Remains of one house three storeys high bear signs of a balcony. It may have belonged to a rich sea aptain, since it is so much larger than the others. Paintings found in the house include one of a naked fisherman holding mackerel. In another, children are boxing: the first known painting of someone wearing a gloves.'

Archaeologists found much broken pottery.

'Intact pots had been placed under beds for safety. Window frames also survived. But no human remains were found. We suspect, people had a warning. They fled, only to be killed by huge tidal waves, hundreds of feet high.'

One modern grave is situated within the precincts.

'An archaeologist died when an empty space collapsed. He's interred in the place he loved.' Dilys pointed out the oval roofs of whitewashed houses. 'They help to withstand earthquakes. Many are painted brilliant blue, along with the local churches' amazing domes. Harsh winds sweep across the barren island. Dotted with black basalt and pumice stones, it grows few trees. But viticulture thrives, an industry specialised to a degree not necessary in temperate climes.'

Dilys showed us grapevines grown only to the height of cabbages. 'Each plant is a living basket, formed by training one long tendril into a circle. Within, the bunches of fruit are protected from the harsh climate.'

No rain falls in summer.

'The vines gain moisture from the humidity, and water leached out of the pumice stones, from winter downfalls.'

Barbara and I recalled the superb Santorini wine we had enjoyed on board the *Triton*.

Dilys went on, 'The island dates to the Bronze Age. A time of female deities. Nothing was known of the role of males in procreation.'

Women were revered as life givers, goddesses of the universe. Priestesses used special rituals to bless food, fruits, seeds, grain and eggs to guarantee a good harvest.

'When people understood that it was the change of seasons which produced crops, the veneration of females ceased. Three thousand years ago, male gods took over.'

We wandered around the narrow streets of Thira enjoying the view of the bay and volcanic cliffs, I fell into conversation with an elderly American man. Long, daggy shorts, bald. We shared delight over the vista.

His wife glared at me. 'Why are you here without your husband?'

'I'm a widow.'

'Oh! I'm sorry.'

A cable car took us to the shore to resume our cruise. A splendid meal of salad and strawberries ended a fascinating day.

I wrote a postcard: 'Enduring the panorama of sun-drenched islands and blue Aegean sea. At Crete, we viewed the remains of the ancient Minoan city of Knossos.'

Dilys told us, 'The writings of Homer led archaeologists to this site. It dates from the third to first millennium BCE. The kingdom of Minos, the prehistoric ruler of the seas. Minos was a title like Pharaoh. An original palace was devastated by the earthquake and tidal wave that destroyed Akritori. Rebuilt a couple of centuries later by Daedalus, it was destroyed by fire about 1200 BC.'

Sir Arthur Evans unearthed the remains of this palace in 1900.

'Partially restored, decorations included the double-headed axe. It's a ritual symbol of the Minoan religion. Mythological birds, symbolise royal power.'

We recalled the ancient Greek legend of a half-bull, half-man who roamed the Labyrinth. 'King Minos kept his enemies to a minimum by feeding them to the beast. Every nine years the animal was said to require the sacrifice of seven maidens and seven youths.'

Theseus was meant to become another victim. 'A handsome young man, lover of the king's daughter, Theseus must kill the Minotaur, then return through that maze. The princess obtained a reel of thread from Daedalus. He unwound it on his way in, then used it afterwards to make his escape. You'll recall that Daedalus was imprisoned for revealing the secret of the labyrinth. He constructed wings for himself and his son, Icarus. The boy ventured too close to the sun, melting the wax. He fell into the sea. Daedalus flew on.'

Nightly performances and dancing on board ship made the cruise one big party. My favourite was a Greek show put on by the crew. Passengers wore blue and white in honour of the occasion. The girls and boys whirled, leapt and gyrated in their wonderful national costumes. Haunting strains of folk music. Free tastings of ouzo. At every high point of the amazing and delightful show, the audience rose, shouting 'Oom pah.' Wild clapping for their energy, skills and enthusiasm.

Dilys warned, 'Beware of imbibing too much ouzo. One glass and you feel like a bird. Two glasses and you are a mad bird. Three glasses and you're a dead bird.'

Breakfast coffee on deck. The golden glitter of yet another morning danced on every wavelet. The beautiful harbour of Rhodes. Ancient stone windmills. Magnificent walls.

'Built by the Knights of St John of Jerusalem about 1306. A Christian bastion against the Turks. Minarets are all that remain of the Ottoman occupation.'

Rodos, island of roses.

Dilys said, 'The main maritime power in the eastern Mediterranean, back in 2 BC. Famous for fine arts and gold jewellery. Ceramics were decorated with stylised plants and animals. The Turkish influence produced the Rhodes faience style of pottery, with brilliant enamels. Rodos was renowned for sculpture. You'll recall the masterpiece the *Victory of Samothrace* at the Louvre. Another, the *Laocoön* at the Vatican, is a complex work of twisting serpents and figures. But in 265 BC, Chares of Lindos produced the most magnificent statue of all.'

She went on, 'The huge Colossus of Rhodes was one of the seven wonders of the ancient world. It depicted the sun god, Helios. A goliath, thirty metres high, it stood on two sides of a harbour inlet. Sailing ships passed between its legs. Toppled by earthquakes, it was melted down and transformed into coins or guns.'

Barbara spoke for all of us. 'A sad fate for such a treasure.'

In the old town, we chanced upon a group of university students. Clad in blue jeans and T-shirts, international uniform for the young, they performed a spontaneous folk dance or Horus. It was a delight to witness their verve and enthusiasm.

I mused, 'The only Australians of a similar age with a tradition of dance are our Indigenous folk.'

A pleasant drive through the perfumed pine forests. Lemon and orange groves, vineyards and quaint villages.

'The little town of Lindos was once the capital of Rhodes.'

Wiser folk than me hired donkeys for the climb up the winding paths towards the top. Hadn't I walked to the top of Ayers Rock? This one looked easy. It wasn't.

Tablecloths, crocheted doilies and other napery were spread out across rocky outcrops. Nature's open-air shops, a perfect means for enterprising locals to gain some of our tourist dollars . So why did we find it amusing?

Dilys had said, 'It's worth a look. The summit's a rocky promontory, with a sheer drop of four hundred feet to the sea. There's a splendid view of St Paul's Bay. That's where the apostle landed in AD 51. You'll see fortifications of the Knights Templar, remnants of a Byzantine church and the fourth century BC Doric temple of Athena Lindia.'

Gosh, I thought, this place has everything.

Fiona and I fancied a dip.

Dilys said. 'A taxi to the beach should be four hundred drachmas.'

The first driver suggested a distant one. 'Seven thousand drachmas.'

I attempted to argue in Greek.

'Out, get out. Now.'

Laughing, we approached a Greek moustache.

'Four hundred drachmas.'

'That's more like it,' I said.

We took our places.

That driver extolled the virtues of a beach fifteen kilometres distant. Costing – you've guessed it – seven thousand drachma. With my limited Greek, I insisted on the initial price and original destination. The picture of gloom, he dropped us off.

'We've saved $40 dollars. It only cost $2!'

Fiona chuckled. 'Still, the joke's on us. We could've walked.'

The cool water offered a carefree interlude. Pleasant, except for the sharp stones.

Fiona groaned. 'Wish I'd packed my swimming shoes.'

'Me too. They'll either massage our feet, or cripple us for life.'

14

Graham declared, 'Ephesus is the highlight of all the archaeological sites.' He stressed the importance of being first on the scene. 'Crowd-free, you'll really appreciate it .'

A six a.m. breakfast at anchor, in the Turkish port of Kusadasi.

'No matter which group they call, you just go.'

Graham's instructions worked. We piled onto the first bus.

Yusuf, our local guide, took the microphone, 'Turkey is the treat we enjoy with Christmas dinner. The name of the country is pronounced, Tur-key-ay.'

Lush countryside, bright sunshine. Glimpses of men in bright local costumes driving donkey carts. Tantalised, I wondered why I hadn't taken the whole tour of this colourful land.

Graham's strategy worked. He received a round of applause. Unimpeded by crowds, we admired Ionic, Doric, Corinthian and mixed style marble columns.

Yusuf smiled. 'Carved by the skilful hands of ancient craftsmen. Ephesus represents the most extensive archaeological excavations in the world. It will take about a thousand years to unearth completely.'

Once the most important city and port of the Mediterranean for wealth, art and culture, it dated back to about 1000 BC.

'Ephesus had a population of 300,000. A succession of rulers included the Persians, and the legendary king Croesus.'

The city was destroyed by an earthquake in AD 17.

'Ephesus was rebuilt and enlarged under the Roman emperor Tiberius, later made capital of the Asian province.' Yusuf added, 'Hadrian added shrines and remarkable buildings such as the Library of Celsius. At one time, St John and St Paul lived and worked here. During a riot by the Ephesians, St Paul probably advocated destruction of the statue of Artemis, the goddess of fertility and protector of the city.' He said, 'In time, the harbour silted up. Malaria took its toll. People died or left. Earthquakes completed the devastation.'

Dark red poppies danced in a slight breeze. Long grass sparkled with dew. We slapped away the odd mosquito. Hundreds of tiny black frogs hopped across the marble road in front of us, oblivious to the danger.

Ruts worn by the wheels of Roman carriages bore testimony to archaic history. The road was grooved to make them less slippery.

Yusuf: 'The Arcadian Way once led directly to the ocean. Now it's far distant. What a sight this avenue of columns must have been when statues graced each of them.'

Here stood a carving of twisted serpents, symbol of medicine. There a fallen angel lay among yellow fennel and pink wildflowers.

Violet hyacinths grew beside the communal marble toilets.

Yusuf said, 'Once a roofed building with flushing cisterns. An open-air pool allowed the escape of noxious gases. Here, perhaps twenty men shared their most private moments. On cold mornings, a slave was used to warm the seat for his master.'

Chuckles.

The double-storey library of Celsius.

'Note the impressive façade. Excavated and reconstructed, statues were restored to their niches.'

Opposite the library was the bordello. His cheeky grin.

'Inscribed marble tablets in the street indicated the way for sailors and other male visitors. Underground passages led directly from the house of ill-fame to the library.'

Don guffawed. 'Giving the phrase, going to the library, a new significance.'

We fell about laughing.

'And now we reach this imposing theatre. One of the oldest in existence. It survived thousands of years of earthquakes and natural disasters, relatively intact. But look at it now. Loutish fans and loud music of a Guns and Roses concert caused enormous structural damage and cracking. It's now closed for expensive restoration.'

Dismayed glances. Anger that such things could happen.

Back in Kusadasi, we sipped Turkish apple tea. Gazed at fabulous designs in the finest silks and wools. Turkish carpet experts gave us a demonstration. A flick of the salesman's wrist. Rugs twirled hrough the air. It was easy to imagine them in full flight.

Yusuf said, 'Long hours and hundreds of knots are necessary to produce such masterpieces Young children lost their eyesight over the task.'

Fiona sighed. 'One needs to be as rich as Croesus to buy one of any size.'

Triton sailed through the golden afternoon towards Mykonos. Sad that our adventure was drawing to an end, Don, Barbara and I reclined on deckchairs. Sipping a final G&T, we watched the sea and islands slip past.

Small craft dropped us ashore. Strolling around the picturesque harbour, we gazed at a whitewashed town. Brilliant blue and green shutters adorned houses. Blue-domed churches and white windmills marked the horizon. Stopping for a beer in a small café, we admired the sparkling bay. Red and blue boats rocked to and fro in a teasing breeze, reflected in the clear water.

Narrow, winding streets brought the tantalising aroma of souvlaki and other exotic Greek food. Red geraniums spilled over balconies. A cactus reached skywards, a giant candelabra in the white-walled courtyard of a small restaurant. Water trickled into an attractive carved drinking fountain. Marine pictures jostled for space with trinkets in shop windows.

Wine flowed in one open-air taverna. Waiters rushed to and fro, serving delicacies to dozens of guests. A sombre-faced musician, coaxed haunting Greek tunes on a bouzouki. A patriarch with white beard and weathered face, spun and undulated. Moving hands, arms and body in dancing patterns older than him. Outside, a basket-laden donkey offered rainbows of spring flowers. A twirling moustache waited patiently beside his source of income.

Twilight. Back on board the ship, Graham gave instructions for dis-embarkation. Details competed with a noisy room.

Barbara and I made a toast with the remainder of our Santorini wine. 'To our trip. And many more.'

Farewell drinks spoke with nostalgia of all we has seen and done.

I gave a small koala and some postcards to our waiter. 'You've been especially kind. Thank you for keeping our Santorini wine safe.'

He smiled, kissing my hand. 'A pleasure, madame.'

Barbara giggled. 'You'd think he was French.'

Triton ploughed through the star-spangled darkness towards Athens. Tired smiles waved. Drifted away to pack.

Up at six, I sat in the half-light on the foredeck. Awaiting orders to disembark. The *Triton* felt sombre, or was it me? Multicoloured bunting hung forlorn and still in the crisp morning air. Big ships plied to and fro. The ghostly shape of Rodos passed from view. *Queen Odyssey* drifted across our bows.

Confused about Graham's details, I heard the loudspeaker screech, 'Go Ashore.' I took it as an order. My feet hit the gangway, made it to the wharf.

Grahame's eyes bulged. 'You were told to leave with the group, not individually.'

Meekly, I retraced my steps.

At the Grande Bretagne, another beautiful room. I'd miss those high ceilings, elegant furniture, and the marble bathroom. Peckish at five, I sampled one of the restaurant's elegant afternoon teas. In smart green silk slacks and top, I lingered over their strawberry liqueur shortcake with custard cream and lemon tea. It cost me the equivalent of twenty-five dollars, expensive in those days. It felt deliciously extravagant.

I mentioned my splurge to Don and Barbara.

He grinned, 'And did you scrub up for it?'

I chuckled, 'Of course,' thinking it must be some quaint and archaic American expression denoting smart clothing. Later I realised that he must have heard it in *Crocodile Dundee*.

Amazing the difference four days can make. Don seemed thirty years younger, adopting the carefree persona of his youth. Barbara as always, gentle and kind. I'm sure she was a credit to the nursing profession.

15

Thirty-first of August 1997. I'd barely settled back into my shift at Wattle Grove than a tragedy shattered the royal family. Unfolding on the lounge room TV, and on screens around the planet. Staff and residents watched in shock. Lady Diana, Princess of Wales, was critically injured in Paris.

Young, charismatic beautiful. Surely, she'd survive? Devastated for her young sons, the Princes William and Harry.

Eyes brimmed. 'Dead at only thirty-six. Icon of our time.'

The world poured out its grief, in cards, letters and floral tributes. She had mothered her boys to perfection, the fun mum everyone deserved.

The two young princes walked behind her casket, in the full glare of cameras and public scrutiny. Eyes brimmed. It seemed cruel and unnecessary, a time of unbearable grief. Harry was only thirteen. His card, to 'Mummy', touched me deeply.

Our DON, Ninette, took the podium. 'Documentation is crucial to justify our claims for funding, and subsidies.' Adding, 'No back-up documentation, no funding.' She indicated five folders of information. 'All RNs are required to read these.'

Menik's eyes met mine. Five folders? Impossible at the weekend, given the raft of duties of an eight-hour shift. Medications, dressings, monitoring residents, supervision of staff. Half-a-dozen folk might each be listed for half-an-hour's exercise daily. It looked good on paper. Until one did the sums.

I put up my hand. 'Can we borrow the folders to read at home?'

'I'm afraid not.'

At that moment, Liz pushed a petition towards Ninette. 'Signed by all the weekday staff.' Written in circular form, it concealed the identity of the instigator. Her eyes glittered. 'It asks that weekend staff write care plans.'

Ninette hesitated. 'Care plans should be shared by all staff.'

Trin's hand shot up. 'I second that.'

'Except,' continued the DON, 'weekend sisters.'

The room grumbled.

She continued, 'I remind you that weekend sisters have no support staff. Weekday RNs complete paperwork in a timely manner, thanks to extra staff working a half day each week. As you all know, we employ four occupational therapists. One answers the phone. Our nursing unit manager (NUM) deals with the doctors' visits, consults with the relatives, arranges for the ambulance. We also have Liz, our deputy director, to lend a hand. Also, I'm there to help.'

She continued, 'Clara and Elsie are entirely on their own. They take care of supervising and arranging replacement staff. Dealing with emergencies, equipment breakdowns, locating tradesmen, arranging an ambulance for hospital transfers. In addition to all the usual duties.'

Trin's hand jiggled, high in the air. 'What about Sister Menik?'

Matron hesitated.

I jumped in. 'Menik doesn't have any support either. She is my pillar in any emergency situation. By the way, we both work through our meal breaks. None of the weekday staff do that.'

The meeting seethed to an end.

Juggernauts rattled my cottage windows. I sought three realtor opinions. Estimates varied from $ 90,000 to $220,000.

Elsie said, 'Cottages on a highway aren't the best investment.'

I laughed. 'Tell me something I don't know. Thank goodness I've savings.'

My father arrived at Stacey Street. The journey from Hunters Springs took two days, instead of one. He grinned. 'The old Valiant suffered all sorts of mechanical problems.'

Wry smiles, recalling our journey through Victoria, years earlier.

Druce had turned fifty: my kid brother. I found it hard to believe.

'Like a lot of unmarried folk, I fear he's waiting for his life to begin. Aren't we lucky, Dad? Good marriages. Children and now grandchildren.'

A proud grin. 'And my great-great-grandchildren.'

Dad planned to stay a while. He hated being alone on the farm since Mum and Victor had died. He'd never noticed the downside of isolation until old age. Healthy and busy, surrounded by a wife and family, life had been the way he liked it.

We mostly got on well. Yet it wasn't easy living at the beck and call of an aged parent. The moment my feet hit the floor each morning, Dad was up scrabbling for slippers and cane. I craved a few minutes quiet. Space to sort myself out.

He looked gloomy. 'It won't be long now, dear, before I'm gone.' The next day, 'I'll live to be a hundred. Or well beyond it.'

Thin but wiry, I figured he'd see me out.

I asked Dad about his early life. How this or that was done in the olden days.

He confirmed details of when, how and why Hunters Springs was bought. Told of his difficulty to arrange a loan, despite having a large deposit. 'I practically had to get down on my knees and beg.'

His tales of family history were vital for books I had underway.

Mum's death had brought Dad one blessing: the freedom to confide secrets. Forbidden for a lifetime to speak of it, he confirmed rumours of Mum's abortion. He also shared a tale of one dear old family friend. It seemed she'd long fancied him.

One day she said, 'Joe, there's something I've always wanted you to do.'

'Just ask.'

They'd shared a long and tender kiss.

I did my rounds.

Annie, one of my favourite residents, had been feeling poorly. She said, 'I'm not afraid of dying, you know, sister. I did that once.'

I sat on her bed. 'Really? What happened?'

'I collapsed in hospital. Unconscious.'

'Did you see anything? '

'I whooshed through a tunnel. Arrived at the most wonderful place you could ever imagine. I walked in a park with blue and white flowers. Vibrant colours you could never imagine. A lovely, glowing light. I saw my mother as a young woman. My father looked older than her. Everything was so relaxed and peaceful. I didn't want to come back. But a voice said it wasn't my time.'

'Do you recall returning to your body?'

She shuddered. 'It was horrible. They used those paddle things with jolts of electricity. Resuscitation brought back all the pain. It took me a while to recover. Then I learnt that my niece was getting married. I offered to make her wedding gown. It was a lot of work but made me very happy. Her mother had died of cancer when the children were very young. I'd promised to do what I could. Glad that I was able to create something very special for her. The bride declared, "Your designer gown made my day."'

I patted her shoulder. 'I'm grateful you told me, Annie. That's a powerful near death experience.'

My father urged me, 'Give up work. Live with me at Hunters Springs. It would only be for about ten years.'

I chuckled. 'Dad, that's more than people get for murder.' I'd fought hard as a teenager to escape his rural paradise. 'I'll help you, Dad, but I can't give up everything.'

'I wouldn't expect that of you, dear.'

Like others of his generation, my father anticipated a daughter's unstinting support. He'd approached widowed friends, seeking a companion. None were prepared to give up the comforts of civilisation.

My father's closest friend offered a solution. On his deathbed, he said, 'When I die, Joe, you can have my wife.'

His wife, Hazel, had no say in their arrangement.

Dad made his pitch. But by then, Hazel had hooked up with an old flame, in the mixed tennis doubles, and as a partner.

RN Huang joined Wattle Grove staff, boasting a brace of degrees. His role was NUM or nursing unit manager.

Deputy Liz gritted her teeth. 'I've seen a lot of educated fools come and go. This one lacks both practical experience and common sense.'

Doone, usually kind and gentle, seemed angry. 'You won't believe what I've heard about Huang.' Her eyes sparked. 'Mabel, poor old soul, was at death's door. Semi-conscious. Weak pulse, laboured breathing. RNs and family had said their goodbyes. But not Huang.' She trembled. 'He took up her walking frame. She needs motivation.'

I've heard tell that Liz shouted, 'Put that away, Huang. Can't you see Mabel's condition?'

'Another lady could no longer manage food, her life measured in days. One daughter's eyes brimmed. "I'm glad you're letting Mum go peacefully." Nurses attended her basic needs. Oral hygiene, mouth moistened for comfort, regular pressure area care, the caress of clean linen. You all know the drill. Huang took it upon himself to force-feed her fluids with a syringe. She developed aspiration pneumonia. Died in hospital. Spare us idiots in our declining years.'

I sighed. 'Hear, hear.'

Some claimed a new age of nursing had dawned. On paper, a halcyon place of continuous improvement. On paper, all was well. On paper, rhetoric took over.

Anonymous white-collar workers and government number-counters in distant offices made the rules.

Somehow, Ninette had coped with the dramatic increase in her workload. Pressured to reduce costs and cut staff numbers, she developed arthritic problems. Bad knees. High blood pressure.

Government minions kept her busy monitoring care plan results. One aspect of patient care brought too many points? Next time around, the rewards from that area would be negligible. Something else would be substituted. Nobody could keep up in that dance of funding catch-up.

Doone brought more worrying reports of Huang. 'He asked the GP to check Mrs Mort's toe. Claimed it was infected. Her doctor found no inflammation, redness or heat. Pointed out healing areas. Said it looked good. "Carry on Betadine."'

Menik chuckled. 'Huang must have lost a lot of face over that.'

I asked, 'But has he learnt anything?'

Doone shrugged. 'I doubt it.'

That Saturday I found Mrs Mort's foot encased in enough crepe bandages for an Egyptian mummy, held firmly in place with a criss-cross of tape. Yet the treatment sheet stated, 'Paint with Betadine.'

Hairs prickled on my neck. Someone wanted to ensure the dressing remained intact over the weekend. But why? I unrolled the bandages. Removed thick Duoderm, taped in place. Called Menik. 'Look. It's riddled with small ulcers.'

She frowned. 'Pale and wrinkled, too.' She added, 'Moist for several days.'

Suffering from dementia, Mrs Mort couldn't name the culprit.

I groaned. 'Healed on Thursday. The deterioration since then. Doubtless, Huang planned to show it to her GP on Monday or Tuesday.'

'Vindicated over the need for antibiotics?'

'Doone's right.' I seethed. 'He's not only incompetent, but dangerous.'

She frowned. 'Will you tell matron?'

'You bet.'

Elsie and Menik witnessed the treatment sheet orders.

'Should it disappear, we'll present a united front.' I wrote an explicit report to DON.

Mrs Mort's GP looked shocked . 'I'll report this to Ninette. Action must be taken.'

Huang resigned that very week.

Antoine had recently returned from teaching French in China. We shared a dinner in Sydney's CBD.

He asked, 'What's the latest on Stacey Street? You've got to get away from there. Petrol fumes will kill you.'

'Ah, but you haven't heard my news. Naomi's expecting.'

'Well, well, well. That deserves a toast.'

We clinked glasses.

'I've put aside Stacey Street woes until after the UK.'

He knew that my daughter, Naomi had moved to London and married a Brit.

'I can't wait to hold my first grandchild.'

A grandfather several times over, he grinned. 'All the fun and none of the hassle. What do you want?'

I laughed. 'It's a cliché…'

'So long as he/she is healthy, eh?'

A bus dropped us back at Gladesville.

Antoine told me, 'Here's my shortcut.'

Victoria Road traffic thundered past.

'I'll use the pedestrian crossing.'

'Scaredy cat. I always cross here.'

Was I being excessively cautious? A break in the traffic. We set off.

I'll never know why Antoine shouted, 'Run.'

Expecting to be mown down by some juggernaut, I ran. On reaching the footpath, I glanced back for Antoine. Crashing like a wall of bricks. My right ankle collapsed under me. I held the throbbing foot in both hands. Mad at Antoine. Angry with myself for ignoring my gut feeling.

Only weeks away from England and my number one grandchild. Suppose I couldn't travel?

Antoine returned with a tea towel and washer.

I spluttered, 'Where are the bandages?' Slipping off my pantyhose, I wound them around the ankle.

He helped me hobble to his apartment. The ankle was bruised, and badly swollen. I couldn't sleep for the pain.

Next morning, Antoine drove me home. He'd sold his vehicle some time earlier.

I gripped the seat. 'Make up your mind on your lane, man. Don't straddle two at once.'

Grateful for my safe arrival at Stacey Street, I rang Wattle Grove to cancel my shifts.

Liz said, 'If the ankle's fractured, you'll be off for six weeks. Four for a sprain.'

I took a cab to the medical centre. X-rays ruled out a fracture.

The GP shook his head. 'Nothing can be done for the swelling and bruising.'

Next morning, Liz arrived on my doorstep. Checking to see if the injury were genuine, I supposed. A curt greeting.

She blinked at the colour and degree of ankle swelling. 'I'll take the medical certificate so you'll get paid.'

Was she kidding? I didn't need one for the first two days of an illness.

A visit to the medical centre followed each week. It puzzled me why the doctor didn't write me a certificate for longer. The ankle remained bruised and swollen.

He said, 'You need to start exercising your foot.'

'Good,' I said, 'I'm flying overseas in four weeks. My first grandchild.'

He blinked. 'Such a trip is ab-so-lute-ly out of the question. How could you help your daughter?' Adding, 'You've a bone chip. Could float around forever. It may never heal. There might be torn ligaments – nothing can be done for those.'

I blinked. Bone chip? Torn ligaments? Never heal? What nonsense.

'You might need CAT scans. Tests. Problems likely for the next six months.'

I seethed. Clearly, the idiot had been counting on weekly visits – and for months.

Using dear old Uncle Bill's walking stick, I tottered to the health food and vitamin shop. 'Is there any natural remedy to reduce swelling and bruising?'

The young woman had had a badly broken arm. 'Traffic accident. Bruised and painful for months. Doctors had nothing to suggest. Arnica tablets were my turning point.' She examined my ankle. 'Arnica tablets hasten dispersal of fluids, bruising and toxins. They also help ligaments and tendons.' She added, 'Take two, three times daily. Dissolved under the tongue, Arnica goes straight into the bloodstream. I also recommend calcium, a thousand milligrams daily, with Vegetal Sicilia five hundred milligrams three times daily.'

The speed of improvement amazed me. By the following morning, the bruising and swelling were much reduced. For the first time in weeks, I slept and walked pain-free. The recovery continued. Arnica tablets saw the ankle healed. They have continued to prove their efficacy for thirty years. When will research see them available for hospital patients?

Liz frowned over my travel plans. 'Get a second opinion. Make sure you're up to it.'

She was right. I mustn't be a hindrance to Naomi.

The specialist listened to my ankle report with a twinkle in his eye. I avoided mention of natural remedies. 'I can see no reason why you shouldn't fly.' He suggested a physio consult.

I could have jumped for joy – except for my weak ankle. A wobble board helped improve my balance. The physio's exercises strengthened muscles and ligaments.

Our next staff meeting. Palpable hostility, weekend staff the target. Staffing and roster issues had lurked in the shadows of innuendo and gossip.

Now Ninette confirmed the rumours. 'Employee numbers must be downsized. Ten-hour shifts and rotating rosters will be introduced.' She looked at Elsie and me. 'That will end weekend shifts. But your jobs will remain.'

Trin sniggered. 'Now we'll be working your weekends. And you'll be doing our weekly shifts.'

I shot her an icy glance. 'No way. I'll resign and live off my investments.'

The NSW Nurses Association clarified our rights.

I told Elsie and Menik, 'Permanent part-time employees are deemed to have a contract. The employer can't reduce or increase hours without our permission. They must give us two weeks' notice, in writing, of any changes,' adding, 'We may be required to work four days in a week, to comprise our total hours in any one pay period.'

Menik asked, 'Could they bully us into full-time duties?'

I laughed. 'Refusing would lead to the sack. But also make our employer culpable.'

Elsie chuckled. 'Then we'd have to seek redress for unfair dismissal. Maybe the big boss would negotiate a redundancy package?'

'Dream on.'

My holiday pay was meant to be paid in advance. By Tuesday, nothing had reached my bank account. On Wednesday, I called the pay office. Assured, 'It'll be there tomorrow.'

Thursday drifted into Friday. Still no cash. I made yet another call.

The paymaster said, 'It'll be in your bank by the morning.'

'Good. If it isn't, I'll have to put the matter into the hands of my accountant. Keith will ensure I've received my correct entitlements. Penalty rates, Saturday and Sunday salary, Base rate, and so on.'

A long silence.

My salary appeared within the hour. Everything was in order.

Druce drove Dad back to the farm, awaiting my return. Bills paid, mail stopped.

The great departure day. Head-to-tail traffic squished toward Kingsford Smith. I wore my floral black and white skirt, black top and cardigan. The one jarring note was my white Reeboks, given that ankle sprain.

A large suitcase groaned from the weight of family presents. Gifts included a patchwork quilt, my first attempt. Nursery pictures were surrounded by red edging.

The driver of my shuttle bus made a joke a minute. We laughed our way to the airport.

He grinned. 'All the best for your grandchild.'

It felt great being an almost-granny. Savouring a gin and tonic, I watched planes soar into thick banks of cloud.

An immigration official cast a quizzical glance between me and my ten-year-old photo. 'Is this your passport?'

'Well, I hope so.'

'It doesn't look like you.'

'I've changed my hairstyle.'

Doubts followed me through the gate.

At Melbourne, two guys joined my row of seats. Bruce seemed much older than his seventeen years. Markus offered a weak handshake. He plaited and caressed his long, straggly hair as we spoke.

Vistas of ocean gave way to beige desert hues, changing to browns and reds in Central Australia. A lively discussion ensued on dreams and astral travel.

'I'm almost certain my soul has travelled to places like Tibet in sleep,' I said. 'Such vivid images.'

Bruce's face creased concern about meeting his Malaysian relatives. 'It's been ten years.' Raised in Australia, he feared the divide between cultures.

By the end of their journey, I felt quite fond of Bruce. He needed mothering.

A peck on his cheek. 'You'll be fine. Probably long to stay there.'

He laughed.

I sensed that Markus had darker problems. An odd whiff of methylated spirits exuded from his pores.

'You'll be glad to get back to your family in Germany.'

He hesitated. 'Sort of.'

I worried over my arrival at Arsenal tube station. Loaded like a pack-horse, a trolley wouldn't help. Not with two sets of stairs. I hoped some strapping lad might take pity on a granny in need.

Our jet glided into mellow afternoon light. Peaks and shoals of meringue, bathed in gold. The glitter of one tiny sun, reflected on metal. Had Naomi birthed her baby yet? Was I a grandmother?

A plane change at Kuala Lumpur. It would be a miracle if I travelled halfway around the world, arriving in time for the birth. But wouldn't it be lovely?

I recalled Naomi's excitement over meeting her new boyfriend. On a teacher exchange at Dollar, Scotland, she wrote, 'His name is Daniel. Very tall and slim, with dark hair and sensuous green eyes. He's a computer programmer, but he is extremely funny and interesting, not at all like the stereotypical geek. His humour is a bit like Cedric's. He's thirty-five, and his birthday was just the other day. What I really like is that he's not afraid to talk about, love, and commitment. He's coming up to Dollar to visit me next weekend. And I'm going to London next weekend to see him…'

Antoine and I had crossed our fingers. 'He seems keen.'

They'd wed in Devon, a simple ceremony with only close friends and family. Naomi wore a silk dress in gold. I'd felt lucky to be there, sad that Neville would miss his cherished daughter's marriage. I'd delivered the nuptial speech, a father's role. Made poignant by his loss.

The perfect match? A volatile pair, they had lots of spats.

Purple shades of evening sea – or was it sky? Head wind quiver. The last glimmers of a dying day. Banks of clouds, blanket stitched to night. Wingtip blinks… One dawn followed another. Sleep and waken. Breakfasted, buffed and becalmed for a perfect landing.

The ordeal of border control. A train sped me from Heathrow to London. I switched to a suburban line, worrying about my luggage. At Arsenal, I took a big breath. '

A smiling older man saw my dilemma. 'May I help you up the stairs?'

Profuse thanks. 'Blessings on you and your family.'

We were no sooner outside than Daniel arrived.

'Give me that suitcase.'

Naomi, heavily pregnant, heaved along behind him. Hugs all around.

Chez Naomi. 'I feel fine. Slept the first leg. Not a hint of jet lag, thank goodness.'

We talked non-stop for hours.

Naomi's expected confinement date, 11 April, came and went. Nana Jane, my fellow gran-in-waiting, arrived for what the Jarvis-Webbs called supper.

I daren't share George Orwell's joke about the upper-lower middle class's preference for the word.

Naomi said, 'I'm so excited. Can't wait for the baby.'

Next day, we stopped by a hardware shop. The brown dog panting beside the counter was also expecting.

An elderly assistant eyed Naomi's bulge, then his bitch's tummy, teats swollen. He declared, 'I reckon you'll drop before she does.'

What could one do but laugh?

16

They had chosen not to know our baby's gender. I liked that: it brought added excitement to a birth.

One day slipped into another. What was keeping baby? I bit my nails.

Naomi sighed. 'I just want to have it all over.' She perused manuals on pregnancy and labour. 'Braxton Hicks contractions are nature's rehearsal for the real thing.'

A succession of false alarms came and went.

My frown. 'I can't recall this.'

She chuckled. 'Mum, your pregnancies were a long time ago.'

I'd done the practicals but not midwifery. The complexity of hormones which precede labour fascinated me. 'I had no idea.'

Naomi read, 'Some labours…extended periods between contractions. Others quickly proceed to full intensity. Waves of contractions from the fundus (top) allow little time to rest between them.'

'I do recall that.'

She continued. 'When the cervix reaches full dilation, the adrenal glands produce adrenalin. It triggers the expulsive process of birth. A time of maximum intensity, for both mother and baby.'

Daniel tried old-fashioned remedies to hurry things along. A chickpea curry. Long walks. A hot bath.

I put a hand on her tummy. 'Wow! Baby's moving around like mad.'

Finally, the little one settled.

'Our miracle. Probably asleep.'

On the evening of Wednesday, 22 April, Naomi's contractions became regular. The first, intense pangs.

Her nervous smile. 'Much stronger than previously, Mum.'

'It's happening, darling.' I gave her a hug. 'You'll be fine,'

Ironically, we were watching a BBC program on human birth at the time.

Daniel packed sandwiches. 'It might be a marathon.'

Shortly before midnight, we reached the London University College Hospital. The pleasant antiseptic aroma took me back to training days.

Daniel grinned. 'I was born here, you know.'

'A family tradition, eh?'

My daughter had opted for a water birth. 'Helps with contractions.' A new and almost experimental approach to childbirth in a hospital setting, with midwives in control. 'It's safer than a home birth. A doctor's on standby, should problems arise.'

Naomi took long gulps of gas, helping her cope with the intensity of contractions. Splashes. 'The buoyancy feels good.'

The midwife, Tammy, said, 'Your cervix is dilated to seven centimetres. Shouldn't be long now.'

Despite her pain, Naomi grew anxious about our welfare. 'Why don't you go home and get some sleep?'

'Don't worry about us, darling. 'I squeezed her hand. 'I wouldn't miss this for anything.' I felt so alert. It surprised me.

Daniel chuckled. 'Your adrenalin is pumping, like mine.'

Tammy brought me a welcome cup of tea. I devoured one of Daniel's sandwiches. He opted for a doze.

I listened to the monitor. Baby's heat galloped.

Around four a.m., Tammy did another examination. 'Your cervix is fully dilated.' She ruptured Naomi's waters. A flicker of concern crossed her face. 'Your baby has passed meconium. Usually it occurs shortly after birth. It's not uncommon, though, when a baby is overdue. It rules out giving birth in the pool.' Tammy said, 'Your baby's mouth and nose must be suctioned immediately the head presents. Before baby takes a breath.'

We heard the moans of other labouring mums. Raw cries from newborns. Exchanged glances. How long before it was our turn?

The nurse told Naomi, 'Keep walking. Speeds things up.'

My daughter paced, resting during contractions. She breathed in rhythm, to lessen the pain. Resumed pacing, Daniel at her side.

The second stage, in a standing position. I marvelled at her energy. Daniel gave her physical support. Women of my generation had pushed against gravity.

Tammy's guarded calls to doctors. I bit my nails. Suppose Naomi needed a Caesarian?

A paediatrician checked equipment, ready for the suction.

Seconds dragged. My fears gained wings. Suppose they didn't clear the baby's mouth properly? Healthy newborn infants died from ingesting meconium.

A stronger contraction.

Tammy urged, 'Push, now. Keep going! Keep going! Well done.'

Naomi panted. I wiped her brow with a damp cloth. Her eyes told me that she craved a good sleep.

Tammy said, 'Baby's head is close.'

Medium-brown hair appeared, edging towards the light.

At moments when Naomi's task seemed impossible, Tammy's input was vital. 'You can do it.'

Closer. Millimetre by millimetre. A tiny face appeared, eyes closed.

Tammy snapped, 'Stop pushing! Hold it there.'

Naomi panted, strain written in every cell of her face. I guessed the effort it must take, resisting Nature's powerful expulsive forces. Her excruciating pain while they suctioned the baby's nose and mouth.

Seconds ticked by. An eternity for both of us.

Later, she told me, 'Every fibre of my body wanted to push that baby out.'

Suction over, everything happened fast.

Naomi yelped, 'I can't hold it any more! I can't hold it!'

The baby slid out like a fish.

On Thursday 23 April 1998, Imogen Chloé joined the world – not that she was yet named. Tammy caught the slippery baby in a towel. Cries of protest.

'A girl! A healthy girl!' echoed around the room.

'Congratulations. Well done!'

'My beautiful granddaughter,' I babbled. 'Thursday's child, like me. Has far to go.'

A group hug between the three of us.

The intense part of Naomi's ordeal had lasted barely half an hour. Only five hours for the entire labour, short for a primapara. Naomi flopped onto the bed, a shipwreck survivor. Exhilaration and joy floated on the air.

Tammy clamped and cut the cord. Gave an injection of Syntocinon in Naomi's thigh, a synthetic version of oxytocin. It helps contract blood vessels, prevents post-partum haemorrhage, and ensures quick delivery of the placenta.

The midwife examined the ugly, but marvellous organ. 'During the nine months from conception to birth, it acts as liver, stomach, kidneys, circulation and everything else.' Hers was a healthy, oval shape. Nurse smiled. 'Excellent. No breaks or bits missing.'

Naomi trembled in every limb. I didn't know whether it was from the injection or shock or both. Later she confided, 'It was sheer exhaustion.'

Daniel had a first nurse of his tiny daughter. Chloé blinked in the bright morning light. We marvelled at her alert expression.

Tammy smiled. 'I'll borrow your beautiful baby to be weighed and measured.' At eight and a half pounds, and twenty-three centimetres long, Chloé enjoyed her first bubble bath.

'Isn't she a darling? Love her white jumpsuit.'

Nurses brought us toast and tea.

Naomi cradled hers. 'For some reason, I'm ravenous.'

I laughed. 'No wonder, after all your efforts.'

Daniel gave her a kiss. 'I'm so proud of you, darling.'

Settled in her new room, the warmth of love shone in Naomi's eyes. She gave baby her first cuddle and breastfeed. 'I hadn't expected this depth of maternal feelings. Not so soon.'

Early light crept over the city. Daniel's mother, Jane, and his sister, Durga, arrived, exhausted from sitting her osteopath exams. Her real name was Eris, but she'd renamed herself after the goddess of time in Hinduism.

Jane proudly cuddled Chloé.

Daniel and I took a taxi home.

'This one's on me. We deserve a little luxury. It isn't easy, being a caring team.'

He laughed.

Back at Riversdale Road, I planned to make phone calls. My brain refused to function. The moment my head hit the pillow, I slept. Amazed by the restorative powers of six hours sleep.

Following the British midwife system, Naomi and her baby went home the same day.

A triple certificate nurse appeared daily. She weighed Chloé and assessed her progress. Supportive and knowledgeable, she told us, 'Disposable nappies keep urine away from the skin. That old bane of babies, nappy rash, has almost ceased to exist.' A big plus, environmental issues aside.

Chloé suckled well at the breast, sleeping for long periods.

Naomi's eyes shone. 'She's such a sweetie.' My daughter complained of aches and pains, weary from night feeds, yet to recover from the birth.

The last time we'd cuddled such a delightful creature had been a decade earlier: our beloved Siamese cat. More than once we called the baby 'Samantha', then chuckled. Our feline friend was never far from our hearts.

<h1 style="text-align:center">17</h1>

We welcomed my niece, Caitlin, on a European holiday. She maintained large flower and vegetable gardens at the Kerry Packer estate, at Ellerston, near Scone. I felt proud of her achievement, having topped the NSW horticultural exams.

I hugged her. 'A garden tour of England and Europe is a perfect way to hone your skills.'

The manager of the station had told Grandfather Joe, my father, 'What a fine young woman she is.'

I could only agree.

Caitlin shared our delight in Chloé. We did the Big Bus tour of London to show her the lie of the streets. Impressed how Caitlin found her way around the city with ease.

Taking the tube to Hampstead, I found my way through lanes and byways. We arrived just after one p.m. the appointed hour for lunch.

Jane seemed flustered to see us. 'Oh! Oh, you're here already. Where are the others?'

We stood on one foot then another while she dithered.

'Should I sit you outside or in?'

Daniel knocked, Naomi and Chloé in tow.

Jane counted heads. I suppressed giggles. You'd think a multitude had invaded her flat. She gave us the obligatory garden tour.

A grumble of clouds squabbled with patches of sunshine.

A salad lunch, and fine red.

Jane said, 'Now we'll take an afternoon walk around Hampstead Heath.'

I made the unforgiveable error of calling it a park.

Jane wailed, 'This is just the sort of thing we're fighting against.'

Caitlin and I exchanged a glance. Jane didn't grasp the Australian concept of a national park, an area of untouched natural bush. One only had to glance around to see that Hampstead Heath was a developed site. New plantings thrived, not the untamed wilderness Jane imagined.

Sunday's downpour delayed our visit to Kew Gardens. We left at a midday, bathed in gold. Another shower caught us unawares. We rushed for shelter, sheets of water soaking the gardens.

Munching our sandwiches in a faux temple, I mused, 'Is it too late to choose an indoor attraction?'

Caitlin said, 'This may be my last chance to see these gardens.'

Naomi breastfed Chloé.

The glitter of clear skies crept back.

'Go ahead, girls. I'll join you shortly,' said Naomi.

Caitlin and I tackled slick paths, under dripping leaves. Delighted by foreign trees and flora, she identified most of them.

Naomi joined us, very pale. She carried Chloé in a sling, with a backpack for baby stuff. 'I'm exhausted. Guess this day out is a bit soon for me.'

Caitlin left with a boyfriend on her exploration of Europe. We hugged.

'Have fun. I'm off to Ireland. A country I've always longed to visit.' A dream voice told me, you're going home. I had at least two Irish grandmothers and a host of other Celtic ancestors, later confirmed by DNA: fifty-five per cent Irish. Yes: I was going home.

Still, I'd miss my darling granddaughter. But her parents needed an opportunity to bond, and to enjoy family time.

A taxi sped me to Heathrow airport. A flight to Dublin. It surprised me to discover that the Irish use a different currency. Pleased by the dual-language street signs – English and Gaelic.

Geraldine, our guide, explained, 'There's been a resurgence of language learning the in recent years. It engenders respect for a unique culture.'

I took an immediate liking to my twin-share roommate, Sandra.

It was all downhill from there. Fifty, going on seventeen, every conversation began and ended with sex. I'd change the subject. Invariably, she drifted back to her carnal adventures. Husbands. Lovers. One-night-stands. I tuned out the gruesome details. Did she really imagine anyone would be interested in the mechanics of how she did it?

She asked a group member old enough to be her father, 'Are you seeking a physical relationship?'

He was visibly taken aback.

Sandra recounted juicy titbits on other travellers. 'He's that old. Would you believe he's still at it?' This person in the group wore funny clothes. That one was rather a snob. 'And Hilda does go on so.'

Hilda's conversations were far more interesting than hers. We discussed our mutual Fitzgerald heritage.

Friday, Saturday and Sunday's all-night parties in Dublin saw forlorn stacks of glasses leaning drunkenly around the streets. The smell of urine hung heavy on the morning air. In small towns, pubs were tiny and numerous. Many could only accommodate a dozen drinkers at most. An Irishman's favourite pastime seemed to be a pub evening. Celebrating with mates over a pint or seven of Guinness.

Window displays?

Hilda chuckled. 'A coating of dust, and a dead fly or two, seem neither here nor there.'

The guide said, 'Dublin has Norse, Viking and Danish roots. The capital of Ireland, it's a university and cathedral city. Monks established an earlier settlement at Wicker Crossing in the sixth century. Mentioned by Ptolemy in AD 149, called Iblana, later Hibernia.' She drew our attention to the Georgian Mile, fine buildings of three or four storeys, plus basement. 'These houses were built between 1730 and 1830. They belonged to the Anglo-Irish gentry.'

Sandra enjoyed teasing Monty, a shy fellow with a stutter. Surprised when he touched her leg. 'I wasn't flirting. Didn't mention sex.'

I laughed. 'Of course you were. Flirting is an intellectual exercise. Subtlety is what makes it all the more tantalising.'

Hilda chuckled when I told her. 'Subtlety? One word, I fear, not in Sandra's vocabulary.'

On the second day of our tour, Geraldine explained the procedure. 'We move forward two rows every day.'

A few individuals refused to give up their front-row seats. Despite her pleas, they showed no sign of moving.

A suave gentleman with trimmed silver beard took control. 'Anyone fancy a cup of tea?'

The rest of us trooped off the coach.

'I fancy things will settle when they realise the tour isn't going anywhere.'

We chatted and laughed for the next half an hour. On return to the coach, the recalcitrant few had taken their correct places.

Geraldine thanked us for ending the impasse.

Hilda looked thoughtful. 'On my next tour I'll start day one by sitting halfway down the bus, left-hand side.'

'To travel forward quickly?' I could see her point. 'Excellent idea.'

We crossed the River Liffey via the Halfpenny Bridge.

Geraldine asked us 'Can you guess how it earned its name?'

Someone said, 'A toll?'

'Exactly. A halfpenny was charged to cross. It replaced the ferries. It's one of our most photographed bridges, for its elegance.' She pointed out the O'Connell Bridge. 'This one's famous for a number of reasons. Firstly, it's wider than long. Named after Daniel O'Connell, one of the heroes of liberation in 1823. You'll find it mentioned in a number of books, including James Joyce's *Ulysses*.

She pointed out bullet holes in the post office. 'Damage from the Easter Rising, way back in 1916. The insurrection failed. Subsequent events led to the War of Independence. 'Dublin University and Trinity College go right back to Queen Elizabeth I. Founded for the education of the sons of the ascendancy classes – the gentry.'

Sandra paid cursory attention to the wonderful Oliver Goldsmith Library. Hilda and I drooled over the amazing repository of ancient volumes, and the exquisite Book of Kells, an illuminated manuscript.

Geraldine said, 'It dates to the ninth century. Celtic monks used black, red, purple and yellow ink to decorate over eight hundred magnificent vellum folios or pages. It's one of the greatest treasures of medieval Europe.'

Hilda's eyes gleamed. 'How lucky we are to enjoy this marvel.'

Geraldine continued, 'Lavish illustrations of the four gospels – Matthew, Mark, Luke and John – were completed in Latin about AD 800. It's bound in calfskin and written, they say, with the quill of a swan.'

Or several quills, I thought.

'It was brought from Iona to the manuscript department of Trinity in the 1600s.'

In our room, Sandra's words thundered down. Hail clattering on a cold tin roof. 'My latest husband left me. He's an alcoholic. But I miss him.'

'Isn't his loss a positive?'

'I guess.' She blinked. 'I do have a guy who's sweet on me back home.'

'There you are.'

Hilda told me, 'Castlebar is the home of my Fitzgerald ancestors.'

Proud that my grandmother hailed from the same noble family, we discussed the Fitzgerald/MacGerailt line over a coffee.

'They were one of the greatest families who came to Ireland after the Anglo-Norman invasion.' She told of two main divisions, Desmond (among whom are the holders of two ancient titles: Knight of Kerr, and Knight of Glin) and Kildare. 'Their leaders held almost regal sway, up to the rebellion of Silken Thomas. He and his close relatives were executed by Henry VIII in 1537.'

Hilda had me write down, Bibl. IF. Map Cork, Kerry. Kildare and Limerick.

'Geraldus, 1060–1275, was born a Fitzgerald, formerly called de Idea of Gurtens and Cadiz in Spain. Descent was through barons of Offaly from Othus. Records included Charlie, William and Ormon Fitzgerald.'

'I've a lot of reading to do, Hilda.' I told her, 'Florence née Fitzgerald was my favourite grandmother. At seventy-five, she danced the Irish jig in my bedroom at Hunter Springs.'

She laughed. 'I can see why you loved her.'

'I'm also interested in exploring the Conolly line of my great grand-mother, Marion.' Variations of the spelling surprised me. O Connolly, O'Conghaile (from Connacht and Monaghan) It's spelt Connelly in County Galway. 'The name is widely distributed in the provinces. My great-great-grandfather, Henry, spelt his name Conolly. I believe the name is found in Galway, Fermanagh, Meath and Monaghan.'

'Goodness, you've some work there.'

We admired Dublin's famous Phoenix Park. Nearly two thousand acres, it boasts icy water springs and herds of wild deer. There's a monument to the phoenix bird, for which it's named. Deerfield, the US ambassador's residence, is located in the park environs.

Geraldine told us, 'A light burns in a window, day and night. A farewell and welcome to the Irish scattered throughout the world. The house boasts a ha-ha, a deep ditch, to keep wandering cattle from the formal garden.'

Our driver, Jack, always had a twinkle in his blue eyes. A quip at the ready, he sent us into gales of laughter. It pleased me how the Irish make jokes against themselves. He looked like a senior version of the Australian politician Tim Fischer.

At night, Sandra's clatter continued. She boasted, 'I look so young. People think I'm half my age.'

'Good for you.'

She giggled. 'I fit in perfectly with all the twenty-something guys at work.'

Yawning, I took a sleeping pill. Donned an eye mask. Put off my light.

Sandra rattled on. Surprised at my silence. 'Oh! You're asleep?'

A visit to the National Gallery took one's breath away. Hilda and I gazed at the splendid Impressionist paintings. She shook her head. 'Geraldine said the collection began with a hundred works.'

'Yes, it's hard to believe.'

The George Bernard Shaw bequest – royalties from the success of *Pygmalion* – allowed purchase of many works. Geraldine told us that one of his ancestors was Lord Elwood Fitzgerald, associated with Leinster House, the Irish parliament.

Hilda's ears pricked up. 'He must be related to us.'

I laughed. 'You, anyway. Don't know about me.'

The cobbled streets reminded me of period movies. I pictured the trot of horse and squeak of carriage wheels. Ironically, St Patrick's Church of Ireland, dating back to 1191, was Anglican.

'It unites all Christians and converted people,' Geraldine said, 'It's the largest church and tallest Gothic spire in Ireland. Boasts medieval towers.' She added, 'Jonathan Swift, Dean of the Cathedral, wrote *Gulliver's Travels*, a satire on the government of his day.'

Sandra knew that I worked in an aged nursing facility. Her eyes glittered. 'Careful, or you'll become like one of your oldies.'

I laughed. 'You may have a point.'

'Sandra makes every aspect of life a contest, or put-down,' I told Hilda, 'No matter what I've seen, done or bought, Sandra's experience tops mine.'

Hilda laughed. 'I've noticed.'

Geraldine told us, 'The Irish midlands have over forty hues of green in crops, grasses, and trees. Land varies from good to marginal.'

Elderflowers combined with Celtic twilight in my dreams. I wondered what it meant.

At Limerick, delta of the River Shannon, fields danced with yellow buttercups. Farms ranged from deer, to poultry, sheep and pigs.

'Kerry potatoes and Donegal praties survive in the fields. Lettuce, tomatoes, cucumbers, carrots, celery, zucchini and peas grow in glasshouses. One farmer used three hundred and sixty gallons of oil in one night to maintain the temperature,' Geraldine said. 'Apple, pear and plum trees grow well, and organic farming is emerging.'

Hedgerows protected animals from wind and rain.

'A haven for wildflowers, they shield fields from erosion. Mechanised farming and larger fields spell danger for wild birds and animals. By the way, one farmer dug up a priceless sixth century gold chain in his field, not far away from here. It's exhibited in the National Museum of Ireland.'

Silver Beard chuckled. 'Where's my metal detector?'

'The Moon River is the longest in Ireland. In the eleventh and twelfth century, Normans and Danes navigated the Shannon estuary in their longboats. Donegal and Galway were the last parts of Ireland to be colonised on the western seaboard. Gaelic was the main language spoken until the middle of the twentieth century.'

Toothed stone fences surrounded cottages. Hilda deplored the bare, concreted yards. Adored vistas of wildflowers white daisies, yellow buttercups, purple foxgloves and yellow iris.

'People of Mayo say, God help us in winter,' Geraldine said. 'A grey eiderdown of cloud hangs low over the countryside. Sixty inches rainfall, the highest in the country. Absence of the sun brings worrying levels of anxiety and depression.'

Someone asked about their Irish and Scottish heritage.

'Towns like Dollar and Stirling, Donegal, Dingle and Kerry had Gaelic roots. Celts arrived from the Rhineland in Central Europe. In 700 BC. Scots, Welsh, Manx and Brittany formed the five nations of shared culture, language and music.' Geraldine told us, 'A pirate queen, Grace O'Malley, dubbed Grahnia, lived hereabouts. A political and military leader, she led fleets of ships against Turkish, English and Spanish pirates. Made useful alliances.' Adding, 'Wars to pacify the Irish had almost bankrupted the English crown. It's thought that Elizabeth I was ripe for a solution. Grahnia gained the support of Gaelic chieftains. Then she set off to breach the English court. Her biggest gamble: she risked death as pirate and traitor. After a long voyage, from the east coast of Ireland, she sailed up the Thames to Hampton Court. Grahnia didn't bow, or apologise. She declared the meeting was queen to queen. Fascinated by this powerful and charismatic woman, Elizabeth granted a private audience. The two monarchs conversed in Latin, their common tongue. Elizabeth confirmed her visitor's right to ancestral lands. Gave Grahnia permission to impose taxes on her subjects. After matching swords with Good Queen Bess, Grahnia divorced her third husband, Sir Rupert Bingham, having him thrown from the castle battlements.'

Our Atlantic drive brought bright red fuchsias with purple centres, and a profusion of purple rhododendrons. Abandoned stone cottages, gave the countryside a forlorn air.

Geraldine said, 'A deserted villages stabilisation fund has been established. Note those trim thatched roofs. Some restoration projects are under way.'

Hilda liked the idea of renovating old cottages. Modern conveniences with all the charm of antiquity.

The peat industry flourished in the rocky landscape of Ahol Sound.

'Peat contains chemical preservatives which mummify bodies. It burns with a soft, sweet smell. Before refrigeration, people cooled food and wine in the peat water. And, believe it or not, monks hid their gold collections in peat bogs. Retrieved centuries later.' Adding, 'By the way, have any of you tried Mountain Dew?' Geraldine's eyes twinkled. 'I thought not. People around here brew illicit liquor. It's also called White Lightning. Believe me, it has a kick like a camel.'

Silver Beard guffawed. 'Bring it on.'

A soft Irish day. County Clare led us towards the Burran. Purple foxgloves undulated in the breeze. Creeper-clad vistas of distant mountains were jewelled by the sparkle of lakes. White cottages with slate roofs nestled among bracken, stone fences topped with river stones. Light rain turned into a downpour, with gusty winds. Our driver gripped the wheel, his road clouded by fog. Secondary roads were of gravel.

'The Irish call this chippings.'

County Mayo, skies hung low and heavy. Forbidding peaks rose above Kylemore Abbey, a private college. Nestling among trees and flowers, it's mirrored in a lake.

'Kylemore, the founder, is an astute business woman and entrepreneur. She produces limited editions of bronze sculptures and carved bog-oak artefacts and jewellery. Over thousands of years, the wood became hard, coloured black or light brown. Comparable to the world's best tropical hardwoods.' Geraldine said, 'Employment for twenty people.'

In the Connemara Valley, wild ponies grazed and galloped, tails and manes flying with the wind.

'Famed for their docile temperament, they're born black. Dappled grey on maturity.' Geraldine added, 'They reach a height of only fifteen hands but sell for 1,500 to 3,000 pounds sterling.'

Galway, a medieval city, once traded with Spain. Ships could enter the harbour, called the Clara.

'You'll notice that the architecture reflects a strong Spanish influence.'

Hilda and I tried the famous Irish drink, Black Velvet, half champagne and half Guinness.

She grinned. 'Hmm. Not bad.'

I laughed. 'Not bad at all.'

Galway Cathedral, impressively named the Cathedral of Our Lady Assumed into Heaven and St Nicholas.

Geraldine took up her microphone. 'Building commenced in 1958, completed in 1965. The last great stone cathedral to be built in Europe, on the site of an old prison.' She told us of one son of Galway, who offered a place for his tomb in front of the high altar, saying, 'I wouldn't let anyone walk over me in life and don't propose to do so in death.'

Hilda chuckled. 'He had a point.'

'Interest in Gaelic has increased among actors and writers of the Irish theatre, including Samuel Beckett. George Bernard Shaw, who won the Nobel Prize for Literature. And W.B. Yeats famously wrote his own epitaph: "Cast a cold eye / on life, on death / Horsemen, pass by!" People are divided about what this means. I feel it just says to look dispassionately on life and death. We are all going to die. Get on with your life.'

It may not have been the moment, but we laughed.

Galway Bay and the Cliffs of Moher were cloaked in fog, and battered by gusting rain.

Geraldine warned, 'Gales blow up to force eleven.'

A sore throat had sapped my energy. I thought, why push yourself? There's little chance of glimpsing Aran Island. I lingered below.

Sandra returned. 'Did you make it to the top?'

I grinned. 'There's nothing to see in this fog.'

Her eyes glittered. 'Oh, I went. The fog cleared. I had a perfect view.'

'Well done.' Surely Sandra was lying?

Hilda later confirmed my suspicions. 'We couldn't see a thing.'

I laughed. 'Thought as much.'

I wondered aloud how Naomi and Daniel were managing young Chloé.

Hilda smiled. 'You must miss her.'

18

I resorted to Cointreau on ice. 'It's perfect for a sore throat.'

Before long, the whole coach had adopted my Dr Cointreau cure.

In County Clare, Geraldine told us, 'You'll all be amazed by the wonderful diversity of flora. Perhaps it's something to do with it the limestone country.'

Hilda's face shone. 'Wild orchids, edelweiss, wild geraniums.'

An English lady added, 'Hazelwood, primroses, cowslips, gentian purple, foxgloves.'

I joined in the fun. 'Isn't that Queen Anne's Lace? Buttercups. Wild Judah roses.'

The count went on.

Silver Beard chuckled. 'No wonder it's a popular spot for painters, sculptors and photographers. Geraldine says even musicians are inspired.'

At Liscannon. a post and dolman structure appeared.

'It dates to pagan times, used for Celtic sacrifices.'

Visible from the road, but barbed wire and No Trespassing signs abounded.

Geraldine shook her head. 'It's a mystery to me why the landowner doesn't cash in. He'd be a millionaire.'

Luckily for us, someone had cut the wires. Giggling, we took our chances on a closer look.

The coach chuckled over Irish logic. 'Later this afternoon, I can get it for you this evening, and, if you want a dearer phone card, you'll have to pay more money.'

Hilda said, 'Don't you just love it?'

I wiped my eyes. 'As the old saying goes, half the world are Irish, and the other half wish they were.'

The golden veil of evening brought woods, and pine plantations. A black cat licked its paws in the doorway of a stone cottage. Bunches of elderberries hung, ripe for the picking.

Innistymon Hotel had perfect views of cascades on the Inagh River. White water surged and roared, almost in the shadows of the Magilly Cuddy Reeks.

Hilda and I searched the town in vain for the Fitzgerald story. I'd love to have had a copy. Alas, it was not to be.

She told me, 'No visit to Ireland would be complete without a toast to medieval St Brendan, known as the Navigator.'

'What's his claim to fame?'

'Goodness, there are so many. He was one of the twelve aApostles of Ireland, patron saint of two Irish dioceses, Kerry and Clonfert. He's also a Celtic patron saint of mariners, travellers, even whales.'

Geraldine said, 'Perhaps you've heard of St Brendan's voyages? Legend has it that he build a currach, an Irish boat of skins stretched over a wooden frame. Discovered America before Columbus.'

Glances of surprise. I liked the idea of a sixth century Irish monk making such a momentous voyage. 'But could it be true?'

Geraldine said, 'Remember, Brendan was a colourful figure who travelled widely in Europe. His exploits are listed in the annals of Ireland. Some little while ago, modern adventurers set out from Ireland in a similar craft. They arrived in Newfoundland thirteen months later.'

Hilda clapped. 'So, it's entirely possible that St Brendan made that voyage.'

'Why not? A millennium before Christopher Columbus in 1492.'

An article in *National Geographic* gave this 1,500-year-old tale new wings.

Twelfth of June dawned. My fifty-eighth birthday. I'd have appreciated good wishes, even from Sandra. Not much likelihood of that, I thought, given her constant put-downs.

I ached to see my family. To cuddle darling little Chloé. Lingering in the shower, I silently mouthed, 'Happy birthday to me,' thinking,

'You're pathetic.' Why did I feel so vulnerable? I carried the burden of my secret celebration all day.

Only half-listening to Geraldine's tales of the Spanish Armada.

'Lost off the west coast. Stories abound of buried treasure in Mayo, Sligo and Kerry.' The area was famous for ring circles, usually over burial sites. 'Some people believe they're inhabited by spirit ancestors, going back to pagan times.'

Poor man's orchid, wild iris, and purple foxgloves transformed hills into a vision of beauty.

Geraldine said, 'Over a million Irish died from starvation during the potato famine from 1845 to 1847. Crops were sent to absentee English landlords. Some people may have believed that the heartbreak was over. But the terror of the Irish clearances followed. People were evicted from land they'd occupied for generations. Thatched roofs were set aflame. People fled the smoke and fire. Some were beaten by the constabulary. Many emigrated to Australia and America. It halved the Irish population.'

Blarney is both a town and castle.

'Built six hundred years ago, by one of Ireland's greatest chieftains, Cormac MacCarthy. Kissing the Blarney Stone is said to bring eloquence. But it's imperative do so leaning backwards, and upside down.'

The coach rippled with laughter.

'People have been performing this rite for over a hundred years. You can either climb the many steps to do so, or kiss someone who's already performed the rite.'

Hilda chuckled. 'That sounds like a cop-out to me.'

Geraldine told us, 'Blarney goes back to the time of Elizabeth I. She was struggling with her conquest of Ireland. Talked into leaving by sweet words from this town, Queen Bess wasn't fooled. "It's blarney. Nothing but blarney."'

Limited time made our group anxious to reach the top. A gaggle of Americans gawked out the windows of every landing, blocking us from moving forward.

I explained our urgency. 'We only have forty-five minutes.'

A big Yank twirled his salt-and-pepper moustache. 'It'll take you all an hour at least.'

I simmered. 'For goodness sakes! Let us pass. We haven't time to look out every porthole.'

Other members of our party joined in. Mutters of selfish, and darned cheek. Faced by our angry mob, the Yanks moved aside.

The Blarney feat performed, we all laughed, helping our friends do so.

Outside, Hilda commented on a tall shrub. 'Is it the tree of heaven? I've seen it everywhere.'

We admired the clusters of yellowy-green flowers.

We returned to Dublin by six that evening. I felt determined to enjoy Doyle's Irish cabaret at the Burlington Hotel, a real birthday treat.

Hilda and I nabbed the front seat of the bus. A quick get-away then enabled us to occupy the best cabaret seats at the head of the table. Sandra took the equivalent position on the opposite side, beside Monty and Stephen.

The boys had brought neither cash nor cards. 'We expected drinks to be included.'

Given Sandra's unrelenting attempts to be top dog, I bought them champagne. I smiled and clinked my glass with theirs. 'To a great night.'

Sandra gave me a filthy look, having to buy her own.

Excerpts from *Riverdance* brought wild applause. Comedians had us rocking in our seats. A very attractive man played the squeeze-box. Oh, those sexy Irish eyes, glancing into mine. Or was it my imagination? His wink, my shiver. He seemed familiar. Had we met in another life? Or did he just remind me of someone from my childhood?

A birthday call during the performance. Too little, too late. The show ended. Players assembled to sell their records. And who should be standing behind the table?

He grinned. 'I saw you making eyes at me.'

I laughed. Gushing about my Irish family. 'Irish grandmothers and great-grandmothers. Cousins.'

'Why, that's grand. Grand.' He grinned. I've travelled all around Australia. Loved every minute.' He helped me to choose a tape. 'Give us a hug and kiss before you go.'

Doubtless, he flirted with some lady in the audience at every performance. Yet the embrace from a lovely, special man made a miserable day perfect.

On the way to the Blooms Hotel, the coach reverberated with birthday wishes. I floated somewhere above the others. Neither a noisy disco crowd downstairs, nor Sandra's bedtime antics spoilt my mood.

Smiling, I donned my eye mask. Put in earplugs.

Next morning, I felt disorientated. Almost jet-lagged.

At breakfast, Hilda sighed. 'All our activities these last eight days have caught up with me, too.'

Sandra chose to remain in Dublin for another day.

Hilda said, 'Heaven be praised. We're spared her little games at the airport.'

Our flight was delayed. We strolled around, exploring the shops. I carried Hilda's things on my trolley. A lovely lady, she reminded me of my grandmother, Florence née Fitzgerald.

We hugged in farewell. I could hardly wait to see baby Chloé.

19

I cuddled my granddaughter. 'My! How Chloé has grown.'

Naomi smiled. 'If babies' growth rate continued throughout child-hood, they'd be the size of an elephant.'

We all chuckled.

Daniel had prepared a chicken cacciatore with real tomatoes in a chunky sauce and fresh herbs. Creamed potatoes, julienne honey carrots and broccoli completed a wonderful meal.

I said, 'You can't beat home cooking.'

The proud new mother confided, 'We did miss your help, Mum.' She added, 'A tidy of the house, washing the dishes, or just rocking Chloé when she's fretful. An extra pair of hands makes a huge difference.'

Daniel nodded. 'I never dreamed a young baby could take so much work.'

Jane brought me fresh flowers from her garden for my birthday. I felt touched. Naomi did a sketch of Chloé, as her gift.

'It's a real treasure.'

'Yippee! We're off to Normandy for eight days.' Naomi hugged me.

Our smart green hireling, a Fiat 10, boasted a sunroof. Three adults, heavy suitcases, and one baby crossed the Tower Bridge, headed for Dover.

At half-ten, we reached the Western Docks. A queue of motor ve-hicles hummed, waiting to board the hovercraft. Daniel's tomato and blue cheese sandwiches took the edge off our appetites.

A monster emerged from the mist, riding on a metre of air and rub-ber, a cushion for our voyage across the English Channel. Speeding to-wards Calais, the powerful Rolls Royce engines barely whispered.

Wide-eyed, giggling, two sweet little boys sat beside me, celebrating their first hovercraft ride. The younger one reminded me of Cedric at that age, intelligent and lovable. 'Seven, almost eight.' He gravely introduced his brother, nearly eleven.

Feeling almost like his mummy, I put my arm around the seven-year-old, to afford him a better view. Pointing out the shapes of ships and freighters.

His wriggles of excitement. 'Two more Sea Link ferries.'

'Look!' I cried. 'The French coast.'

'I hoped to buy maps of Normandy at the wharf. None for sale.' Daniel took a compass reading, heading south.

Naomi acted as Daniel's guide and navigator. She kept a sharp lookout. Traffic approached from his blind side, and at 110 kilometres per hour.

I bit my nails and prayed.

She ordered, 'Go. Now!'

Daniel sped into the freeway.

'Watch that semi-trailer,' she said. 'That fool. He changed lanes without indicating.'

He'd blundered into our lane, almost causing a crash.

The kilometres sped away beneath our wheels.

'Aha, a service centre.' Daniel stopped to buy maps. 'Large and unwieldy. But the only ones available.'

Naomi said, 'I'd love some strawberry- flavoured milk.'

I told her, 'It's *du Lait Parfumé avec fraise,*' or simply, '*Du lait fraise.*'

At the last minute, she lost confidence, buying an ice cream.

I chuckled. 'But you're breastfeeding. You need milk.'

I found a large bottle labelled, *Yaourt framboise pour boire.* Raspberry yoghurt to drink.

Naomi said, 'Delicious, but too sweet.'

We helped her finish it.

My role was group interpreter, cursing my poor pronunciation. Naomi and Daniel spoke French perfectly, but lacked vocabulary. I consoled myself. Dammit, what's a language all about? Communication. And discovered fascinating aspects of French culture along the way.

We adored the magnificent countryside around the Somme. Nature had largely healed the carnage of World War I. Forests of what Daniel thought contained oaks, cypress, beech and spruce were reminiscent of those in French paintings. We glimpsed half-timbered houses.

'Look! Irises grow along the ridge of those thatched roofs.'

Daniel said, 'Grown in clay,' I believe. 'Iris produce a dense root system, protection from leaks.'

At Rouen, he made the courageous decision to drive into la Centre Ville.

'This town is infamous for burning Joan of Arc, The maid of Orleans, in May 1431. The French consider her a heroine for her role in the Lancastrian phase of the Hundred Years' War.'

Naomi winked at me. Trust Daniel to remember all that, I thought.

Wonderful old houses and ornate cathedrals delighted me. 'Don't I know that one?' I cried. 'I'm sure it featured in Impressionist paintings, showing the effects of light at different times of the day.'

Naomi hesitated, 'You could be right.'

The streets surged with Saturday crowds. We longed to stop and walk those rues. To join people relaxing over beers in little bistros.

Daniel groaned. 'Parking is chock-a-block.'

The Fiat crawled forward, narrowly avoiding pedestrians with a death wish.

He vowed, 'We'll return.'

Relieved to put the city behind us, we took to a highway. Nobody had a clue if it was the right one.

Daniel yelled, 'Are we going the right way?' Expecting an immediate response. Repeating the question.

Paper crackled. Naomi struggled. 'These darn maps.'

Daniel shouted. 'What's wrong with you? Only a fool could take so long to sort this out. Can't you read a map?'

I snapped. 'A nasty attitude won't solve anything. Naomi's doing her best.'

At last she found the correct route.

Daniel sped along the freeway. Distracted by our screaming baby but thankfully silent.

Naomi stroked and kissed Chloé. 'It's all right.'

I bit my nails. Things couldn't get worse.

Until they did. A tunnel swallowed us whole. A burst of multi-coloured lights flashed into my eyes. They flickered and blazed around us, an almost overwhelming attack of illumination.

It terrified Chloé. Her screams reached a crescendo.

Naomi stroked her baby's scarlet face. 'There, there, little one.'

Chloé was bathed in a lather of perspiration. She grabbed her one lifeline. At last, exhausted, the baby fell into a deep slumber. Blonde strands of Naomi's long hair, pulled out at the roots, were entangled in her tiny hands.

Dozens of Intriguing villages met our delighted eyes. At twilight, we reached Gennville, deep in the countryside. The first glimpse of our rented cottage.

Naomi seemed enchanted. 'Oh, look. Our very own irises on the thatched roof.' My daughter looked around. 'Comfortable, with all we're likely to need.' Her sudden thought. 'Where will Chloé sleep? There's no crib.'

I laughed. 'My parents solved that problem for me, all those years ago. *Voila*! An empty drawer makes a perfect bed for a young baby.'

They chuckled. 'Well done.'

We explored the quaint little town. Ancient stone church, cemetery full of floral tributes. Milk, butter and other essentials were on our list. But the only business still open was a boulangerie, the local bakery.

Daniel bought French bread and a pear tart. 'Tomorrow, we'll search out provisions.

We dined at a garden restaurant, and took an early night.

A grey day dawned. We devoured the delicious pear tart. I shuddered at black tea.

Naomi chuckled. 'How do you say it? *Pas de choix*. No choice.'

Bathing revealed another problem.

Daniel frowned. *Madame* has left us only one towel.'

'For three adults? Oh, dear.'

I checked with *Monsieur*, our neighbour. He wasn't acquainted with the owner of our rented maison. My apologies in French for disturbing him. Friendly occupants on the opposite side were also unable to help.

We pondered our next move.

At that moment, *Monsieur*-next-door's black Citroën drove up to our gate. 'I've made some calls. Would you like me to drive you to the house of Madame Gilles?'

'*Merci beaucoup,*' I said.

Daniel, Naomi and Chloé drove along behind. We reached a large house and farm. Knocked. No response.

'I'll call her later.' Adding, 'Oh, is there someone local who sells milk?'

Our benefactor offered to show us a nearby farm.

We sped off through the Normandy countryside along narrow roadways. I loved the way trees formed a canopy, pruned into tunnels for passing traffic.

At the farm gate, a big, bewhiskered farmer shook our hands. I enjoyed a friendly chat.

A wide grin. 'You speak very good French.'

'*Merci beaucoup, monsieur.*'

Two mastiffs strained at their chains. Ferocious barks, baring their fangs.

'*Méchant chiens de garde,*' the farmer chuckled. 'Wicked guard dogs.'

I kept my distance.

The farm bore an air of cheerful neglect. Discarded, rusting equipment lay in disarray. At least thirty cats lounged about outside *la maison*, more glimpsed within. The farmer and his wife were friendly, signs of a hard life writ large on their tired faces, and in their patched clothing.

The milk appeared to be rich and creamy.

'It's way better quality than that bought in supermarkets,' I said. 'Do you sell butter?'

The farmer's wife smiled, revealing missing teeth. 'No. But we've eggs. Or perhaps you'd like a chicken?'

'Both, please.'

The friendly *camion* driver offered to deliver it that evening.

Naomi chuckled. 'Still no extra towels, but progress.'

Daniel cooked tasty scrambled eggs on toast for lunch. Then we drove to Honfleur, about eight kilometres distant. A charming town, full to overflowing with tourists and locals. We sat enjoying ice creams, beside a pretty lagoon. Colourful yachts and other craft bobbed at anchor.

At the baker's we bought bread, brioche and a couple of small pizzas. I asked the *patronne* about other provisions.

She directed us down a side street. '*Tout droit*: straight ahead.'

A grocery sold everything we required.

Back at the maison, the truck driver handed over our chicken. Daniel made us a delicious *poulet au vin*, with lobster soup, white beans, vinegar and spices.

I giggled. 'Love this French food.'

We made a latish start on a walk into the country. Chloé bounced on Daniel's back.

Naomi juggled an awkward map. 'I can't find the path. It's not clear.'

Daniel smirked. 'You just don't know how to use the darn thing. Give it to me.'

We delighted in vistas of cow parsley, dandelions, buttercups and other wildflowers. Blackberries of two varieties bloomed. Both white and pink flowers.

I spied a *lavoire*: water from a natural spring had been collected in a concrete pool. 'That's where country women once washed their linen.'

Daniel chose the perfect spot for our picnic. Trespassing in a farmer's deserted field, we munched on ham sandwiches. Naomi breastfed Chloé.

My daughter mused, 'This scene reminds me of Impressionist paintings, *En Plein Air*.'

We trotted in Daniel's wake. His navigation led us over a river, up a steep hill, past a farmhouse. Perplexed, he stopped at a road. Consulting the map.

We giggled. 'You're the expert. Where are we?'

He looked sheepish. 'We may need to retrace our steps.'

'*Mignonne,*' declared a nearby farm lady, admiring Chloé. It meant cute.

I seized the opportunity. 'I think we've mistaken the route.'

Daniel pointed out our desired *randonnée* on the map.

Madame explained, 'You must hike back to the river.'

'Before the river?' I asked, not sure if I'd understood.

'*Oui*, well before the river.'

We enjoyed a stroll past yew, weeping beech, and trees.

Daniel pointed at a flutter of birds. 'Look, finches. And I think that's a woodpecker.' Back at the car, he grinned. 'I enjoyed that.' He drove to the address of a woman who made cider. Madame sold him several bottles, pointing us in the direction of a calvados supplier.

A longish drive followed, through tunnels of clipped trees, dappled by the bright and shade of a summer's day. We passed all sorts of quaint maisons.

I could never have navigated the twisting network of narrow country roads. Somehow, Daniel stopped right outside Monsieur Gilles' garden.

A riot of orange, red and blue blossoms. A strong handshake.

'*Bonjour.*' His speech with a strong regional accent.

It pleased me to understand a good deal. Monsieur's displays showed the fabrication of pommier. cider, calvados and so on. After an extensive tasting – *le degustation* – Daniel made his choice.

Back at our maison, Naomi fed the baby.

Daniel made a big pot of soup from vegetables and chicken bone stock. Boiled a few young potatoes. Succulent peaches for dessert.

Bemused by a word game, I lost my turn. Happy to look on. Daniel came up with all sorts of obscure words. I'm sure he'd made many of them up on the spot. We lacked a dictionary to settle disputes. Lots of laughter. I could see they took winning seriously.

20

Morning brought that fine drizzle which the French call *bruine*. Daniel and I spun into town for bread and milk. I made another attempt to phone Madame Gilles about our towel problem. No answer.

A pleasant drive through beautiful countryside, with appropriate stops. When Chloé became restless, we drew to a stop for mum to offer her a meal.

Daniel grinned. 'Avoiding a full-throated roar is the name of the game.'

Tailed by *un flic*: a cop, Daniel did the sensible thing and pulled off the road. In the a small shopping centre, we enjoyed low-cal beers.

'The last thing I need is to be booked for some trivial infringement,' Daniel mused. 'They'd frisk the car for the obligatory red safety triangle, first aid kit and so on.'

Flushed with success, I said, 'Good news, guys. I've made contact With Madame Gilles.'

She was full of apologies. 'I'll bring the towels around this evening.'

Naomi delighted in the famous Bayeux Tapestry. 'It's a most remarkable work of art.'

We gazed at a miracle of horses, stylised trees, animals, erotic scenes and battles.

'The depiction seems just as extraordinary today as it must have been in the 1100s when it was embroidered.'

Daniel said, 'Hmm. The story of King Harold, and his seizure of the English crown. Death by an arrow piercing his eye at the Battle of Hastings. William the Conqueror gained the throne of England. Before them, it was King Alfred the Great.'

Naomi caught my eye.

Another masterpiece was Bayeux Cathedral, built in the eleventh century. It stands on the site of an ancient church, part of which remains in the crypt.

Wandering around the town, I savoured the atmosphere. Exquisite food. Fine wines. Chic window displays. Tantalised by the snatches of French conversations. 'I seize every chance to practice.'

Naomi laughed. 'I've noticed.'

Happy and carefree, we stopped at a supermarket. Buying all sorts of goodies for a barbecue.

On the drive home, Daniel lost his way. Panic. Shouts. Sarcasm. Bagging Naomi's navigating skills. I seethed. And recalled Neville acting in the same crazy way.

Madame Gillies arrived at our maison with our towels and profuse apologies. 'I'm devastated.'

We reassured her, 'No problem, madame.'

The moon hung low in the evening sky. I sipped a superb local red wine, watching the golden vapour trails of passing aircraft. Daniel cooked us a delicious barbecue. Steak. New potatoes. Honeyed carrots. Peaches with crème fraiche our final delight.

Next morning we planned a visit to Monet's famous maison and garden.

I noticed a glint of determination in my daughter's eye. She planned to forestall further episodes of *J'Accuse*. 'Right, guys, here are the maps. Everyone must have some idea of routes we need. Towns we'll pass through, and so on.'

Daniel blinked. An argument-free journey followed.

A busy road runs between Monet's flower and water gardens. Probably it was a quiet country lane in his day. We adored the flowers, grown in nuances of shades, the long columns and trellis effects. Huge thistles – at least six feet high – jostled for space with tiger lilies, poppies, day lilies, roses and snapdragons.

Sitting on a bench in the garden, we devoured sandwiches. Sternly rebuked by an attendant. 'Oops! It's forbidden to eat in the garden.' We should have known.

After she'd gone, we finished, at speed.

A subway took us under the road.

'*Voici*!' I said. 'The Water Garden.'

A meandering stream. Pink weeping willow roots undulated in the current. Bamboo stood tall. Water lilies smiled from pools. Flowers of every kind nodded in the breeze, colours ranging through pinks to reds, to blues and purple.

Naomi's eyes widened. 'We're standing on the green bridge made famous in Monet's paintings. The green rowing boat is over there, caressed by water lilies.'

Monet's maison was a treasure of Japanese prints, source of his inspiration. Blue tiles chatted to shining copper in his kitchen. The atelier, his studio, displayed copies of his most famous works. The yellow dining room boasted a wide table. It could seat two friends at either end, and ten either side.

I mused, 'Picture the conversations and delicious meals, those glasses of fine red.'

Trouville and Deauville, famous resorts in the era of Coco Chanel, were a must-see.

'Imagine the rich and famous promenading along the seafront.'

But with the tide out, we had ugly stretches of mud. Barely a hint of *la plage*. A blustery wind blew scudding grey clouds and teased shrubbery. We hugged ourselves into puffer jackets.

Naomi chuckled. 'Can you believe it's midsummer?'

An air of excitement rippled along crowded streets.

Naomi tutted at the kitsch and way over the top houses. 'A haven for rich poseurs.'

'Maybe.' I shivered. 'Yet there's a certain aura about it. The essence of a bygone era. Imagine Coco and her friends having a flutter in the huge and ornate casino.'

Near Buzi, a local restaurant caught Daniel's eye. The cool décor and delicious aromas lured us. Naomi took precautions to make our dinner a success. She fed and changed Chloé. Confident of another evening of French culinary delights, we took our seats. Daniel studied the menu.

Chloé's eyes flicked open. One glance, and she howled. Naomi tried cuddles and coos. Chloé's yells grew louder. Diners glared and muttered.

Daniel sighed. 'C'mon, guys. It's plan B.'

He bought a quality bottle of local red. Cooked a cassoulet. Served with new potatoes and broccoli, it was a simple, but perfect, meal.

A grey day greeted our Chartres visit. We drove along the Chateau de la Loire Road. Glimpsed the green copper roof of the famous cathedral from miles away. It rose like a beacon from fields of wheat. Excitement grew.

'Two completely different spires. Magnificent flying buttresses,' Naomi said, 'Twice destroyed by fire, I believe.'

We felt lucky to enjoy the rose window and stained glass. It dated from the twelfth century, a miracle of colour and diffused light.

'Removed to safety and stored, during the two world wars,' I recalled.

We admired the Gothic architecture. Intrigued by the floor maze.

Naomi said, 'A site for meditation and prayer.'

We walked hundreds of steps of the spiral staircases, reaching the dizzy heights of the summit. Enchanted by every aspect of that extraordinary building. UNESCO had given the cathedral World Patrimony, calling it, 'The richest and most complete medieval monument conserved in Europe.'

Candles flickered for the lost. I lit ones for Mum, Neville, Cousin Polly, My brother, Victor.

Daniel tackled the long drive to our maison. Everyone felt tired and hungry. At twilight, in the crepuscule, fog descended. The *bruine* made it damp and chilly.

He groaned. 'Dare we try another restaurant?

Chloé slept soundly in her car seat.

Naomi's sudden brainwave. 'Let's find a restaurant where we can park right outside. We'll watch Chloé in her car seat, and enjoy our supper in peace.'

21

We found the perfect place to dine, deep in the countryside. Daniel parked right outside the large window of *un petit restaurant*. The excellent menu and a delicious local cheese platter brought a gleam to his eyes.

We took turns strolling outside to check on our baby. Chloé slept on.

Ready to leave, it emerged that *la patronne* had thought we were checking on *un chien*, a dog! We all chuckled. Relaxed and happy after an interlude of superb French food and fine wine.

A slow drive home, battling low visibility of a fog.

Chloé spent her usual restless night. A quick tidy of *la maison*. Daniel made soft cheese sandwiches. Naomi did her magic, packing the car with remarkable efficiency. There was barely an inch to spare, given Daniel's boxes of wine.

'We've been lucky with the weather.'

He drove away. Fog and rain obscured the countryside. At a small village, Daniel bought cheese and wine of the region, *du fromage et du vin* for Jane, and his stepmother, Ros.

The weather hung low and chalky over Calais. White caps teased the waves. Our hovercraft arriving half an hour late.

Daniel shook his head. 'We're in for a rough crossing.'

My ginger capsules weren't needed.

Back in London, it felt good to be in familiar surroundings. Chloé seemed pleased, too, despite her evening tears. Fed and put to sleep, adults watched a French movie, *The Horseman on the Roof*. An electrifying historical epic, this French drama moved between life, death and love.

An exhibition lured us to the Royal Academy. The works were from Chagall's Moscow and Russian period. Living in Paris, he had returned to his homeland for three months. World War I erupted, trapping him for the duration. His family doubted he was a famous painter. He gave the world his answer, a wonderful series of paintings and drawings from that period.

I liked his saying, 'Who of us can see in its entirety, his path, whether in life or art? And who can tell where it can end?'

Time for my return to Australia. A London tube strike spoilt my plans for a leisurely departure. Naomi and I took a taxi ride into the centre of town.

She frowned. 'The Piccadilly Line is packed. New passengers are being refused entry, Mum.'

'That's a help.'

'Red airport buses are meant to depart every twenty minutes, though.'

A young Japanese man groaned. 'I've been waiting more than forty minutes. Not one.'

A glance at my watch. 'I have to be at Heathrow in an hour. I've fifty quid. Join me with a taxi.'

The Japanese man frowned. 'I can't contribute my half. Sorry.'

'We both have planes to catch. Be my guest.'

A long taxi queue made my hopes sink.

Naomi had a brainwave. 'Wait here, Mum.' She ran around a corner, hailing a cab where they turned for Kings Cross Station.

Heathrow. A long queue snaked towards the Malaysian Airlines check-in. An official checked passports and tickets. I headed for the loo, under the delusion that I'd checked-in. Another queue. Heavens, I thought, I've forgotten to tell them about my Frequent Flyers points.

An official told me, 'When you book in...'

I glimpsed my forlorn and abandoned suitcases. Gosh, I must be spaced out. How could I have forgotten about my boarding pass, and the roll-away process?

Naomi appeared. 'I was worried. They blow up unattended suitcases.'

Glad for a cup of tea and a Danish pastry, we enjoyed chatting with an American from New York. 'I lived in Sydney during the Second World War.'

'Never!'

Naomi confided, 'My marriage feels stronger since you've been here.'

'I'm so pleased.' We embraced. 'Maybe Daniel's father had a word?'

She shrugged. 'Maybe.'

Farewells. Hugs for Naomi and the little one. Chloé was full of giggles and laughter, waving her chubby hands. We blew kisses. I'd had a cuddle and sleep with her earlier that morning. She'd whimpered, maybe from a pain in the tummy. My gentle massage helped. We had both drifted into a deep sleep. I'd dreamt of travelling with the baby.

My plane headed towards Mannheim, Germany. Innsbruck. Multiple valleys. Peaks of the alps, glittering crystal snow in the early morning light. In forests, I imagined walking paths. Farms. Small villages. Rome, direction Lake Balaton. The temperature outside was minus forty-four degrees centigrade.

We glided over jagged mountains, glimpsed through a veil of evening gold. I'd hoped to sleep on the thirteen-hour marathon from London to Malaysia. Lord save us from noisy neighbours.

The palm and rubber trees of Asia.

Malaysia's modern airport had just opened. No-nonsense white columns were mirrored in the polished floor. Names like Gucci, Burberry, and Chanel – it could have been anywhere. I missed the unique flavour of the old one. A motley collection of shops had sold everything from perfume to tie-dyed tablecloths.

Glittering Sydney Harbour, the Bridge and Opera House welcomed me home. I guessed that Dad would be back soon, bless him.

Good old Antoine met me. 'How was it, pet?'

'Fantastic!' Groggy and jet-lagged, I yawned. 'Can't wait to tackle those renovations, though.'

He laughed. 'It may be wise to wait a week or so.'

The End

About the Author

Decima Wraxall, née Wright, was born in Newcastle, NSW, Australia. She spent her early years in the alpine region of the Upper Hunter Valley. A graduate from RPA Hospital, Sydney, Decima worked as an RN for over thirty years.

Her passion for the French language resulted in a diploma, accredited by the Alliance Française de Paris and the French Ministry of National Education. She later spent a month honing her skills at ELFCA, as a paying guest of a French family at Hyères, in the south of France.

Decima has received prizes for poetry and short stories. Her fictional memoir *Black Stockings, White Veil, A tale of Adversity, Triumph and Romance* was a finalist in the 2009 New Generation Indie Book Awards for historical fiction. She has co-edited two anthologies, *Our Womens' Work*, a finalist in the 2014 New Generation Indie Book Awards for women's issues, and *Bare*.

Recent successes include the publication of three poetry collections, *Bloom*, *Flame* and *The Mists of Time*, and a coming-of-age novel, *Stolen Fruit*, all published by Ginninderra Press, thanks to Brenda and Stephen Matthews OAM.